Dear Reader,

I love antiques, especially the family heirlooms that have found their way into my home. My favorite keepsake is a book of family folklore that was compiled and edited in 1955. This amazing book recounts the true experiences of a group of people from Pennsylvania who settled near the town of Dawson, Nebraska, in the 1870s and 1880s. Some of the compelling stories in the book include: *The Grasshopper Years*, *The Mad Dog Scare*, *Christmas at the Grandparents*, and *Love Takes a Hand in Destiny*.

My love for antiques and heirlooms is one of the reasons I'm so excited about the *Mysteries of Silver Peak* series! Sadie Speers owns an antique shop in the town of Silver Peak, Colorado, a place full of history. In *A Mountain of Mystery*, Sadie makes the startling discovery that her own family history may need to be rewritten.

I hope you enjoy *A Mountain of Mystery* and the characters you meet in Silver Peak. You may even be inspired to write down some of your own family history to share with future generations.

Blessings,
Kristin Eckhardt
writing as Carole Jefferson

Mysteries of Silver Peak

MYSTERIES
of SILVER PEAK

A Mountain
OF
Mystery

CAROLE JEFFERSON

Guideposts
New York

Acknowledgments

Every attempt has been made to credit the sources of copyrighted material used in this book. If any such acknowledgment has been inadvertently omitted or miscredited, receipt of such information would be appreciated.

Scripture quotations marked (NIV) are taken from *The Holy Bible, New International Version.* Copyright © 1973, 1978, 1984, 2011 by Biblica, Inc. Used by permission of Zondervan. All rights reserved worldwide. www.zondervan.com

Cover and interior design by Müllerhaus
Cover illustration by Greg Copeland at Deborah Wolfe, Ltd.
Typeset by Aptara, Inc.

Printed and bound in the United States of America
10 9 8 7 6 5 4 3 2 1

Prologue

Silver Peak, Colorado
June 15, 1897

Dear J.,

He is arriving three days hence and I can do nothing to stop the wedding. My terror grows with each passing moment and I would rather face death than the prison that awaits me in marriage to such a man.

I shall leave tomorrow at midnight, just as we planned.

I want nothing from here, save my father's photograph and my dear mother's wedding dress. They are all I have left of my old life. She has locked these treasures away from me as it gives her great pleasure to witness my distress.

But no more.

My fear is that she knows of our plan and waits in secret to stop me. I was so foolish to ever trust her and I have suffered dearly for it. Only you and God know my pain, as I dare not reveal it to another living soul.

You are my only hope.

I shall wait for you by the place where we hide our letters. If you do not come before the dawn, then I shall be lost.

Yours,

R.

1

─────

SADIE SPEERS TOLD HERSELF NOT TO PANIC.

Her wedding ring had gone missing. For the past hour, Sadie had looked around the nooks and crannies of the Antique Mine, her antique store in the historic mining town of Silver Peak. She'd taken her ring off to protect it from the paint thinner she'd planned to use to strip the peeling paint off of an old wooden rocking horse she'd been asked to restore.

Now that the job was done, she couldn't find her ring. Sadie examined every inch of her long mahogany desk that doubled as the store's front counter, looking under the cluttered surface for some sign of her ring. She was certain she'd set it there before starting her project. The man who had given her that wedding ring, her late husband, T.R., had also made this counter. He'd refinished the elaborately scrolled mahogany front of the antique desk and varnished it to a high polish. Then he'd added a dark granite top. Silver veins ran though the granite, adding to its richness.

"Where is it?" Sadie said out loud, looking high and low for the silver wedding band that had been on her finger for over four decades. She could only assume that it must have rolled off the desk and was now lost somewhere in the store.

Sadie planted her hands on her hips and looked around the shop. She loved the high pressed-tin ceiling and the way the sunlight streamed in through the plate-glass front window, but there were too many places where the ring could disappear.

She'd already searched behind the vintage quilt rack and in the dark recesses beneath the antique sleigh bed. Her gaze moved to the labyrinth created by the vast array of hand-carved wood chairs and tables that wound its way throughout her beloved shop.

Sixty-two years of living had taught Sadie that, most of the time, there was little sense in worrying. But that ring meant so much to her—the symbol of the love she'd shared with T.R., especially now that he was gone. She couldn't imagine never seeing it again.

The brass bell above the door jingled and Rosalind Putnam walked inside. The two women were almost nothing alike on the outside, but had been kindred spirits since kindergarten. Sadie was petite at five feet four, with short, salt-and-pepper hair and twinkly brown eyes. She embraced her mountain girl heritage and found herself most comfortable in the outfit she wore today: hiking shoes, blue jeans, and a sky-blue North Face vest over her pine-green cotton turtleneck.

Her best friend, Roz, was tall, often joking that she stood five feet twelve, with straight, shoulder-length gray hair that framed her cheerful face. Today, her long legs were hidden by the knee-high leather boots and the patchwork denim skirt she wore. A bright yellow tunic top was cinched at the waist with a vintage turquoise belt that matched the turquoise-blue frames of her stylish glasses. Roz often looked more like a time-traveling flower child from the sixties than a retired schoolteacher, and Sadie loved her all the more for her eccentric, bohemian sense of style.

"Am I glad to see you," Sadie exclaimed, walking over to greet her friend with a big hug. "I lost my wedding ring and I can't find it anywhere."

Roz's groomed gray eyebrows rose in alarm. "Oh no! How did that happen?"

Sadie explained the situation. "I thought I left my ring on the desk. If I did, I suppose it could have fallen off when I was gathering supplies to take into the back room."

Roz looked around the crowded shop. "So it could be anywhere?"

"Yes." Then an idea popped into Sadie's head. "You know, I decided to have a cup of tea on the back patio before I started my project. Maybe I took it off there."

Sadie moved quickly to the back room of the store. She opened the door and glanced around the small fenced yard where she'd set a white wrought-iron patio table and two chairs. Silver Peak was nestled high in the Rocky Mountains, and the wide blue sky provided the perfect backdrop to the snowcapped peaks and the untamed wilds of the Rockies. Sadie could see breathtaking mountain vistas in nearly every direction.

But she didn't see her wedding ring on the patio table.

Roz appeared in the open doorway. "Did you find it?"

"No." Sadie walked back inside and started looking around the vintage pie safe that stood next to the back door while Roz began searching behind the front desk.

Sadie smoothed one hand over the polished oak wood of the pie safe and carefully wiped a small smudge off one of the punched tin door panels. Her ring wasn't on the floor, so she checked the inside of the pie safe just to be certain it hadn't found its way there.

The telephone rang on the desk.

"I'll get it," Roz said, reaching over to grab the phone.

Sadie rounded the pie safe and picked up the copper washtub setting beside it.

"Sadie," Roz said, her brown eyes wide as she held the telephone receiver against her chest. "It's for you."

Sadie set the washtub back on the wooden floor. "Just give me a minute to catch my breath," she said, chuckling. "I haven't exercised like this in quite a while."

Roz leaned toward her and whispered, "It's Edwin."

Sadie stared at Roz, trying to figure out what she was talking about. "Edwin who?"

"Marshall," Roz whispered, a slow smile spreading across her face. "He wants to talk to you."

Sadie's heart skipped a beat. She hadn't talked to Edwin Marshall for decades. They'd gone steady together as teenagers until Edwin left Silver Peak to attend college and went on to a successful career as a circuit judge in Chicago. Why would he be calling her now?

Sadie took a deep breath and then reached for the phone. "Hello?"

"Hello, Sadie," he said, his deep, resonant voice carrying over the line. "Edwin Marshall here. How are you?"

"I'm fine, Edwin," she said, aware that Roz was watching her. "Long time, no speak. How are you?"

"I'm good. Happy to be back in Silver Peak."

"You're in town?"

"Yes—I actually moved back two days ago and I'm still settling in."

"Well . . . ," she said, struggling for words. "That's a surprise."

"Someone told me they call you the Antique Lady now," Edwin said.

Sadie laughed. "That's true. I just hope it's not a reference to my advanced years."

It was Edwin's turn to laugh. "You always did have a great sense of humor. I'm sorry to bother you on such short notice, but I need your help."

"Oh?" Sadie couldn't imagine what help Edwin might need from her. She rested one hand against the desktop to steady herself. "What can I do for you?"

"Well, you might remember the old family home on Monroe Avenue. I've just moved into it and I was wondering if you might be able to stop by today. There's something I want to show you."

"Sure." She wanted to ask him more questions, but something in his tone made her hesitate. "Is now a good time?"

"It's perfect," he said.

"Okay, then, I'll see you soon." Sadie ended the call, then looked over at Roz. "Do you mind watching the store until Julie gets back from lunch? It shouldn't be long." Julie Pearson worked part-time at the Antique Mine while her twin boys were in school.

"I'd love to." Roz moved closer to her. "But you can't leave until you tell me what Edwin said."

"He didn't say much." Sadie was still shocked that Edwin had contacted her after all these years. "But it sounds like he's back in Silver Peak to stay. And he wants to show me something."

"Well, that's intriguing," Roz said, amusement dancing in her brown eyes. "So what are you waiting for? Scoot!"

Sadie laughed as she headed for the door. "I'll be back soon."

"Take your time," Roz called after her.

A few minutes later, Sadie drove up the steep incline that led to Jefferson Avenue, one of the nicest streets in town. In the late 1800s, Silver Peak had been a boomtown with a population of more than fifty thousand people. That was when most of the town's huge Victorian houses had been built, along with many of the brick storefronts that still lined Main Street.

The Marshall family home was a three-story white Victorian with a large turret in the front and the original gingerbread trim all around. The porch wrapped around one side of the house and was bordered by large purple lilac bushes that Edwin's grandmother had planted herself.

Sadie parked in the driveway, then took a glance in the visor mirror. She took a moment to fluff her short hair before climbing out of her red Chevy Tahoe.

Edwin might not even recognize her, Sadie thought to herself as she walked to the wide front porch of the Marshall house. But then again, she might not recognize him either. When she thought of Edwin, she still pictured a tall young man with broad shoulders and laughing blue eyes.

"I wonder what he wants," she murmured, lifting the brass knocker and rapping it twice against the heavy oak door.

The door opened almost immediately and Edwin Marshall stood on the other side. His solid, powerful frame filled the doorway. His hair was an attractive steel-gray now, but the twinkling steel-blue eyes and patrician nose both belonged to the boy she remembered.

She would have known him anywhere. "Hello, Edwin."

He smiled. "Sadie, you haven't changed a bit. Please come in."

As Sadie walked inside the house, she felt as if she were stepping back in time. The Marshall house had been built by Edwin's grandparents and had stayed in the Marshall family all these years. She'd often visited here as a young girl whenever her grandfather, Jacob Wright, had come to play a game of chess with Edwin's grandfather, James Marshall. The two men had been good friends for more than sixty years.

"This brings back memories," she said, looking around the front hall. Nothing had changed, not even the furniture or the artwork on the walls. If she closed her eyes, she could almost hear her grandfather cheerfully calling out "Checkmate" in the next room.

"It's wonderful, isn't it?" Edwin said. "I spent so many happy times in this house. I couldn't think of a better place to enjoy my retirement."

Sadie met his gaze. "So you really are back for good?"

"I am," he replied. "My wife passed away five years ago, so there was nothing to keep me in Chicago. I was ready for small-town life again."

"Small-town life is all I've ever known," Sadie said with a wistful smile. "I'm sorry about your wife. I lost my husband, T.R., a few years back."

"I know," he said softly. "I've had a subscription to the Silver Peak *Sentinel* ever since I left here, so I've kept up with the joys and sorrows of all my old friends. You have a daughter, don't you?"

"Yes," she said, touched that he'd kept track of her. "Alice recently moved here from Denver with my two teenage grandchildren, Theo and Sara. It's nice to have them so close by."

"That's wonderful. My daughter, Noelle, lives in Atlanta, Georgia, with her husband, Carl, and my five-year-old grandson, Sam. I visit as often as I can."

"Grandchildren are a blessing, aren't they?"

His eyes shone with pride. "They sure are."

Sadie couldn't take the suspense any longer. "So what did you want to show me?"

He chuckled. "You always did like to get right to the point." Then he motioned her toward the stairs. "It's in the attic. I hope you don't mind a bit of a climb."

"Not at all," she said cheerfully, following him up the stairs. "If I did mind, I wouldn't be living in Silver Peak."

When they reached the attic, Sarah saw several old trunks and assorted boxes scattered across the crowded space.

"I've been sorting through some of my grandparents' and parents' things," Edwin said, leading her toward an open trunk, "but it occurred to me that I might want to bring in an antiques expert before I start handling a few of these items." Then he pointed inside the trunk. "Especially something like that."

Sadie moved closer and saw an old dress box with the lid partially dislodged. Curious, she lifted the box out of the trunk and removed the lid.

"Oh, Edwin," she breathed, "this is lovely."

Inside the box was a gorgeous Victorian wedding gown with the delicate lace sleeves neatly folded across the silk-and-lace bodice.

"The fabric looks pretty fragile," Edwin said, "so I didn't want to do anything that might damage it."

"It's in excellent condition for its age," Sadie told him, admiring the detailed hand-stitching along the neckline. She lifted one sleeve for a closer look at the lacework, then she noticed something else on the dress.

There was a small hole in the center of the bodice. Ash-gray smudges surrounded the hole, along with some small, rust-like streaks. "Well, this is interesting."

"What is it?" he asked.

"I think it might be—" Sadie leaned closer to the hole. "It looks like a bullet hole." She sniffed the gray smudges and recognized the unique odor right away. "This gray stuff is gunpowder."

"You're sure?" His wiry brows lifted.

"Pretty sure." She saw him glance at the trunk before turning back to her. "Where did this dress come from?"

"I don't know," he said slowly. "It was in the trunk and, as far as I know, this trunk has been in the attic since before my father was born."

"What else was in the trunk?"

He hesitated. "There were some old photographs of people I don't know. And a packet of old letters with only initials used instead of names."

"How strange," she said, staring at the wedding dress.

Then he pointed to the rust stains around the bullet hole. "Is that blood?"

Sadie shrugged. "I'm not sure. You'd have to get it tested to know for sure. Rust stains are common on vintage fabrics and they're almost impossible to differentiate from old bloodstains just by the naked eye."

When he didn't say anything in response, Sadie looked up at him. "Is anything wrong, Edwin?"

"To be honest with you, Sadie, there is another reason I asked you to come here."

Something in his tone made her skin prickle. "What reason is that?"

"There *was* something else inside the trunk with the wedding gown," he said, his deep voice almost gentle now. "Something I removed before I brought you up here."

Sadie stared at him, not sure what to expect. "What was it?"

"A gun," he said, then he looked at her for a long moment. "And your grandfather's name is engraved on the handle."

2

───────

SADIE FOLLOWED EDWIN OUT OF THE ATTIC AND DOWN THE STAIRS to the parlor on the main floor. Her heart pounded in her chest as she watched him set the dress box on the antique coffee table.

"Please have a seat," he said, turning toward her. "I'll get the gun out of the gun safe and be right back."

After he disappeared into the hallway, Sadie sat down on the red velvet divan. The dress box was on the table in front of her and she reached out to run her palm over the lid, almost certain that she knew the origin of the wedding gown inside and the story behind it.

A tale known around Silver Peak as the Legend of the Runaway Bride.

Back in 1897, her great-aunt Rachel Wright had been engaged to a man named Wallace Marley. The betrothal had been arranged for sixteen-year-old Rachel by her stepmother, Hester Marley Wright. Rachel's father had been dying from tuberculosis and too ill to realize that Rachel wanted no part of such a marriage. But Hester wanted to cement the bond between the wealthy Wright family and the struggling Marley family.

Sadie still wasn't sure how much of the runaway bride story was fact and how much was fiction. The one thing she did know for certain was that Rachel had escaped on horseback on the day of her wedding and shot herself near the old family silver mine. Somehow, Rachel had managed to take off her wedding dress and wander into the creek, possibly hoping to wash the blood from the wound.

After seeing the smeared blood on the boulders lining the swollen creek, the search party had determined that the rushing creek waters had carried the injured girl away and, sadly, her body had never been found.

That incident had caused a rift between the Wright and Marley families that had never been fully healed. It didn't help matters that Hester Marley Wright had accused Rachel of theft shortly after the girl had turned up missing.

Sadie breathed a wistful sigh as more bits and pieces of the tale started coming back to her. Rachel's tragic end hadn't been discussed much in her family. Sadie's grandfather, Jacob Wright, always refused to speak of his deceased younger sister. Everything Sadie knew about Silver Peak's most infamous runaway bride she'd learned from town folklore and the occasional details shared by other family members.

There wasn't even a photograph of her great-aunt in the old family album. Hester had destroyed all the photographs of her stepdaughter after Rachel had embarrassed the Marley family by choosing death over marriage to Wallace.

The sound of footsteps broke Sadie's reverie and she looked up to see Edwin walk into the parlor. He held an antique revolver in the palm of one broad hand.

He approached Sadie, taking a seat next to her on the divan. "Don't worry, it's not loaded." He held it out to her. "I've checked it twice."

Sadie took the revolver from him, feeling the weight of it in her hand. The silver barrel was rounded and the trigger guard made of brass.

"Well?" Edwin asked, curiosity swimming in his steel-blue eyes.

She smiled, knowing that her old boyfriend was well aware of her antique firearms expertise. "It looks like a Colt Army Model, 44-caliber, like the kind they manufactured during the Civil War and for a few years afterward."

Sadie's father had collected antique guns and when she was a teenager he'd often taken her with him to various sales and shows. He'd taught her to respect firearms, and she'd eventually learned to recognize the make and model of most antique guns and rifles. Sadie had soaked it all in, but she'd usually found the stories surrounding the antique guns more interesting than the guns themselves.

That was certainly true about the revolver in her hand. It had a six-shot, rotating cylinder and looked to be in excellent condition for its age. Her father would have been thrilled with such a find and she wondered if he'd ever known of its existence.

"There wasn't any ammunition with it," Edwin informed her.

"I'm not surprised. To load a revolver like this, you'd need to measure gunpowder into a chamber and then place a lead ball at the front of that chamber. And you'd need some lard."

A smile tipped up one end of his mouth. "Lard? Seriously?"

She smiled. "Yes. It was often used as a chamber lubricant to prevent more than one chamber from being ignited when another chamber was fired."

Then her gaze moved to the letters carved into the varnished walnut grip: *Jacob Silas Wright*—her grandfather's full name.

The fact that a pistol with her grandfather's name had been found in the same trunk as a bloody antique wedding gown made her believe that the gown probably *did* belong to her great-aunt Rachel. And, sadly, that Rachel had used her older brother's gun to shoot herself.

That was part of the story that Sadie had never heard before. And the fact that her grandfather's revolver wasn't included in her father's gun collection made her believe that sad fact of Rachel's death had been kept secret even from the family. Sadie had always known the subject of his sister's death was painful for Grandpa Jacob, and now that his revolver had been found with the wedding gown, she realized how deep that pain must have been.

Edwin sat silently beside her, letting her continue to examine the revolver without asking a lot of questions. Even after all the years that had separated them, she still felt comfortable around him.

"It has to be my great-aunt Rachel's dress," Sadie said at last. "I just don't understand what it was doing in your attic."

"My grandpa's attic," Edwin reminded her. "He and your grandpa Jacob were best friends."

"Yes, they were," Sadie said softly. "It's just so strange. I first heard about the legend of the runaway bride when I was about eight years old. It never quite seemed real to me. But now . . ."

"I know," Edwin said gently. "That story is part of Silver Peak's folklore."

"That's right." She looked up at him. "A lot of people in town know about Rachel's story. So it is possible this isn't really her wedding gown or my grandfather's gun."

Edwin arched a skeptical brow. "You think someone planted them in the attic?"

She smiled. "No, but they might be props. There was a play written by one of the Marleys about the incident. It was even performed at the opera house years ago, back when we were just starting high school."

A gleam of recognition shone in Edwin's eyes. "I remember that play! Now, what was it called . . . ?"

"*The Treasure in the Wedding Dress*," Sadie told him. "Not that I ever saw it. I was forbidden to attend. No one in my family saw the play, since they'd heard that the playwright had branded my great-aunt Rachel as a thief."

"Yes, that's right," Edwin said with a slow nod.

"To make matters worse," she continued, "the play was a success and traveled to Denver and other towns in Colorado. The Marleys certainly got their revenge, even though no one had ever proven that Rachel stole anything."

"I remember that part of the story now. Didn't they accuse her of stealing some jewels?"

Sadie nodded. "And some stock certificates to a silver mine— one that is still operating today and is quite prosperous."

He whistled low. "I wonder what those stock certificates would be worth today?"

She shrugged. "I can't even imagine. That mining company has diversified since 1897 and now calls itself Moose Creek Industries and owns several other corporations. That's one of the reasons the Marleys and Wrights still don't get along. The Marleys believe they've been swindled, even though those stock certificates had belonged to Rachel's father—they were supposed to be part of her dowry."

His gaze moved to the box in front of them. "So you think the wedding gown and the gun might just be props from the play?"

"I don't know what to think. This revolver is authentic, so someone went to a lot of trouble if it was just a prop." She looked up at him. "And we still don't know why this box was in your family's attic."

Edwin looked thoughtful. "I don't remember my parents or grandparents being involved with that particular play, although they were patrons of the opera house."

Sadie glanced at her watch, surprised at how much time had passed since she'd arrived. "I'd better get back to the shop. Do you mind if I take the wedding gown and the revolver with me?"

"Not at all," he said without hesitation. "As far as I'm concerned, they belong to you."

"Thank you." She found herself looking into his steel-blue eyes. Then she realized she was staring and felt a warm blush bloom on her cheeks. Sadie turned away from him and opened the lid of the dress box to place the revolver inside.

"Let me carry that for you," he said, waiting for her to replace the lid before he picked it up off the table. "It's been so nice seeing you again, Sadie."

"You too," she said sincerely. "I just wish we'd had more time to catch up. So many years have passed since we were in high school."

He chuckled as he headed toward the front door. "They sure have."

Sadie followed him, noting that the passing years hadn't changed his tall, athletic frame or broad shoulders. His voice was a little deeper, and he had a dignified, yet humble manner that spoke well of his years on the bench as a circuit judge.

When they reached her Tahoe, Sadie opened the rear door so that Edwin could set the box inside. Then he straightened and closed the door before turning to Sadie. "Let me know if you find anything out about that dress."

"Oh, I will." She smiled and held out her hand. "Thank you again for inviting me over to see the dress. I never could have imagined spending my afternoon this way."

He laughed. "Well, I'm glad you weren't disappointed. Although I meant what I said earlier about catching up. Maybe we can have coffee sometime soon. I hear there's a nice coffee shop in town."

"You bet. It's called Arbuckle's and it's actually located right next door to my antique shop."

His eyes widened with delight. "That sounds perfect. I can take a tour of your shop and then we can have coffee together."

She opened the driver's door. "Please stop by anytime. I'm sure you're busy getting settled in, so don't hurry on my account."

"I'll be there before you know it," he said with a grin. "Having coffee with an old friend will be a nice break from all the unpacking I still need to do."

Sadie bid him good-bye and then climbed into her Tahoe and started the engine. Edwin stood on the sidewalk, watching her pull out of the driveway and then gave a jaunty wave as she turned onto the street. Sadie waved back, still finding it hard to believe that Edwin Marshall was back in town after all these years.

As she drove back to the shop, she wondered why she hadn't heard about his impending return to Silver Peak. She hadn't even read about it in *The Chatterbox*, which was Silver Peak's own online social blog. The anonymous author of the blog seemed to have an uncanny sense of ferreting out information about the town and the people in it.

Sadie cracked her window open during her drive back to the Antique Mine. She enjoyed the fresh autumn breeze and the way it cooled the flush on her cheeks. The faint aroma of wood smoke drifted into her nostrils, and she gave thanks that her woodpile was fully stocked at home and ready for the cozy fires that would burn brightly in her hearth during the cold months ahead.

Sadie parked her Tahoe in front of the Antique Mine and then grabbed the dress box out of the backseat before entering the shop. The bell over the door tinkled as she walked through the door. "I'm back," Sadie called out.

A moment later, Julie appeared from the back room. "Hey, there." At thirty-six, Julie was married to the town pediatrician and was the mother of ten-year-old twin boys, Logan and Brody. The tall blonde had green eyes and was as active as her boys, busy training for 5K races and always looking for ways to put her interior design degree to good use.

"Am I back in time?" Sadie asked, glancing at the clock. "I know you need to take the boys to soccer practice after school today."

"Just in time," Julie said with a smile as she hitched her purse over one shoulder. Her gaze moved to the large dress box and her eyes widened with curiosity. "Did you find something for the shop?"

"I'm not sure," Sadie said. "It's kind of a long story, so I'll tell you about it later."

"Sounds good," Julie said as she headed for the door. Then she turned around. "Oh, Roz told me you lost your wedding ring. I looked around the shop, but I didn't find it." Her brow furrowed. "You don't think someone took it, do you?"

"No," Sadie assured her. "It turned up missing this morning before I even opened the shop. I'd come in early to work on restoring the rocking horse."

Julie wrinkled her nose. "That reminds me. Marge Ruxton called earlier and wanted to know if the rocking horse was done."

Sadie laughed. "Done? I've barely started. She only brought it in two days ago."

"I don't know why you agreed to do the job," Julie said with a small shake of her head. "No matter how it turns out, Marge won't like it."

"Just call me an optimist," Sadie said with a wry smile. She knew Julie was probably right, but Marge was a paying customer, no matter how much the woman got under her skin. She'd tried to befriend Marge in the past, but they seemed to mix like oil and water despite Sadie's best efforts.

"I hope I'm wrong," Julie said. "And don't worry about your ring. We'll keep looking. It's got to be around here somewhere."

"I hope so," Sadie said as Julie headed out the door. "Have a nice evening."

After Julie left, Sadie placed the dress box on the desktop and began humming along to Hank Williams singing "I Saw the Light" over the store speakers.

She opened the lid and pulled the wedding dress out for a closer look. She held it up to herself, noting that the hem of the long dress fell just to the top of her feet. That meant Rachel had been about her height, although judging by the narrow waist of the dress, her great-aunt had been thinner. Of course, women had worn boned corsets back then, Sadie reminded herself, often squeezing their torsos so tightly that fainting was not uncommon.

Sadie retrieved a padded hanger from the coat closet and then carried the wedding dress over to the antique wardrobe that stood near the window. She slipped the dress on the hanger before placing the dress on a wooden peg on the side of the wardrobe. The sunlight shining through the shop window illuminated every small detail of the wedding dress.

Aware of the damage that the sun could do to vintage fabrics, Sadie didn't intend to let the dress hang there for long, but she wanted to take a closer look at that bullet hole.

The bodice was made of ivory silk and adorned with delicate lace. The bullet hole had torn through both. But as she examined it more closely, she saw a tiny run in the lace that extended several inches. She turned the fabric in her hand and examined the inside of the bodice. That was when she saw another small tear in the fabric, at least three inches from the original bullet hole.

Sadie carefully fingered the tear, wondering how it had gotten there. Had it been caused by the bullet too? That would possibly explain the part of the Runaway Bride legend that had always troubled her. How could Rachel, after taking a gunshot to the chest, have been able to remove her wedding dress and wade into the creek?

But if the bullet had only grazed her, causing a flesh wound, the story made more sense. Most likely, Rachel would have removed her dress to examine her wound. Still dressed in her corset and underclothes, she might have waded into the creek to wash away the blood. Or even to let the water carry her away since the bullet had missed its mark.

Sadie shuddered at that thought, feeling as if the story was so much more real now that she had Rachel's wedding dress in front of her. Although she still couldn't be certain it was the real thing.

But perhaps the box could give her a clue.

Sadie left the wedding dress hanging on the wardrobe and returned to the desk. She'd given the box just a cursory glance at Edwin's house, so shocked by the sight of the dress inside of it. Now, as she approached the cardboard box and the lid beside it, Sadie studied them both. The box was gray with age and the corners looked battered a bit, but the sturdy construction of the box had held it together for over a hundred years.

Things had been made to last back then, Sadie thought to herself as she ran her fingertips over the gray satin lining inside the box. It was frayed at the edges and a little loose in places, but when she turned the box over and shook it, only a bit of dust fell onto the desktop.

Then Sadie turned her attention to the lid. It had the same satin lining on the inside as the box. But as she ran her fingers over the lining, she noticed an odd, flat bulge that had been invisible on visual inspection. Then her fingers moved into the seam at the inside corner of the lid and she felt a small, three-inch slice in the lining. The slice was in the seam and barely visible, so she wasn't surprised that neither she nor Edwin had noticed it earlier.

Very carefully, Sadie tucked her fingers beneath the lining to examine the mysterious bulge—curiosity bubbling inside her. She felt a piece of paper and snagged it between two fingertips before slowly pulling it out from the open seam. It barely fit and she found herself holding her breath, hoping the satin didn't tear as she finally pulled the paper free.

It was an envelope, the paper faded with age. On the front of the envelope she saw the name *James* handwritten in a neat, black scrawl on one side.

A letter to Edwin's grandfather?

Her heart skipped a beat as she pulled out the letter inside and began to read it.

> *Dear James,*
>
>   *The loss of my sister still haunts me. I must leave here or go mad. I cannot bear to see her wedding gown or my gun, yet I cannot bring myself to destroy them. Please keep them for me until I return—if I return.*
>
>   *Your friend,*
>   *Jacob*

Sadie thought the handwriting looked like her grandfather's, but she couldn't be sure. This could still be a ruse of some kind—or simply props from the play. She'd known nothing about a letter written by her grandfather to James Marshall. However, she did recall that Grandpa Jacob had left Silver Peak as a young man to work on cattle drives in Montana and Idaho. He'd eventually returned and settled down, marrying Sadie's grandmother.

Had Jacob left because of Rachel's death?

It made sense, especially given the bad blood between the Wrights and the Marleys. From the sound of the letter, he'd been haunted by both the dress and the fact that his revolver had caused that bullet hole.

But were the revolver and the dress and the letter authentic? That was the question Sadie needed to answer. She folded the letter in half again and started to put it back in the envelope when she saw something shiny in the bottom of the envelope—something she hadn't noticed in her excitement to read the letter.

She turned the envelope upside down and a brass key fell onto the granite desktop with a tiny clinking sound. Sadie picked it up, her fingers shaking a little. It was a small key, too small to be a house key. It looked more like a key to a jewelry box or even a small safe.

Sadie had never believed the folklore about a treasure in Rachel's wedding dress. Now, as she held the antique key in her hand, she wasn't so sure. Where had it come from? And why was it in the envelope that had been hidden beneath the satin lining?

Had she just found a key to this century-old mystery?

3

SADIE PICKED UP HER CELL PHONE AS QUESTIONS ABOUT THE key swirled in her head. The first step to answering them seemed obvious—find out if the antique wedding dress had really belonged to Rachel.

She dialed the number for Dr. Conroy's office. His receptionist, Rita Dodd, picked up on the first ring. "Hello, Sadie."

Sadie smiled. "That caller ID gives me away every time, doesn't it?"

"It sure does," Rita said with a chuckle. She'd gone to high school with Sadie and had started working as a receptionist in Dr. Conroy's office one year after they'd graduated. "But every once in a while the screen says *caller unknown*, so that adds a little mystery into my life."

"Well, it's probably no mystery why I'm calling. I'd like to set up an appointment with Doc."

"Any certain day or time?" Rita asked.

"The sooner, the better," Sadie said. "I'm not sick. I just want a consultation."

"Well, you may be in luck. Our five o'clock just cancelled if you'd like to come in today. It's Doc's last appointment, so you'll have all the time you need."

"That's perfect." Sadie glanced at the clock, noting that it was almost three. She could close the shop a few minutes early that afternoon and make it to the doctor's office in plenty of time. "Thanks a bunch."

"You're welcome," Rita replied. "See you at five."

Sadie ended the call and slipped the cell phone into her purse. She had a bad habit of setting it somewhere and losing track of it—just like she'd lost track of her wedding ring. That thought pulled at her heartstrings and she intended to keep looking for it, in between helping customers. But first she needed to get the dress ready to go.

She walked into the back room and retrieved a roll of plastic bubble wrap. Then she returned to the front of the store and retrieved the wedding dress from the wardrobe. She carefully folded it up and then wrapped it in the bubble wrap, securing the loose ends with tape. The dress had been fairly well-preserved for all these years so she didn't want to take the chance that something would stain it now. Then she pulled out one of the zippered, clear plastic bags that she used to transport antique quilts. She placed the wedding dress inside the bag and zipped it closed.

She intended to take it to Doc Conroy's office and ask for his help in obtaining some tests. First, to see if the dark-brown stain on the wedding dress was actually blood and, if so, to see if the DNA on the dress matched Sadie's own DNA. That would prove a familial connection to the dress and provide the proof she needed that the wedding dress truly had belonged to Rachel.

After another fruitless search for her wedding ring, Sadie spent the next hour in the back room with the rocking horse. She used the spacious room as a break area, a storage space and as her workshop. The open doorway allowed her to hear the bell above the front door in case any customers stepped inside the shop. She studied the rocking horse, able to give it a good evaluation now that the thick layer of white paint had been removed.

The craftsmanship was incredible, with fine, artistic details carved into the wood that she'd seldom seen before. Sadie still found it hard to believe that Marge Ruxton had picked this up at an estate sale in Arvada for only a few dollars.

Sadie had sensed that Marge didn't want to spend much more than a few dollars when she brought the horse in for Sadie to restore. But Sadie had known Marge long enough to set a firm price with her before she'd started the job. Not that the money really mattered to Sadie, certainly not as much as restoring such an exquisite antique back to its original beauty, but Marge could be a genteel bully when the mood struck her, as Sadie had learned from past experience.

Now that she'd stripped the rocking horse down to the bare wood, she could assess it for possible damage. Sadie carefully checked all the joints to make sure they weren't loose and was happy to find them quite secure. There were a few narrow cracks in the wood, but those could be filled and smoothed over.

The rocking horse's mane, however, was another matter. Made of white sheep's wool, it was a gray, matted mess. She picked up a comb and tried to separate some of the strands, but the comb just got tangled in the wool. How would she ever smooth it out?

The bell above the front door jangled, startling Sadie. She set down the comb and gave the rocking horse a gentle pat, planning to return to it soon. As she walked out of the back room, she saw Anita Slattery, the wife of the town sheriff, entering the shop.

Anita and her husband had moved to Silver Peak two years ago after he'd retired from his job on the Denver police force. The opening for the sheriff's position in Silver Peak had appealed to both of them, according to Anita, since her husband was looking for a slower way of life. Since the crime rate was so low in town, the sheriff spent much of his time searching for lost hikers in the mountains and helping stranded motorists.

"Hello there," Sadie called out. Anita was a frequent patron, often coming in just to browse, but she seemed like a nice, if quiet, woman. The Slatterys tended to keep to themselves.

"Hello," Anita said with a small smile. Her curly brown hair was threaded with silver and she had dark-brown eyes. "I'm just here to browse a bit."

"That's fine," Sadie assured her, taking another peek at the clock. There was a good forty-five minutes before she had to leave for the doctor's office. "Let me know if there's anything I can help you with."

"Thanks, I will."

Sadie watched Anita round the antique potbellied stove and disappear behind the long bookcase that held vintage books and maps.

Sadie turned her attention back to the dress box. The pistol was still inside as she placed the lid on the top. She'd take it home with her tonight and place it in the gun safe with her father's collection of antique guns and rifles. She placed the letter and the brass key in her purse, also planning to take them home for safekeeping.

Then she picked up the feather duster and began to make her way around the shop. As she dusted, Sadie kept her eyes open for her wedding ring. She knew her husband, T.R., would have laughed and teased her mercilessly about misplacing her ring. His sense of humor had always brightened her day.

Her mind drifted to her meeting with Edwin earlier. His manner was so different from T.R., yet there was much to admire about both men. Her husband had been well-loved by the folks in Silver Peak, the church pews overflowing at his funeral.

Sadie was so lost in her thoughts that she almost bumped into Anita as she dusted a tall, antique armoire. "Oh, excuse me," Sadie said, coming to an abrupt halt. "I wasn't watching where I was going."

"Oh, that's all right," Anita said with a smile. "I was so busy looking around I didn't even see you."

"Are you looking for anything in particular?"

Anita hesitated a moment. "I was wondering if you have any pioneer clothes. I hear that people wear pioneer garb for the Founder's Day Picnic."

"Some do," Sadie told her, "although it's not required. I don't have any ready-made clothes on hand, but I do have some vintage fabric and some pioneer dress patterns if you're interested."

Anita gave a slow nod. "I'll take a look at them."

Sadie led her over to the vintage fabrics and notions, pointing out the patterns with pioneer-style dresses and bonnets. The Founder's Day Picnic was an annual event to celebrate the founding of Silver Peak by William and Antonia Tate when they settled here in 1878, near the start of the silver rush. Prospectors soon followed, populating the makeshift town with tents and hastily constructed cabins.

"I just don't know," Anita said, fingering a bolt of yellow calico in front of her. "Maybe we won't dress in costume. Mac started grumbling almost the moment I suggested it."

Sadie smiled. "Well, you don't have to decide today. The picnic is still three weeks away, and I'm sure I won't run out of fabric."

Anita nodded. "Yes, I'll think about it. Thanks for your help, Sadie."

"You're welcome." They chatted for few minutes more before Anita took her leave.

Sadie began to close up shop, eager to talk to Doc Conroy. She carried the wedding dress and the box to her Tahoe and placed them in the backseat. The afternoon sun warmed the mountain air and cast a lovely golden glow over the tree-lined main street. Sadie took a deep breath, feeling a little nervous as she locked up the shop and headed for the doctor's office.

She arrived with five minutes to spare before her appointment. The reception room was empty as she walked through the front entrance carrying the bag containing the wedding dress.

"Hi, Sadie," Rita greeted her. She sat behind a long desk made of polished pine with a dark marble top. Her long gray hair was pulled back into a neat braid, and a pair of purple bifocals was perched on the bridge of her nose. "Doc is ready for you now if you'd like to go on back to exam room one."

"Thanks, Rita," Sadie replied, heading down the hallway.

Doctor Tom Conroy had taken over the medical practice from his father, Dr. Wesley Conroy. The senior Dr. Conroy had delivered Sadie and been her childhood physician. By the time Sadie had given birth to her daughter, Alice, the junior Dr. Conroy had taken over the practice.

A native of Silver Peak, Dr. Tom Conroy was now pushing seventy, but he was still on top of all the latest technological advances in medicine. His daughter, Lucy, had followed in her father's footsteps and pursued a career as a physician too. Lucy currently worked at the Boulder Medical Center, but everyone in town was hoping she'd eventually come back to Silver Peak and take over for her father when he retired.

Sadie stopped in front of the open door marked with the number one and then walked inside. The exam room was empty, so she set the plastic bag on the exam table before taking a seat on a padded chair near the door.

A moment later, Dr. Conroy walked inside. "Hello, Sadie," he greeted her with a smile that lit up his green eyes.

"Hi, Doc," she replied. "Glad you could see me on such short notice."

"Rita tells me you want a consultation." A worried frown creased his silver brow. "Have you been feeling poorly?"

"Oh no," she said, smiling. "I'm perfectly fine. I was hoping you could help me with a dress. Your stitches are legendary around here."

He laughed. "Well, that's a new one. Are you sure you've come to the right place?"

"I am." Sadie smiled as she rose to her feet. "I need a medical opinion." She walked over to the exam table and unzipped the plastic bag. Then she carefully unwrapped the wedding dress and laid it on the table. "I have something of a mystery on my hands."

He moved beside her. "Looks old." Then he leaned closer, his gaze on the bodice. "Is that a bullet hole? And blood?"

"That's what I'm hoping you can tell me. It's possible that this wedding dress belonged to my great-aunt Rachel."

He turned to look at her. "The runaway bride?"

She gave him a wry smile. "One and the same. Edwin Marshall is the one who found the dress."

"I heard he was back in town. He moved into his folks' house, didn't he?"

"Yes, and it was his grandparents' house before that." She explained the friendship between Jacob Wright and James Marshall, as well as the note she'd found in the dress box. "I want to believe it's Rachel's dress, but I need to know for sure. If that *is* blood on the dress, I'm hoping you might be able to do a DNA test and compare it to mine."

He gave a slow nod. "DNA tests do show family matches, but I don't have the technology to do them here."

Disappointment shot through her, although Sadie wasn't really surprised. "Is there a lab you can recommend?"

He smiled. "As a matter of fact, I can. Lucy works with the DNA lab in Boulder. I can give her a call if you'd like."

"Absolutely," Sadie exclaimed, barely resisting the urge to hug him. She'd come to the right place after all.

"Let me give her a quick call," he said, walking toward the door. "I'll be right back."

Sadie sat down to wait, hoping Lucy would agree to facilitate the test. She hadn't seen Lucy in years, but remembered her as a smart, studious girl who took her responsibilities very seriously. As far as she knew, Lucy had never married. The girl had been two years ahead of Alice in school, which would make her about forty-three years old.

Rita stuck her head in the partially open door. "Hey, I'm going to take off. Can I get you a cup of coffee or anything before I go?"

"No, thanks," Sadie said with a smile. "Love the glasses, by the way. Roz is going to be jealous when she sees them." Both Roz and Rita loved to collect stylish eyeglasses.

Rita flashed a grin. "I just picked them up yesterday. And I've got a pair of hot pink frames on order." She winked and gave her a small wave. "See you later, girl."

"Bye," Sadie said with a chuckle as Rita disappeared. The woman had been so much fun in high school and hadn't changed a bit.

A few moments later, Dr. Conroy walked back into the exam room. "Good news. Lucy will make sure the DNA test gets done right." He walked over to the sink and opened the cabinet above it. "And I'll need a cheek swab from you."

"Well, that sounds painless," Sadie said as he walked over to her. He swabbed the inside of her cheek with a long cotton Q-tip and then placed it inside a test tube. He labeled the tube and then sealed the top of it.

"Now comes the part that might be a little painful," he said with a sigh. "Lucy insisted that I needed to send the dress to the lab, not just a sample of the bloodstain. She said the lab has special techniques to extract DNA and it's best not to take chances with something this old."

"Oh," Sadie said, looking over at the wedding dress. She hated to send it off after just finding it, but she trusted Doc Conroy and his daughter to keep it safe. "Then that's what we should do. I'll need an address . . ."

He held up both hands. "I can take care of it, Sadie. I'll box it up tonight and send it express first thing in the morning. Lucy told me to send it straight to her and she'll deliver it to the lab."

"Well, I appreciate it. Just let me know the shipping cost and I'll reimburse you."

"I'll add it to your tab," he said with a smile. "Although I wish all of my patients were as healthy as you."

"I am doing well," she said with a smile. "The shop keeps me busy, and it's nice to have Alice and my grandkids in Silver Peak."

"I'm glad to hear it." He moved toward the door. "Lucy says the test results should be back in two to three weeks. I'll let you know as soon as I hear something."

Sadie picked up her purse and the empty plastic quilt bag and followed him out of the exam room. "Thanks so much for your help. I can't wait to find out if that is Rachel's dress."

"Neither can I," he said, his green eyes twinkling as he walked with her to the front entrance. "Although you can be certain that doctor-patient privilege means I won't say a word about it—no matter how tempting."

She smiled. "I know. I'm trying to keep it quiet myself, at least until I know more. There are enough rumors about the runaway bride. I don't want to add to them."

He opened the door for her. "Well, let me know if you need anything else in the meantime."

"Thanks, I will." They bid each other good-bye and then Sadie headed out the door.

As she climbed into her Tahoe, she breathed a happy sigh, eager to get home. Hank, her loyal golden retriever, would be excited for his evening walk. She was ready to do some walking and thinking and praying herself—especially when she considered that the contents of that dress box might contain new pieces of an age-old family puzzle.

4

On Tuesday morning, Sadie sat at her kitchen table and read her devotional. The blueberry muffins she'd baked that morning still filled the air with their sweet aroma. Hank lay under the table, his head resting on her slippered feet.

She cherished the peace that filled her heart when she read God's Word. After the events of yesterday, she welcomed that peace. Last evening had been busy with phone calls to Alice and Roz, letting them know the details of finding the wedding dress and her plans to have it tested for DNA. Alice had been excited by the discovery, certain it was Rachel's dress, while Roz had shared Sadie's skepticism. The most difficult part would be waiting for the test results to know for sure.

"Lord, give me patience," she prayed out loud. Then she turned her attention to the Bible verse at the end of the day's devotional, Galatians 6:9: *Let us not become weary in doing good, for at the proper time we will reap a harvest if we do not give up.*

With a sigh of contentment, Sadie closed the devotional and then rose from the table. She carried her breakfast dishes over to the stainless-steel sink, giving them a quick rinse before loading them into the dishwasher. Then she wiped the dishrag over the pearl-white granite countertops. T.R. and Sadie were the fourth generation to live in her family's ranch house and T.R. had remodeled the kitchen only a year before his death. Now it looked like it belonged in a showroom. She loved the large chef's oven and the stainless-steel appliances, as well as the dark-cherry cupboards that reached all the way to the ceiling. Best of all, T.R. had restored the original antique leaded window over the sink, adding scrolled cherrywood trim that made it a showpiece.

The once prosperous Wright family ranch had struggled with financial hardships during the Great Depression, forcing Sadie's father to sell off huge chunks of land so they could survive. Now, only the ranch house and the two acres of forested land surrounding it remained in the family, but Sadie counted that as a blessing.

She treasured her home and all the memories it contained. She'd grown up in this house and then moved here as a new bride. Her daughter had been raised here and her grandchildren had played in the yard, chasing each other around the towering fir trees in the summer and building snowmen in the winter.

Hank followed her around the kitchen as she gathered and prepared the ingredients for the beef stew she planned to have for supper and placed them in the slow cooker. When she turned off the kitchen light, his tail started wagging in anticipation of their morning walk. He knew her routine so well that he arrived at her bedroom door first and then patiently waited as she dressed for the day.

Ten minutes later, Sadie ran a comb through her hair and then pulled the blue North Face vest over her white long-sleeved shirt and zipped up the front. Then she sat on the side of the bed and slipped into her brown leather hiking boots, double-knotting the laces. Hank stood in her open bedroom doorway, watching her with his soulful brown eyes.

"Are you ready to go?" she asked, rising from the bed. She laughed as he turned and bounded down the hallway toward the mudroom at the back of the house. Sadie grabbed her cell phone off the dresser and slipped it into her vest pocket before following him.

Once outside, Sadie glanced at the small thermometer tacked to the back of the house. It read fifty degrees, but the light breeze and bright morning sun made it feel warmer.

She knew the first freeze was imminent, but she always waited until that day to take in the potted plants. Soon she'd replace them with decorative copper tubs of pumpkins and gourds in celebration of autumn.

Hank bounded ahead of her and then turned in circles, his tail waving behind him as he waited for Sadie to follow. She smiled as they made their way toward the forest behind the house, aware that Hank was better than any exercise machine she could ever buy.

Their mountain hikes were the perfect venue for her to pray and to relish so many precious memories. She'd retired from teaching business and history at the local high school about ten years ago, but still kept in touch with many of her former students and colleagues. She'd opted for early retirement so she could fulfill her dream of opening the Antique Mine, and the experience had been better than she'd ever imagined. Her love of history had only grown since she'd opened the shop.

Hank ran in wide circles around her, chasing rabbits under trees and barking at birds. He stayed close enough to Sadie so that she could call him to her, but she usually let him run to his heart's content. Then he'd spend most of the day sleeping while she was at the Antique Mine, giving him plenty of energy for the evening walk.

She paused on the hiking trail, taking in the glorious beauty of the aspen trees ahead of her. The cooler weather had turned their green leaves to a vibrant shade of gold. "Thank You, Lord," she prayed out loud, "for reminding me every day of the blessings in my life. The blessings of family and friends and the beauty that surrounds me, reminding me of Your glorious handiwork in this world. Make me a blessing too, Lord, to both friends and strangers alike. Amen."

She took a deep, cleansing breath of the morning air and then continued her hike. The air filled her lungs and soul. This was where she belonged. Someday soon she'd saddle up her horse, Scout, and take her for a ride through the mountains. She boarded Scout at Milo Henderson's ranch about half a mile away, along with the horses belonging to Alice and her grandchildren. Milo operated a prosperous horse ranch and boarded horses as a side business. He took wonderful care of all of his animals and had a special love for horses.

The sun glowed through the trees as she walked, her thoughts going back to her family history and how little she actually knew about Grandpa Jacob's early life.

She did recall one unguarded moment when Grandpa Jacob told her that Rachel had loved animals. He'd quickly changed the subject before Sadie had been able to reply, but the tenderness of his words still resonated within her.

How strange, she thought to herself, *that the death of a family member more than one hundred years ago could reverberate through the generations.* A death that had been kept quiet among the family, more from sorrow than shame. But, now more than ever, Sadie wanted to learn more about her great-aunt and the events in her life that had led to that fateful wedding day.

As a history teacher, she had a special talent for searching for hidden clues in the past. So often, there was more to a story than met the eye. Maybe it was time to put that talent to use and find out more about her own family history.

After a twenty-minute hike along a gently sloping mountain trail, Sadie turned on the path to head back to the house. "Hank," she called out, unable to see her dog among all the trees. "Let's go home, boy."

In a flash, Hank appeared out of the brush and returned to the trail, trotting just a few feet ahead of her. His tongue lolled out of his mouth and a gold leaf adorned one ear. Sadie laughed as she caught up with him. "Very stylish," she said, carefully pulling the leaf from his tangled fur. "Looks like we need to give you a good brushing tonight."

When they arrived at the house, Hank headed immediately to his water bowl in the kitchen and began to lap up water.

By the time Sadie changed out of her hiking boots and into a pair of black leather loafers, Hank was curled up asleep in his bed next to the sofa. A doggie door in the mudroom opened both ways, allowing him into the fenced backyard while Sadie was away.

After one last look around the room, she grabbed her purse and then walked quietly through the front door, closing it softly behind her. She locked it and then headed for her car, humming a favorite hymn under her breath.

———

Five minutes later, Sadie pulled into an empty parking spot between the Antique Mine and Arbuckle's Coffee Shop. She walked to the coffee shop first, in the mood for a chai latte. She inhaled the aroma of fresh-baked pastries the moment she stepped inside.

The coffee shop was housed in an old brick building that had been remodeled into a cozy space filled with tables and padded armchairs and love seats. Colorful throw rugs covered the wood floor in the seating areas, adding warmth and style to the shop. The high ceiling had exposed ductwork and beams, giving a modern edge to the historic atmosphere.

The only other customers in the shop at the moment were four older men, one of them Roz's husband, Roscoe, all seated at a table near the window. They were so busy debating current events that they hadn't even noticed her enter.

Sadie squared her shoulders as she approached the front counter, determined not to succumb to one of Luz's cinnamon rolls, especially since she'd already eaten breakfast.

Luz Vidal, who owned the shop with her husband, Hector, walked through the swinging door that separated the kitchen from the rest of the coffee shop. She held a pan full of cinnamon rolls between her green oven mitts as she walked over to the glass display case and used a spatula to lift each gooey roll from the pan and place it inside the case. The way the white frosting oozed over the sides of the rolls told Sadie they'd just come out of the oven and she felt her willpower start to crumble.

"Good morning," Luz greeted her. "And how is my favorite Antique Lady?" Her silky black hair was pulled back into a neat braid and her brown eyes sparkled beneath dark eyelashes.

"Wonderful." Sadie smiled. "It's a beautiful morning, and a large cup of your coffee will make it even better."

"How about a roll to go with it?" Luz suggested. "It's on the house."

"I already ate breakfast," Sadie said weakly.

"But I really need your opinion. I'm on the food committee for the Founder's Day Picnic and I offered to bring cinnamon rolls. You only need to take a bite or two and then tell me what you think."

"You know I'd never let one of your cinnamon rolls go to waste, even though it will go straight to *my* waist."

Luz laughed. "Your waist might not like it, but your mouth will thank you—at least I hope so. It's a new recipe and I've only had a small taste myself."

"Well, now I have to try it," she said, telling herself she'd work off the extra calories on her evening walk with Hank.

She waited while Luz plated a cinnamon roll, her mouth already watering. Then Luz handed her the plate and a fork. "Enjoy while I get your coffee."

Sadie cut into the roll with her fork and then took a bite. The sweet cinnamon dough mingled with the warm frosting on her tongue, creating a taste sensation that had her eating half the roll before Luz set her coffee cup on the counter.

"Well?" Luz asked.

Sadie licked some frosting off the fork. "You've got a winner here, Luz. One of the best cinnamon rolls I've ever tasted."

Luz smiled. "I'm so glad to hear it. Good enough for the picnic, then?"

"Absolutely." Sadie forked up another bite. "In fact, you'd better make a huge batch, because these are going to disappear quickly."

They chatted for a few more minutes before Sadie walked through the connecting doorway in the wall that separated Arbuckle's and the Antique Mine. Through the front window of her shop, Sadie saw a small crowd of women gathered near the door. None of the faces were familiar to her, so she assumed they were tourists.

She hurried to the front entrance and unlocked the door, opening it wide enough for them to come inside. "Hello, ladies. Where are you all from?"

"Everywhere," a young woman said with a smile. She looked about twenty-eight and had a sprinkle of freckles across her nose. "We came to Breckenridge for a genealogy workshop and one of the speakers raved about your antique shop, so here we are."

"Wonderful!" Sadie exclaimed, always happy to meet people who shared her love of antiques.

"I'm sure more are on their way," another woman said. "The workshop was nice, but driving around this beautiful country is even nicer."

"Well, I'm so glad you're here," Sadie told them. "Please look around and let me know if you have any questions. I love to talk about antiques."

The next few hours passed by in a flash and Sadie enjoyed every moment. Conference attendees came and went, most of them making purchases before they departed. Sadie engaged in lively conversations with a woman from Kentucky and a man from Minnesota. She talked about Native American artifacts with one customer and gold rush memorabilia with another.

By late afternoon, the stream of customers finally started to thin. That gave her some time to tidy up, keeping an eye out for her lost wedding ring. A woman slowly moved toward her and Sadie wasn't certain if she was just browsing or had a question.

The woman kept looking over her shoulder, as if she was watching for someone. Then she cleared her throat. "Hello."

Sadie moved toward her. "Hello," she said with a smile. "May I help you?"

The woman twisted her fingers together. She looked about fifty years old, with light brown hair cut in a bob and hazel eyes. "I hope so."

Sadie waited a moment and when the woman remained silent, she asked, "Are you attending the genealogy workshop in Breckenridge?"

"Yes." A smile fluttered on the woman's mouth. "I'm from Boston."

"Oh my. That is a long way." She held out one hand. "I'm Sadie. I own this shop."

"Hello, Sadie," the woman said, shaking her hand. "I'm Laura."

"Nice to meet you." Sadie smiled. "Are you looking for anything in particular?"

Laura glanced toward the door and then her gaze moved slowly around the shop. "Yes . . . I am."

Sadie waited, sensing something strange about the woman. Laura seemed apprehensive—possibly even afraid. But there was certainly nothing in the Antique Mine to frighten her. "Are you here with a group?"

"No," Laura replied, as the only other customer in the shop walked out the door. "I came alone. I wanted to meet you."

Sadie blinked. "Oh?"

"I believe we're related."

Sadie arched a brow, surprised and intrigued. "Really? Did you find me on your family tree?"

Laura nodded. "I probably should have called rather than just popping in here unannounced . . ."

"Nonsense," Sadie said with a smile. "I'm glad you did. I've dabbled in researching my genealogy but just never found the time to give it my full attention." She didn't miss the irony that, as a history buff, she knew so little of her own family history. "Did you know I was in Silver Peak before the genealogy workshop or did you figure it out after you got here?"

"Oh, I knew before," Laura said without hesitation. "When I saw the workshop advertised on a genealogy Web site, I thought it would be the perfect chance for us to meet."

"Well, I'm glad you did." Sadie glanced at the clock, happy to see it was almost closing time. She wanted to learn more about this possible long-lost relative. "You must have done a lot of research to track me down all the way from Massachusetts."

A ghost of a smile haunted Laura's mouth. "Years, actually. I wasn't sure I'd ever find this side of my family."

"So how are we related? Are we second cousins? Third cousins?"

"Second cousins," Laura told her. "My grandmother and your grandfather were siblings. Her name was Rachel Wright."

Sadie stopped breathing for a moment, wondering if this was some kind of joke. But she'd only told Alice and Roz about the wedding dress, along with Doc Conroy. And even though she hadn't seen Edwin for years, she didn't believe he'd joke around about something like this. "You must be mistaken. Rachel Wright died over a century ago."

"No, she didn't," Laura said earnestly. "I can see this is quite a shock to you, but it's true. Nana, I mean Rachel, escaped from an arranged marriage and settled in Boston. That's where she met my grandfather."

"Rachel Wright?" Sadie repeated, certain there must be some kind of misunderstanding. "W-R-I-G-H-T?"

Laura gave a fervent nod. "Yes. She ran away on her wedding day."

Sadie's knees felt a little wobbly. "Let's go sit down." She led Laura over to the mahogany desk and they each took a seat behind it. "Now, start from the beginning."

"Well, I don't know all the details. Nana never talked much about her childhood. All she'd tell us was that she was a runaway bride from out west. She never told us she was born and raised in Colorado. I finally figured that out myself after a lot of digging."

Sadie wondered how this could possibly be true. There was the bloody wedding dress. The revolver. The letter. And most of all, the fact that Grandpa Jacob had mourned his sister his entire life—so distraught by her tragic death that he'd refused to speak of her.

Could that all be a lie?

Sadie's mind swam with possibilities. *Rachel's body was never found. Had she stolen the stock certificates and jewels to fund her escape?* Or was Laura's arrival in Silver Peak, the day after the discovery of the wedding dress in Edwin's attic, some kind of scam?

Laura glanced over her shoulder, her gaze scanning the door and front window. "Is there somewhere else we can talk?"

"Why?"

"I'm not . . . comfortable here."

Despite her skepticism, there was something about Laura that reminded her of a lost puppy. She just wanted to bundle her up and take her home. *But she's a stranger,* Sadie reminded herself. A stranger who had entered her shop with a wild story.

"You don't believe me," Laura said, watching Sadie's expression.

"I don't know what to believe," Sadie said honestly.

"Your great-aunt Rachel Wright was my grandmother," Laura said, her chin quivering. "She married my grandfather, Charles Ellis, in 1907, and they had one daughter, Catherine. She was my mother. Rachel Wright Ellis lived to be ninety-six years old." Laura squared her shoulders. "And I can prove it."

5

"WHAT KIND OF PROOF DO YOU HAVE?" SADIE ASKED HER.

Laura dug into the large Coach purse hanging from her arm. A moment later, she withdrew a small, folded piece of newsprint. "Here." She handed it to Sadie. "This is Nana's obituary from the *Boston Globe*."

Sadie unfolded the paper and saw an obituary, dated in 2003, for Rachel Ellis. "Survived by daughter, Catherine Overfield, and granddaughter, Laura Finch." She looked up at Laura. "That's it?"

"No." Laura reached into the envelope. "Here's her picture."

Sadie took the photograph from her. The woman in the photo looked about sixty years old. She had dark hair and brown eyes and a mischievous smile. As she studied it, Sadie could see a slight resemblance to Grandpa Jacob in the shape of the eyes and nose.

"See," Laura said, leaning toward her to look at the photo. "She *is* Rachel Wright."

Sadie sighed as she handed the photograph back to Laura. "She might be. But I've never seen a photograph of my great-aunt at any age. All her pictures were destroyed."

Laura's forehead crinkled. "Destroyed?"

"By her stepmother," Sadie explained. "She must have told you about her." She was eager to see how much of Laura's story matched the family history. That wouldn't necessarily prove the truth of her story, given that Rachel's story was hardly a secret in these parts.

"No, she didn't," Laura said softly. "Nana never spoke of the family she left behind. She said it hurt too much."

Despite Sadie's suspicions about Laura's story, the pain etched on the woman's face looked sincere. Either Laura Finch was an excellent actress or she truly believed that her grandmother had been the runaway bride.

"So she didn't tell you anything about her life in Colorado?"

Laura slowly shook her head. "Only that she'd escaped on the day of her wedding."

The door to the shop opened and Laura almost jumped out of her shoes. She spun around, one hand gripping Sadie's forearm.

"Hello, Sadie," Josh Ralston greeted her. A local woodworker, the handsome twenty-six-year-old was a quality craftsman who consigned several of his pieces at Sadie's shop. "I'm glad I caught you before you closed for the day."

Laura let go of her arm and turned away, walking a few steps toward an antique vanity and placed both hands on the marble top as if to support herself. Sadie hesitated for a moment, watching her, and then turned her attention to Josh.

"I'm glad you did too." Sadie moved behind the mahogany desk. "I've got your check right here."

"Perfect." Josh flashed a smile, his blue eyes twinkling.

She reached into a drawer and retrieved the check she'd written out earlier that afternoon. "Here you go."

"Thanks." His eyes widened as he looked at the amount. "Wow, that's more than I expected."

"I just sold the last of your Adirondack chairs yesterday, so there's plenty of room on the floor for more whenever you're ready."

"I'll get right on it," he said, turning toward the door. "Thanks, Sadie."

"Thank you for doing business with me," she said with a smile. After he left, Sadie looked over at Laura, who still stood at the vanity. "Are you okay?"

Laura turned around, her face pale. "Yes, I'm fine. Your friend startled me."

Sadie nodded, but sensed there was more to it than that. She glanced down at her arm, still able to see the red imprint where Laura's fingers had clutched her. The woman might be some kind of scam artist, but she'd been truly afraid when the shop door had opened. A fear that Sadie couldn't just ignore.

Let us not become weary in doing good . . .

"We still have so much to talk about," Sadie said at last. "If you don't already have plans, we could talk more over supper at my house."

"Oh," Laura said, obviously taken by surprise at Sadie's invitation. "That's very kind." A smile fluttered on her lips. "I'd love to—if you're sure it's not too much trouble."

"No trouble at all," Sadie assured her. "Let me just finish closing up here and we can be on our way."

————

Twenty minutes later, Sadie turned into her long driveway. The sun just barely peeked over the Rockies to the west, casting long shadows as Sadie drove up to the house. Laura followed in her rental car, pulling up behind Sadie as she parked in front of the house.

Sadie waited by the porch steps as Laura climbed out of her car.

"This is lovely," Laura said, her gaze taking in the stone and log farmhouse.

Two stone chimneys protruded from the roof, and the oversize wooden front door was accented with rod-iron fixtures. A pair of white wooden rockers sat beside a small, round table on one side of the front porch. A white wooden porch swing hung from the roof on the other side of the porch. Potted asters and geranium plants dotted the wide plank floor and the wooden porch railing, the blooms starting to fade now that cooler weather had set in.

"Thank you," Sadie said. "It's been in the family for a long time."

"And what a magnificent view." Laura turned in a slow circle, taking in the snowcapped mountains to the west and the colorful, tree-lined slopes to the east. From the front of farmhouse, they could see part of Crystal Lake, which shimmered in the distance. "It's just breathtaking."

"I love it out here," Sadie told her. "My daughter wanted me to move to town after my husband passed away. The winters here can leave me snowed in for days. But this is home and has been since I was born." She smiled. "Besides, I always have plenty of firewood to keep me warm."

Laura looked wistful. "That sounds so peaceful. I'm used to the hustle and bustle of a big city."

"Well, I've got all the modern conveniences." Sadie moved toward the door. "Come on in. I'll give you the full tour."

Hank greeted them at the door. Sadie bent down to pet him. "Hello, boy. Did you have a good day?" She glanced up at Laura. "This is Hank, named after one of my favorite country music singers, Hank Williams."

"He's a beauty." Laura reached out to pet him. "I love large dogs."

"Do you have one in Boston?"

"No. I live in a small apartment and just don't have room. I bet Hank loves to run around outside."

"He does. We both do, although I generally walk while he runs." Sadie straightened. "Now, are you ready for the tour or would you like to eat first?"

"I'd love a tour." Laura looked up at the high, vaulted ceiling. "This room is huge, but so cozy. I love the big stone fireplace and the way you've decorated the place. It has such a Colorado feel to it."

Sadie followed her gaze, seeing the house through her eyes. Oak bookcases bordered both sides of the fireplace, filled with local history books. Two deep, leather lounge chairs sat across from the vintage paisley sofa, a large custom-made oak coffee table, courtesy of Josh, placed between them.

Sadie continued the tour in the dining room, where Laura expressed delight at the rustic, deer-antler chandelier and matching sconces.

"Grandpa Jacob made the table," Sadie said. "He loved working with wood."

"It's gorgeous," Laura said, running one palm over the polished surface. A cushioned bench lined one side of the long table and handsome, high-backed chairs filled the other side.

Sadie confined the tour to the main floor of the house, including the first-floor bedroom that she'd converted into an office and library.

"I've never seen a home filled with so many antiques before," Laura said, looking impressed. "And you've done such a great job of decorating."

"With a little help from my interior designer, Julie," Sadie said with a smile. "She works in my shop and doesn't get much of a chance to use her design skills in Silver Peak. I'm lucky to have her."

"There's such a variety of antiques," Laura said when they reached the kitchen. "Where do you find them all?"

"I attend a lot of estate auctions and antique shows. The hard part is not bringing them all home with me. The house is already full to bursting with them. That's why I love spending my days at the Antique Mine. It gives me more room to enjoy my passion."

"That sounds lovely."

"It's a wonderful adventure," Sadie admitted. "You never know where you're going to find the next treasure, and some of them are buried under a lot of dirt and grime."

Laura smiled. "Nana once said that she left a treasure behind in her wedding dress."

Sadie froze. "She did? I thought you said she didn't talk about the past."

Laura didn't seem to notice Sadie's reaction. "It just slipped out once or twice. She never explained what she meant. Nana was funny that way—she'd drop little comments here or there, but leave them dangling."

"So she was secretive?" Sadie asked, wanting to know more.

Laura shook her head. "No, I wouldn't say she was secretive. She was actually very open and loving. She'd get this twinkle in her eye . . ." A nostalgic smile curved up one corner of Laura's mouth. "She liked a good joke and could give as good as she got."

Sadie thought about the brass key she'd found with the dress. *Did it lead to a treasure?* "It's a strange comment. What kind of treasure could she have left behind with her wedding dress?"

Laura shrugged. "I wish I knew."

So did Sadie. *So did a lot of people*, she reminded herself, especially the Marley family. That was why one of them had written the play about the Runaway Bride, fueling the rumors that Rachel Wright had absconded with those stock certificates.

"Something smells delicious," Laura said, breaking Sadie's reverie.

"Thank you. It's beef stew, an old family recipe." She walked over to the Crock-Pot and lifted the lid. A savory steam rose from the surface of the stew. "It's ready if we are."

"I'm starving," Laura admitted. "I missed lunch today."

Sadie chuckled. "Me too. Although I had two breakfasts to fill me up." She walked over to the cupboard to retrieve two soup bowls. "If you get a chance, stop by Arbuckle's Coffee Shop and try one of their cinnamon rolls. You won't be sorry."

Laura helped her set the table and then Sadie served them each a heaping bowl of stew. Corn bread completed the meal, along with a glass of iced tea for both of them.

"This is delicious," Laura said, blowing gently on a spoonful of stew before taking another bite. "I can't remember the last time I had homemade beef stew."

"Thank you." Sadie picked up her glass and leaned back in her chair. "It's an easy meal to make. I just throw all the ingredients in the Crock-Pot in the morning, set it to cook for eight hours, and supper is ready when I come home."

"I tend to eat most of my meals out." Laura spread a generous amount of butter on her corn bread. "There must be four restaurants on my street alone and it's just too easy to stop in and order a meal to go—especially when I'm busy with work."

"What do you do?"

"I'm in public relations. I do freelance work now, so I can set my own hours. I've cut down to part-time, but I still do some work every day—especially in campaign season."

"Oh, you're involved in politics?"

Laura smiled. "Yes, but strictly work-related. Local campaigns hire me as an adviser. It's all about introducing the candidate to as many people as possible, through Web sites and flyers and such. Most of my work is done on the computer."

"So you can work almost anywhere."

"That's the beauty of it. Telecommuting allows me to travel for events like the genealogy workshop. I've been doing that more and more now that I've cut down my work hours."

"Why did you decide to cut down your hours?"

Laura hesitated. "I was so busy that I didn't have much time for a personal life, so I thought it was the right thing to do. In fact, I'm thinking about stepping away from campaign work and just concentrating on business marketing and promotional work."

"I see." Sadie slid a cooked carrot onto her spoon. Hank lay at her feet under the table, ready for any tidbits that might fall to the floor. He'd already eaten a hearty dinner of his own, but Hank seemed to have a bottomless stomach.

Laura looked around the kitchen. "I can't imagine how you run an antique shop all day and keep up with a big house like this."

"Well, I have help," Sadie said with a smile. "I have a wonderful friend and housekeeper named Claribel who comes in once a week. She keeps the house spotless and organized for me, which is quite a task as you can see from all the things I collect."

Laura smiled. "Are any of your antiques family treasures?"

"Some of them are," Sadie said. "And others are things I've picked up along the way and couldn't let go."

"How long have you owned the Antique Mine?"

"About ten years," Sadie replied, reaching for another slice of corn bread. "Before that I taught high school history and business. I loved working with students, but I was ready for a change. My husband, T.R., knew how much I loved antiques and encouraged me to open my own shop."

"T.R.?" Laura cocked her head to one side. "What does that stand for?"

"Theodore Roland," Sadie told her. "My grandson, Theo, is named after him."

Laura smiled. "So you have a grandchild. How wonderful! How old is he?"

"He's seventeen. And I have a granddaughter, as well. Sara is fourteen. They both moved here from Denver two years ago with my daughter, Alice, after her divorce."

"And how have the kids adjusted to life in a small town?"

"Very well," Sadie said with a smile. "They spend some of their weekends in Denver with their father. Fortunately, Cliff and Alice had an amicable divorce and get along well. I think that makes it easier on the children."

Laura took a sip of her tea. "I agree. I never had children myself." She stirred her stew with her spoon, her gaze on her bowl. "I married once, right after college, and divorced seven years later. Now . . . I'm engaged . . ."

Her voice trailed off as Sadie's gaze moved to the woman's ring finger, but it was bare.

"I might have made a mistake," Laura said softly. "I feel strange even telling you this, since we just met but . . . you're family."

Sadie wasn't ready to make that leap yet, but she stayed quiet and let Laura talk.

"My mom always said I had a broken compass when it came to men. Ray Johnson swept me off my feet a year ago and I thought I'd finally found the love of my life, but now I'm not so sure." She looked up at Sadie. "Maybe I'm just gun-shy."

"Well, there's no hurry, is there?" Sadie said, feeling a little awkward giving advice to a woman she'd just met. "Have you set a wedding date?"

"Not yet. Ray is pushing me to pick one, but I haven't given in yet. He's a man who knows what he wants and he's made it clear that he wants me."

That sentiment might have been romantic, but the anxious expression on Laura's face made it seem a little creepy. Then Laura's face cleared as she smiled at Sadie. "Thank you so much for dinner. It was wonderful."

Sadie scooted back her chair and stood up. "You're welcome. Shall we have coffee in the living room? I thought you might like to see some family photo albums."

Laura's eyes widened with delight. "You read my mind."

They spent the next hour looking at old photo albums. Sadie pointed out each relative starting with Grandpa Jacob. Laura claimed to see a resemblance, even holding up her photo of her nana next to a photograph taken of Grandpa Jacob in 1968, one year before he passed away.

Sadie saw some similarities in their facial features, but that didn't prove anything. "You said earlier that your grandmother never spoke of her childhood or even mentioned that she was from Silver Peak."

"That's right." Laura turned toward her, a photo album still open on her lap. "What can you tell me about her life here?"

"Not much, I'm afraid." Sadie leaned back against the sofa, enjoying the warmth from the logs burning in the fireplace. Hank was stretched out on a braided rug in front of the hearth, still tired from the run he'd enjoyed when Sadie had let him outside after supper.

"I know that Rachel was sixteen when she was engaged to Wallace Marley. She never got along with her stepmother, Hester Marley Wright. Hester was the one who had arranged the marriage and wouldn't let Rachel back out of it. The Wrights were much wealthier than the Marleys at that time, and it was thought that Hester wanted the marriage to elevate the Marley family financially."

"So Nana was from a rich family?" Laura asked.

Sadie smiled. "I suppose so. The family ranch used to be huge, but most of it was sold off during the Great Depression. This house and two acres is all that's left."

Laura gave a slow nod. "That's interesting. Nana and my grandfather weren't wealthy by any means, but she never seemed to mind. She was a hard worker." Then she looked over at Sadie. "What about Nana's father? Why didn't he stop the marriage?"

"He was too ill at the time and passed away shortly after Rachel's death . . . " Her voice trailed off, and she shifted uneasily on the sofa. "After her *apparent* death, I guess I should say."

Laura nodded. "I still can't believe she ran away on her wedding day. That must have caused quite an uproar."

"I'm sure it did. Especially when her stepmother accused her of stealing."

Laura's eyes widened in disbelief. "What?"

Sadie explained the accusations against Rachel. "The stock certificates and jewelry were never found."

Laura leaned forward. "But her wedding dress was left behind, right? That's one of the few things that Nana did say, as I mentioned before. Do you know if it's still around somewhere?" Her gaze moved over the room. "It looks like the Wright family treasures their heirlooms. Surely no one got rid of it—especially if Rachel was presumed dead."

Sadie stared at her for a long moment, finding it interesting that Laura had brought up the dress for a second time. "Well, her stepmother did destroy all the photographs of Rachel," Sadie reminded her.

"But not the dress, surely," Laura said, watching her intently.

"No," Sadie said. "The dress wasn't destroyed. Apparently, the search party found it next to a creek when they went looking for Rachel. It had a bloody bullet hole in the bodice. Everyone assumed Rachel shot herself and that her body was washed away in the creek."

Laura blinked. "That's awful."

"Yes, her death had a profound impact on my grandpa Jacob. He even left town for a few years."

Laura slowly shook her head. "I never knew. And here I was thinking I might be able to wear Nana's wedding dress at my own wedding." She sighed. "Maybe it's a sign."

"A sign?"

"That I shouldn't marry Ray." She swallowed hard. "He's very . . . controlling, Sadie. At first I thought he was so attentive, always meeting my every need and wanting to spend every moment together." A flicker of fear shone in her eyes. "But now I see him . . . differently."

"Can you break the engagement?" Sadie asked, a little perplexed. In her mind, someone well-versed in public relations should be an excellent communicator. Unless . . . "Has he hurt you?"

Her gaze dropped to her lap. "No . . . not yet. But I think he may have followed me here, Sadie. He didn't want me to come alone. And I—"

The sound of the doorbell cut off Laura's next words. Hank hopped to his feet and barked twice. Laura shot off the sofa. "That's him!"

Sadie stood up, seeing the sheer panic on Laura's face. "Don't worry, it's okay," she said, hoping that was true. "Go into the office. I'll handle whoever is at the door."

Laura didn't argue with her, taking off down the hallway like a shot. When she was out of sight, Sadie walked over to the front door, Hank at her side.

Then she took a deep breath and opened it.

6

___

"Hello, Sadie."

Sadie smiled at her pastor's wife, feeling both relieved and a little silly. Laura's fear had been contagious and Sadie's heart still beat faster than normal. "Hello, Jeanne. This is a nice surprise."

"I should have called first," Jeanne said, "but this day has been a little crazy. Do you have a few minutes?"

"Of course." Sadie opened the door wider and ushered Jeanne inside. Hank greeted their guest with a wag of his tail and sniffed the black tote bag hanging from the crook of her arm.

"Hello, boy," Jeanne greeted him, bending down to scratch Hank behind the ears.

Sadie loved spending time with Jeanne, one of the friendliest and organized women she knew. A tall, slender African American, Jeanne had short hair and brown eyes. For a moment, Sadie considered fetching Laura from the office, but decided to let her have some time alone. Surely she'd heard Jeanne's voice by now and knew she was in no danger from her fiancé.

"Let's have a seat by the fire," Sadie told her guest. "Would you like a cup of coffee?"

"No, thank you," Jeanne said, giving Hank one last pat before joining Sadie in the living room. "I can't stay long." She sat down in one of the leather chairs, crossing one long leg over the other. She wore a pair of black slacks and a coral blouse with large, gold hoop earrings. "I'm actually on my way to Fort Collins."

"Tonight?" Sadie asked, a little concerned. The hour was growing late for the two-and-a-half-hour drive.

"Yes, my mother is in the hospital there. She fell and broke her hip this afternoon and has surgery scheduled first thing tomorrow morning."

"Oh, I'm so sorry." She knew Jeanne's elderly mother lived alone in the family home and that they were very close. "Is there anything I can do?"

Jeanne smiled. "That's why I'm here, Sadie. I know this is short notice, but I'll be in Fort Collins for the next month or so while Mom recovers. I was hoping you could take over for me as the director of the Founder's Day Picnic."

Sadie blinked. She'd momentarily forgotten about Jeanne's role as the director this year. It was a big job, but someone with Jeanne's skills for event planning had been the perfect choice. "Of course," she said. "I'll be happy to do it."

"I know it's a lot to ask," Jeanne said, looking visibly relieved, "but most of the planning is already done. You've been involved in putting together the picnic before, so I thought you'd be the perfect choice."

Sadie smiled. "I won't be able to replace you, but I promise to do my best."

"I know you will," Jeanne said with a smile. She reached into her black tote bag and pulled out a blue binder. "You'll find everything you need to know in here, but please don't hesitate to contact me if you have any questions."

Sadie reached over to take the binder from her, impressed by its thickness. "Wow, it looks like you have everything covered."

Jeanne winced. "Well, not quite. I'm afraid the entertainment I'd booked called me yesterday to cancel. I can try to find someone from Fort Collins . . ."

"Nonsense," Sadie told her. "All you need to worry about is taking care of your mother. I'm sure I can find some entertainment for the picnic. Did you have anything specific in mind? Music? A play?"

"Well, I had planned on a barbershop quartet singing popular songs from the boomtown years, but since that fell through I'll leave the choice up to you."

"That's fine. I may even recruit Roz to help me out."

"Good idea." Jeanne smiled. "You two make a great team." Then she glanced at her watch. "Well, I'd better get going. I have a long drive ahead."

"Are you sure you'll be all right?"

Jeanne nodded. "Don't worry about me. I have an Agatha Christie book on CD that should last me the length of the drive. And I'm sure Don will call two or three times just to check on me."

Sadie walked her to the door, Hank on their heels, and bid Jeanne good-bye.

When Sadie turned around, she saw Laura emerging from the hallway.

Laura walked into the living room, a contrite expression on her face. "I'm so embarrassed. I can only imagine what you must think of me."

"Let's sit down and talk," Sadie said gently, leading Laura to the leather chair that Jeanne had just vacated. Then she resumed her seat. "You're truly frightened of him, aren't you?"

Laura hesitated for a long moment, as if searching for the right words. "Ray's never laid a hand on me. He just has a way of making me . . . doubt myself." Her mouth curved into a bemused smile. "That sounds so silly when I say it out loud. But it's like I have to prove myself to him over and over again. And the worst part is that somewhere deep inside, I think that he's right and I'm wrong."

"But you know that can't be true," Sadie said, trying to understand. She and T.R. had enjoyed such a loving, honest relationship. A country lawyer, T.R. had had a big heart and a gentle nature. He'd often barter his services with those in need, or offer them pro bono. Naturally, they'd had disagreements now and then, like all married couples. But they'd been each other's best friend throughout their marriage and he'd always treated her with respect.

"I know." Laura shook her head. "Believe me, I don't have these kinds of doubts in my career. I know what to do and I trust my instincts. I just can't seem to do the same with the men in my life."

"Maybe you just need some time away from him. How long are you planning to stay in Colorado?"

"I'm not sure. I bought a one-way ticket out here because I wanted time to do more genealogy research—and to meet you and other family members, of course."

"That sounds like a wonderful idea. Maybe some distance from Ray will give you clarity."

"Maybe," Laura said, dropping her shoulders. "Only, I know that if he showed up in Breckenridge and asked me to return to Boston with him, I would go. It's like I'm afraid of *myself* almost as much as him." She sighed. "That sounds so pathetic, doesn't it?"

Sadie's heart went out to the woman. Laura reminded her of a small, wounded bird, unable to fly and needing time to heal so she could find her wings again.

"I have an idea," Sadie said at last. "Why don't you stay in Silver Peak for a while?"

Laura fidgeted in her seat. "I don't know if that's a good idea." Then she looked up at Sadie. "Maybe I could stay for a few days. Is there a good bed-and-breakfast you can recommend?"

"I recommend Sadie's old homestead," she said with a grin. "I've got plenty of room and that would give us a chance to get to know each other."

Laura's eyes widened. "Oh, you can't mean it?"

"Why can't I?" Her protective instincts had kicked in, and although she wasn't convinced that Laura was telling her the whole story, she sensed that Laura wasn't a danger to her either. "There's nothing like the peace and quiet out here. I think you'll love it."

"I know I would," Laura said, her thoughtful expression conveying both hope and doubt. "But to intrude on you like this . . ."

"It's already settled," Sadie told her. Laura needed time to find her confidence again and learn to trust herself. Sadie was ready to give her that time.

"If you're sure . . ."

"Absolutely. At least this way, if Ray shows up, he won't know where you're staying. That will give you time to decide what you want to do with your life."

Laura gave a shaky nod. "All right. I accept your kind invitation. And I'm happy to pay for my own food and such."

"Room and board are free at the old homestead. Besides, we're family." Sadie closely watched Laura's face, looking for any indication that the family part wasn't true, but all she saw was relief.

"My bag is in the rental car," Laura said, rising to her feet. "I'll bring it in."

"Good idea." Sadie stood up. "I'll make sure your room is ready. Just bring your bag upstairs and I'll give you a tour of the second floor."

The two women parted, Laura heading outside with Hank while Sadie made her way to the stairs. The second floor of the house had four bedrooms, including the one belonging to Sadie. Her bedroom had a fireplace, thanks to the second stone chimney that had been built to support the coal oven in the kitchen below.

The other bedrooms had each been decorated with a certain theme in mind. One bedroom featured cowgirl décor, another had an evergreen theme, and the third had a mountain theme. She'd had fun finding antiques to fit the style of each room and still looked for knickknacks and other theme-inspired accessories. She wondered which bedroom Laura would choose.

A few minutes later, Laura appeared in the second-floor hallway, slightly out of breath. "I thought I was in better shape."

Sadie smiled. "Don't worry, it's probably the high elevation. It takes a while to get used to it."

"So where do you want me?" Laura asked, suitcase in hand.

"You have three rooms to choose from." Sadie walked to the first room. "Here's door number one."

Laura smiled as she looked inside the evergreen room, her gaze moving over the dark green quilt and window coverings to the pine dresser adorned with an antique basket of pinecones in the center. A large window looked over the tree-lined driveway. Sadie had even placed a pencil tree in one corner and decorated it with small ornamental birds and nests. "This is lovely," Laura said, looking over at Sadie. "You're so creative."

"Julie, my employee, inspires me," Sadie confessed. "She loves to rearrange the shop and try new paint colors on the walls. I've gotten so many good ideas from her."

"I look forward to meeting her," Laura said as Hank poked his furry head inside the bedroom door.

Sadie nudged past him as she headed back into the hallway. "I have two other rooms to show you." She led Laura to the second bedroom. "Here's door number two. If you like cowgirls, this is the place for you."

Laura laughed as she walked inside the bedroom. A hitching post served as a coatrack, complete with a white straw cowboy hat hung from the top of it. The western-style room had a definite feminine touch about it, from the frilly calico skirt on the vintage vanity table to the blue-and-white checked bed quilt appliquéd with horseshoes and stars. The view overlooked a grassy meadow to the south of the house, where Milo sometimes let the horses graze.

"And on to door number three." Sadie opened the door to the third bedroom, revealing the breathtaking view of the majestic Rocky Mountains. A portrait of Pikes Peak, in an antique frame, hung above the four-poster bed, covered with a log cabin quilt that had been pieced and hand-quilted by Sadie's mother. A small antique bookshelf contained mountain-themed books, many of them original editions, such as *Heidi*, *Rocky Mountain Man*, *Into the Wild*, and *The Big Sky*. On the dresser stood a framed photograph of Alice and her kids skiing in Breckenridge.

"They're all so unique," Laura said, "and have such beautiful views."

Sadie smiled, feeling a little like a game show host. "So which door do you choose? And don't worry, there won't be any zonks."

Laura smiled as she considered her choices. After a long moment, she set her suitcase down on the wide-planked pine floor. "Door number three. I love this room, especially the view of the mountains. They make me feel so peaceful."

"I'm glad you like it. You'll find your bathroom just down the hall, and there are extra quilts in the closet in case you get cold during the night." She stepped into the hallway and pointed to the other end. "My room is down there if you need me."

Laura stood on the threshold of the mountain room and then suddenly reached out and gave Sadie a hug. "Thank you," she whispered, her voice shaking a little.

Sadie gave her a warm squeeze. "You're welcome."

———

The next morning, Sadie and Laura both drove their cars into town. They ate breakfast at Arbuckle's, where Sadie introduced Laura to Luz and Hector. She didn't mention their possible family relationship or the fact that Laura was staying with her, wanting to keep that knowledge to just a select number of people. They each ordered coffee and made their way outside.

"Are you still up for a tour of the town?" Sadie asked. Earlier that morning, Laura had wanted directions to the library, where she intended to do some work on her laptop. Sadie had offered to let Laura work at the house and had even given her a spare house key, but Laura had said she was used to the hustle and bustle of a big city and often worked at the library near her home.

"I am," Laura said, "if you're sure you have time."

"I do," Sadie assured her, walking to her Tahoe. "The shop isn't due to open for another hour and neither is the library. So hop in."

Laura made her way to the front passenger door and climbed inside, setting her coffee cup in the double cup holder between them. "This place is amazing. I feel a bit like I've stepped into the old west. I love how most of the buildings on Main Street are made of brick and many of them look like they've been here awhile."

"Oh, they certainly have. The street we're driving on now used to be a dirt road. In fact, I have an old photograph of Main Street when it was full of horses and buggies. Some of the horses were even parked in front of storefronts, their reins attached to the hitching post or rail."

"That's easy to imagine in a place like this." Laura settled back onto the leather car seat with a contented sigh. "I like to think about Nana living here as a young girl." Laura pointed to the brick buildings across the street from the Antique Mine. "Maybe she walked inside that bank or attended a musical concert in that opera house."

"I'm sure she probably did," Sadie replied, looking at her own shop, tucked between Arbuckle's Coffee Shop and Roscoe's hardware store, which he'd named Putnam and Sons. "She may have even been in my building, since it's as old as the bank and the opera house. I believe it was a dressmaker's shop at one time, although some of the old town records are a little fuzzy."

Laura leaned forward to peer through the windshield. "It looks like most of these buildings have more than one floor."

"Most of them have three floors, including mine. I rent out the upper two floors, one to an insurance agent and the top floor is a residential apartment, although it's currently empty."

"That's nice." Laura picked up her coffee and took a sip. "Does the building take a lot of upkeep?"

Sadie smiled. "Old buildings always do. But as long as you stay on top of repairs, it's not too bad. And there's something special about all the history here that makes people want to preserve it."

Sadie began to drive slowly down Main Street, which ran east and west, pointing out various buildings and businesses, including the only grocery store in town called The Market and Los Pollitos, a family-run Mexican restaurant.

"I love Mexican food," Laura stated.

"So do I." Sadie pointed to a building across the street. "And that's ABC Pharmacy, which carries almost everything a person might need, including rattlesnake antivenin."

Laura gulped. "There are rattlesnakes here?"

Sadie smiled. "Yes, but you'll seldom see one. They don't like us any more than we like them."

"I could go my entire life without seeing a rattlesnake."

"Don't worry, I can't remember the last time someone around here needed rattlesnake antivenin. But at least it's there if we need it."

Laura's face relaxed into a smile. "I guess that's a good thing."

Sadie drove along Water Street and Lincoln Street, as well as the five avenues named after the first five presidents, Washington, Adams, Jefferson, Madison, and Monroe.

"Is that a working water tower?" Laura asked, pointing to the west side of town. The tall tower had the words *Silver Peak* painted on it, along with a sign that proclaimed the town as the home of the 1953 state basketball champions.

"It is," Sadie replied, turning north off of Lincoln Street. "And up here is the old train depot. It's home to an ice cream parlor now and a restaurant called the Depot."

"Aptly named," Laura said with a smile. She watched the passing houses through her passenger window. "There are some lovely homes, aren't there? And so many stately Victorian houses."

"There are some beautiful houses here. We'll have to extend the tour later so I can show you some of the houses that have been here since the silver rush days."

"I'd like that."

Sadie headed back to Main Street, pointing out the library along the way. When they reached the Antique Mine, Laura climbed into her rental car and gave a wave before heading off. Sadie watched her drive away, noting she didn't seem as skittish as she had yesterday.

Had it all just been a ruse?

Sadie shook that thought from her head and turned around to head to her shop. That was when she saw him.

Wade Marley stood by the locked front door of the Antique Mine with a sour expression on his face and one cowboy boot tapping impatiently on the sidewalk. Sadie was surprised to see the fifty-year-old Marley in front of her shop, considering he'd never even stepped inside before.

"There you are." Wade's dark brows pressed down in a fierce scowl. "We need to talk."

7

———

WADE MARLEY CONSIDERED HIMSELF A BIG MAN AROUND TOWN. He owned several rental properties, including vacation cabins and resorts in and around Silver Peak. Twice married and divorced, Wade could be cordial although Sadie had never experienced that side of him herself.

Judging by the expression on his face as she approached him, today wasn't going to be any different.

"About time," he said, his green eyes narrowing. "I have an important meeting soon and don't have time to waste."

"You're the one who wants to talk," Sadie said, keeping her voice cool but polite. "So go right ahead. I'm listening."

"You must know why I'm here."

"I haven't a clue," she said, reaching into her purse for her shop key and then opening the door. "Why don't we go inside? Then you can tell me why you're here."

He hesitated a moment and then followed her into the shop, his black cowboy boots clomping on the pine floor.

Sadie walked to the mahogany desk, circling behind it before turning to face him.

"I'm here for the wedding dress," Wade said bluntly.

Sadie stared at him, trying not to show how startled she was at the request. "What wedding dress?"

One corner of his mouth tipped up in a skeptical smile. "You know exactly what wedding dress. The one that your great-aunt absconded with when she ran out on her own wedding."

Sadie shuffled some papers in front of her, momentarily at a loss for words. *How in the world did Wade know that she'd found a wedding dress? And that it might belong to Rachel Wright?*

"That dress," Wade continued, "and anything else you found with it belongs to the Marley family, so I'm here to lay claim to it."

She looked up at him and smiled at his audacity. "That wedding dress belonged to Rachel Wright and her mother before her. The Marleys have absolutely no claim to it."

"Not according to the law books I've read," Wade countered. "Rachel Wright broke the marriage contract that would have transferred all her property to her husband. That contract did not become null and void just because she got cold feet. The laws were different back then. Women couldn't just run off on a whim."

She stared at him for a long moment, struck by the cold way he talked about a teenage girl who had chosen death over marriage to a man she didn't love. At least, according to everyone except Laura Finch. But surely Wade didn't know Laura or about her version of the story of the runaway bride.

Or did he?

Sadie wasn't sure whom to trust and, for that reason, she planned to give him as little information as possible. She was certain that he was wrong about the law. In her experience, Wade tended to leap first and look later. But he possessed enough bluster to often get away with his bully tactics.

"I don't have the dress," Sadie said calmly.

"I don't believe you."

"It's the truth." As far as she knew, the dress was now on its way to a DNA lab in Denver. "But even if I did have it, I wouldn't give it to you. You have no claim to it."

"Look, Sadie," Wade said, his expression relaxing. "I have no beef with you. I'm just trying to do what's fair."

Sadie searched his face, trying to determine if he knew about the brass key and if he suspected it was with the dress. "I don't have a beef with you either, Wade. But I don't have the dress."

A muscle flexed in his jaw. "The Marleys are owed restitution, even after all these years. I'd hoped you would see that, Sadie, since you're known for your fairness around town. It's time to settle this unpleasantness between our families once and for all."

"I have nothing against you or any other Marley," Sadie said honestly. "All of that is in the past. But that doesn't mean I'll hand over something that doesn't belong to you."

"You should know that I don't back down easily," Wade warned and walked toward the door. He opened it, then glanced at her over his shoulder. "And I'm not about to back down now."

Sadie watched the door close behind him and then released a breath she hadn't realized she was holding. Wade might not be the most pleasant person she'd ever met, but today he was downright nasty.

He had to want more than an antique wedding dress, that much was clear. Sadie was almost certain that he wanted the treasure connected to it—especially those valuable stock certificates that had vanished the same day as Rachel. But none of the folk-lore about the runaway bride had ever mentioned a key. Did Wade know about it or was he hoping the dress itself would lead to the treasure somehow?

The front door opened again and Sadie steeled herself, assuming Wade was coming back inside to argue his case again. Instead, Roz appeared on the threshold.

"I just saw Wade leaving and he looked as mad as a wet hen." Roz hurried toward the desk. "What was that all about?"

"*Wet hen* is an apt description," Sadie said with a wry smile. "I think he's trying to play a game of chicken with me, crowing about his family's legal right to Rachel's wedding dress."

Roz's mouth gaped. "How does he know you found it?"

"He didn't tell me and I didn't ask, although I probably should have. But he's not one to reveal his sources—especially to a member of the Wright family."

Roz shook her head. "The Marley and Wright feud is almost as bad as the Hatfields and McCoys. You'd think after all of these years, the dust would have settled."

"Not when there's money involved," Sadie said with a sigh. "I don't care about the stock certificates or the money connected to them. I just want to know the truth about what really happened to Rachel." She met Roz's gaze. "I was going to call you this morning about the latest twist in the story. And when I say twist, I mean a real shocker."

Roz leaned on the counter, her eyes wide with anticipation. "What is it?"

"A woman showed up in my shop yesterday." Sadie told her about Laura and her claim that Rachel had faked her own death and escaped to start a new life in Boston. By the time she was finished, Roz's mouth gaped open.

"Did you just say that you're letting this woman stay at your house?" Roz asked.

"Yes. It just felt like the right thing to do under the circumstances."

"But she's a complete stranger—and her timing is suspicious to say the least! You find the wedding dress on Monday and she shows up the next day?"

"I know," Sadie agreed. "Just like Wade's timing. Somehow, the word is out about the wedding dress. I just want to know who's been talking about it."

"Maybe Edwin let something slip," Roz suggested.

"Maybe," she mused, "although that doesn't seem like the Edwin I used to know."

Roz smiled. "I saw him at the Market yesterday. He's as handsome as ever. Very distinguished."

Sadie nodded. "It was so nice to see him again. And even nicer for him to call me when he found the wedding dress in his attic." She shook her head. "I just don't see Edwin telling anyone about it."

"Well, someone talked. And you know how rumors fly in Silver Peak."

Sadie snapped her fingers. "*The Chatterbox*! That's how rumors fly around here."

"You're right," Roz said as Sadie moved to her computer and turned it on. "I haven't read it for a while. Have you?"

"Not for a couple of weeks." Sadie sat down in front of the computer. The local blog didn't follow any type of schedule. A new post could appear any day of the week. Sometimes a week or more went by before a new blog post appeared.

When the computer was warmed up, Sadie clicked on the Internet and then quickly typed the blog name into the address bar. Roz rounded the desk and stood behind Sadie's chair. A moment later, the *Chatterbox* blog appeared on the screen.

"Here it is," Sadie said, finding the most recent post. She began to read it out loud.

> *Edwin Marshall has moved back to Silver Peak after a pres-*
> *tigious career in Chicago as a circuit court judge. He will*
> *be living in the stately Victorian home that has been in his*
> *family for three generations. A surprise awaited him on his*
> *arrival in the form of a wedding dress. And not just any*
> *wedding dress, dear readers, but that belonging to Silver*
> *Peak's legendary runaway bride, Rachel Wright, circa 1897.*
> *And guess what Antique Lady was seen carrying out of*
> *the Marshall house? A dress box! The scandal that rocked*
> *Silver Peak over one hundred years ago may have a sequel.*
> *Stay tuned to this blog for more information.*
>
> *Yours truly,*
> *The Chatterbox*

"Now we know how Wade found out about the dress," Roz said, "and why he thinks you have it. But how did the *Chatterbox* learn of it?"

"I wish I knew." The identity of the *Chatterbox* writer was one of the biggest secrets in Silver Peak. People had speculated, of course, but no one had come close to solving that mystery. Sadie closed the Web page and then stood up and faced Roz. "As long as the *Chatterbox* writer remains anonymous, we'll have to start from square one."

Roz's brow furrowed. "What's square one?"

"Find out who's spreading the news about the wedding dress—and why," Sadie said resolutely. "It was posted on Monday, which means it's possible Laura saw it too, and that's what brought her here. She did mention Rachel's wedding dress two times yesterday."

"What did you tell her about it?"

"Nothing," Sadie said. "I want to wait for the results of the DNA test before I reveal that I found the dress. And while I wait, I verify Laura's identity and find out who else knows about the dress besides you, Alice, and Edwin."

"What difference does it make now? The news is already out there."

"Because it might help me prove the dress is a hoax. The same person who spread the news about the wedding dress might have planted it in Edwin's attic—either as a prank or with some nefarious purpose in mind."

"But nobody knows the identity of the *Chatterbox*," Roz reminded her. "So the author of the blog must have heard it through the grapevine, since that seems to be the blog's usual source of information."

Sadie met her gaze. "It sure is funny how life can change in less than forty-eight hours. Edwin's back in town, a long-lost cousin arrives and announces that Great-aunt Rachel didn't die at sixteen but lived in Boston and had a family there."

"And now," Roz added, "Wade is trying to ramp up the feud between the Marleys and the Wrights again."

Sadie grew thoughtful, gazing down at her bare ring finger. She used to gently turn her wedding band in circles whenever she was deep in thought. Now her ring finger looked so bare. That had changed in the last forty-eight hours too, and so much had happened that she'd had little time to do a thorough search for her lost ring.

"Ring still missing?" Roz asked, watching her.

Sadie sighed. "Yes. I'm ashamed to say I've forgotten about it a time or two with everything else that's been going on."

"There's nothing to be ashamed about," Roz told her. "T.R.'s been gone for a while now, Sadie. He wouldn't want you to hang on to the past. Maybe it was time to take the ring off."

Sadie looked up at her, a little surprised by her words. "I've never even thought about taking it off permanently." She stared down at her hand again. "And I really can't make that kind of decision now—not with everything else going on. I'll find my ring eventually, I'm sure of it."

"I'm sure you will too," Roz said with a sympathetic smile. "It was just some food for thought."

Sadie chuckled. "I've had so much food for thought lately that I feel like my brain needs an antacid."

"And yet," Roz said, a twinkle in her eye, "I think you're rather enjoying the mystery of it all."

"Okay, I'll admit it," Sadie said, grinning. "I *am* enjoying it. I have a historical mystery right in front of me and I'm itching to solve it."

"And how do you plan to do that?"

Sadie pondered the question for a moment. "I guess the first step is to find some more clues. Maybe I'll start with Edwin. He mentioned something the other day about meeting together for coffee."

"Is Julie working today?"

"She's coming in this afternoon."

Roz nodded. "That's perfect. Give Edwin a call and set up a meeting this afternoon."

"Maybe I will," Sadie mused. Then another thought occurred to her. "I almost forgot! Jeanne Sweeting stopped by last night on her way to Fort Collins to take care of her mother, who is in the hospital with a broken hip."

"Oh dear. That's too bad."

"Jeanne asked me to take over as the director of the Founder's Day Picnic. She's done most of the work already, but I still need to find the entertainment."

"Wow," Roz said, chuckling. "You really do have a full plate."

"I sure do. That's why I'd like your help. We can even be codirectors, if you're willing."

Roz gave her a mock salute. "Ready, willing, and able!"

"Perfect," Sadie said, reaching into her purse. "I made a copy of the to-do list that Jeanne wrote for me. I thought we could split it up."

Roz laughed. "You were pretty certain I'd agree to act as codirector, weren't you?"

"Well, I have known you since kindergarten. You always wanted to be the leader for the day back then. And if the shoe still fits . . ."

"I wore those black-and-white saddle shoes in kindergarten." Then Roz picked up one foot and lifted the pant leg of her bell-bottom jeans to display a golden brown Birkenstock sandal. "I've got fancier—and more comfortable—footwear these days."

"You sure do," Sadie agreed. "Nice sandals, by the way."

"Thanks. Sandal season is almost over, so I'm enjoying them while I can." Then she held out one hand. "Now give me my list. I've got some leading to do."

Sadie handed her the to-do list. "This could be fun."

"It will be fun," Roz insisted as she moved toward the door. "We'll make it the best Founder's Day Picnic yet."

Then she turned to look at Sadie. "Let me know what happens with Edwin."

Sadie nodded. "You can count on it."

After Roz left, Sadie stayed on the computer and searched for information about Laura Finch. She found confirmation that a Laura Finch lived in Boston and worked in public relations. She even found a photograph of Laura with a candidate who had won his election to the county treasurer's office. Everything Sadie found about Laura matched what the woman had told her—except her engagement to Ray Johnson. None of the Web articles Sadie found about Laura mentioned Ray Johnson. Sadie even searched some recent election results, but many of the candidates were listed only by surname, including several Johnsons. Besides, Laura had told Sadie that she'd met Ray through a campaign, not specifically that he was a candidate, so that could be a dead end too.

At least she knew now that Laura had told her some truths— even if she still couldn't completely trust her.

———————

Later that afternoon, Sadie left the Antique Mine in Julie's capable hands and walked over to Arbuckle's Coffee Shop. Edwin was already there, seated at a table next to a window. A few other patrons were seated in the shop, chatting quietly or working on laptops, but none sat close enough to overhear their conversation.

Edwin looked up and smiled as Sadie approached the table. "You're early."

"So are you," Sadie said, pulling out a chair to sit down. "Have you ordered yet?"

"No, I wanted to wait for you. Even though I was born and raised here, Arbuckle's is new to me. So tell me what's good here."

"Everything on the menu," Sadie answered honestly. "I probably drink more coffee than is good for me, but Luz and Hector make the best brew in town."

"Sold," he said with a smile, rising to his feet. "Two coffees? Anything else?"

"You have to try one of Luz's pastries." Sadie looked over at the glass display case.

"Can I get one for you too? As I remember, you used to have quite a sweet tooth."

"I still do," she replied, impressed with his good memory. "Why don't we split one?"

"Perfect," he said with a smile. "Which one would you like?"

"Surprise me," she said, feeling playful.

His smile widened into a grin. "One coffee and one surprise, coming right up."

Sadie watched him approach the counter and engage in conversation with Luz. It only took a few moments before Luz was chuckling with him about something and engaging in an animated conversation.

Edwin had always connected well with people, Sadie thought to herself. That was what had made him so popular in high school. He hadn't lost his disarming charm with the passage of time.

Soon Edwin returned to the table with their order. "One coffee," he said, placing a cup in front of her. Then he grinned. "And one cherry turnover."

"You remembered!" Sadie exclaimed, as he placed the plate containing the flaky pastry in the center of the table.

He chuckled. "I knew you were testing me the moment I saw the cherry turnovers. And it looks like I passed the test."

"With flying colors," Sadie said, picking up a knife and slicing the cherry turnover in two.

Edwin picked up his fork and dug into his half of the turnover, then took a bite. "Mmm. This is incredible."

"And addictive," she warned as she picked up her fork, "but so worth it."

"So what else is new in Silver Peak?"

It was the perfect opening, so Sadie decided to take it. "Well, we've kept up with all the new technology. Silver Peak even has its own blog called the *Chatterbox*. Have you heard of it?"

"No," he said, his blue eyes inquisitive. "Who writes it?"

"Nobody knows. The author is anonymous, but seems to know almost everything that happens in and around town."

He cocked a wiry silver brow. "Intriguing."

"And a little vexing at times, because it veers into a gossip column and the rumors aren't always true." She took a sip of her coffee. "Although, the blog's latest post mentioned your return to Silver Peak and the discovery of a bloody wedding dress."

He stared at her for a long moment. "How did they find out about the dress?"

"I have no idea and because the author of the blog is anonymous, I can't even ask her or him. That's why I said it can be vexing."

"I haven't breathed a word about finding that wedding dress." He set down his coffee, his brow furrowed. "But someone had been in the house before I arrived and may have seen it."

Sadie leaned forward in her chair. "Who?"

"A housekeeper I hired to get the house ready before I moved back. Her name is Miranda Rhodes."

Sadie nodded. "Yes, I know her." Miranda was in her mid-thirties and had her own cleaning business. "If she saw the dress, she might have mentioned it to someone. And that person might have mentioned it to someone, and so on, until the author of the blog heard the news."

Edwin nodded. "I did ask Miranda to check out the attic for me and see if there was furniture up there I might be able to use. She didn't mention finding the wedding dress specifically, but she did say there were some trunks with clothes in them."

Before Sadie could reply, Luz approached their table with a coffeepot in her hand.

"Are you two ready for a refill?" Luz asked.

Edwin smiled up at her. "I sure am."

"Me too."

As Luz refilled Sadie's cup, she said, "You'll never guess who was in here earlier."

"Who?" Sadie asked.

"A travel writer named Lance Ely. He's doing a piece on Silver Peak and plans to stay through the Founder's Day Picnic."

"I've heard of him," Edwin said. "His travel articles have appeared in several prominent newspapers and magazines."

"He's handsome too," Luz said, her eyes twinkling, "and full of questions about Silver Peak."

"So he's mining for information," Sadie joked. "Sounds like he's come to the right place."

"He sure has," Luz said, laughing as she turned and walked away to attend to the other customers.

"I remember reading a wonderful article about Munich a few years ago that had been written by Ely," Edwin said. "It sounded so appealing that my wife and I made a trip there."

"So you two liked to travel?"

"We loved it." Edwin began talking about his wife and the times they spent together, sharing funny stories and poignant memories.

Sadie enjoyed hearing about his life and the affectionate way he spoke of his late wife. "And now you've come back to where you started."

Edwin nodded. "Full circle. Silver Peak gave me such a wonderful start in life. I'd really like an opportunity to give something back."

"I'm sure you'll have plenty of opportunities once you get settled."

"Enough about me," Edwin said with a smile. "Tell me about you."

Sadie shared parts of her life, and the wonderful memories she'd made with T.R. They chatted about old classmates and friends. Then she told him about Laura and the revelation that Rachel Wright might not have died on her wedding day. They discussed the logistics of how Rachel might have escaped from Colorado unnoticed, and Edwin laid out some scenarios that seemed plausible.

Before Sadie realized it, almost two hours had flown by.

"Time for me to go," she said, suddenly aware of the time. "How much do I owe you?"

"Not a penny."

She smiled. "I'm the one who invited you for coffee, remember?"

"And I enjoyed every minute of it. You can treat next time."

Next time. The way he said the words caused a shiver of anticipation to run through her.

"Deal," she said, rising to her feet. "You should stop by my shop sometime soon."

"I will," he promised, "but it's too soon to closing time today and you have a houseguest to entertain. So I'll stop in when we have more time."

Edwin walked her to the door, where they lingered over their good-byes before parting ways. Sadie turned toward her shop, feeling like a schoolgirl. Talking with Edwin had taken her back to the days when they could practically read each other's minds. She'd always considered him a good friend but never expected butterflies, of all things, to return.

The autumn breeze cooled her cheeks as she walked the short distance to her shop, and she tried to turn her focus to Miranda's foray into the Marshall attic. *Perhaps Miranda herself was the author of the* Chatterbox, she thought to herself. After all, a housekeeper did have access into the nooks and crannies of a person's life. She chuckled. Wouldn't it be nice if the mystery of who the *Chatterbox* writer was could be solved that easily? She'd been trying to figure out the voice behind the blog for quite some time now.

Maybe it was time for Sadie to start digging in some nooks and crannies herself.

8

———

When Sadie turned into her driveway that evening, she saw Alice's blue Jeep Cherokee sitting in front of the house. She always loved a visit from her daughter and a surprise visit was even better.

Alice sat in one of Josh's Adirondack chairs on the front porch with a book open in her lap. She looked younger than her forty-one years and was both taller and slimmer than Sadie. Alice's auburn hair and green eyes were both legacies from her father.

Sadie left room for Laura's rental car as she parked next to the Cherokee. She'd stopped at the library on her way home and found Laura working away. Laura told her she'd be on her way as soon as she finished a letter she was composing to one of her clients.

"Hi, Mom," Alice said as Sadie stepped out of her Tahoe.

"Hello there." Sadie joined her on the porch and sat in the matching Adirondack chair. "Reading another mystery, I see."

"I can hardly put it down," Alice said with a smile. From the moment she'd learned to read, Alice always had her nose stuck in a book. Mysteries were her favorite genre. "And you know how much I love reading out here."

"I know." Sadie settled into the chair. "What are the kids doing?"

"Theo's at football practice and Sara's over at Mia's house studying for a science test." Mia Garza was Sara's best friend and they were both at the top of their class in school.

"And I've already finished my study plan for next week," Alice continued, "and picked up groceries, so I thought I could take a little time to relax."

Sadie often wished Alice would carve out more time in her busy schedule for relaxation. Her daughter was always on the go, keeping her house immaculate at the same time she raised two teenagers and taught elementary school full-time. Ever since she was little, Alice had thrived on neatness and organization. Sadie smiled to herself, remembering how Alice's bedroom had usually been the cleanest room in their house.

"What are you smiling about?" Alice asked, setting the book down.

"I was just thinking back to when you were a little girl. Sometimes I miss those days."

Alice stood up and reached out to give Sadie a warm hug.

"Me too. And believe it or not, there are still days when I wish I could climb into your bed and throw the covers over my head." She laughed. "Dad used to tickle me until I'd come out."

Sadie joined in her laughter. "He loved to hear you laugh." She reached out to brush a wisp of silky auburn hair from Alice's forehead. "You do have a lovely laugh, you know. Just like my mom."

"Grandma laughed all the time," Alice said with a wistful smile. She sat back in her chair. "And she was always telling jokes and teasing me about potential boyfriends."

Sadie nodded, missing her mother but treasuring all the warm memories that still lived in her heart. "So are there any potential boyfriends on the horizon?"

Alice smiled, having heard the question before. "No, Mom. I've told you before that I'm not ready to start dating again. Besides, I just don't have time."

"Well, you're still young," Sadie said gently. "There's no reason you can't have some fun once in a while."

"I have a lot of fun," Alice said, holding up her book. "This is fun to me."

Sadie nodded, realizing that her daughter had been gun-shy of men ever since her divorce. She couldn't really blame her, but she still held on to the hope that Alice would fall in love again someday.

But she knew her daughter well enough to change the subject. "So how does Theo like football?"

"He loves it," Alice said. "One of the great things about the kids attending a small high school is that there's not as much competition to make the sports teams. Theo would probably be riding the bench at his old high school in Denver, but it sounds like he'll be a starter for Silver Peak."

"Oh, that's wonderful!"

Alice nodded. "He's thrilled. You know what a big fan he is of the Denver Broncos."

"I do." Sarah chuckled. "He even named his horse Bronco."

"Now it's his turn out on the football field and he loves it. He calls Cliff every night to tell him about their plays and everything he's learned so far."

Sadie had always liked Alice's ex-husband. Cliff worked as a dentist in Denver and Sadie was thankful that he and Alice had maintained a cordial relationship for the sake of the kids. "Will Cliff be able to make it to Theo's games?"

"He'll try, but it depends on his schedule. Will you be there?"

"I wouldn't miss them."

Alice arched a mischievous brow. "And how about your new-found cousin, Laura? Does she like football?"

"I have no idea," Sadie said. "In fact, I decided I want to know a little more about her, so I spent some time today researching her on the Internet."

"And?"

"And, so far, everything she's told me about herself seems to be true. She does work in public relations in Boston and has been involved in political campaigns. I even found a funeral home obituary for Rachel Ellis that matched the one Laura had shown me. I don't know the exact date that my great-aunt was born, but the birth year matched too."

"So you think she's telling the truth?"

Sadie hesitated. "I'm not quite ready to go that far yet. I looked up her fiancé too, Ray Johnson, but there are dozens of men by that name in Massachusetts. And I didn't find any articles or pictures connecting a Ray Johnson with Laura Finch."

Alice's brow crinkled. "Well, that's a little strange. Do you think she made him up?"

"I don't know. It could all be a ruse, I suppose. Her story about Rachel is just so . . . incredible."

"Well, I hope it is true," Alice said. "Imagine a sixteen-year-old girl faking her own death and traveling halfway across the country to start a new life."

Sadie nodded. "Part of me wants it to be true but, if it is, that means our family history is completely different than I've always believed."

Alice smiled. "We may even need a new branch to add to the family tree."

The sound of tires on gravel turned their attention to the driveway. Sadie saw Laura's black sedan making its way toward the house. "Here she is."

Alice sat up expectantly, her eyes on the rental car. A few moments later, Laura climbed out of the car and walked up the porch steps.

"Hi, Laura," Sadie greeted her. "This is my daughter, Alice. Alice, this is Laura Finch."

Alice rose to her feet and held out her hand. "It's so nice to meet you, Laura."

"Thank you," Laura said, shaking her hand. "It's nice to meet you too." Then she tilted her head to one side as she studied Alice's face. "You have Nana's smile."

Delight lit Alice's green eyes. "I do?"

Sadie watched Laura nod enthusiastically, feeling a little disconcerted by the conversation. Was Laura pushing the family connection too much?

"You do," Laura said, answering Alice's question. "Isn't it funny how certain traits are passed down through the generations?"

"I'd love to see a picture of her," Alice said.

Sadie rose to her feet and headed for the door. "Well, come on inside. Laura brought some photographs with her."

"I sure did." Laura followed them into the house. "And your mom has shared photos of you and your kids, as well as other family members."

Sadie closed the front door behind them as Alice and Laura greeted Hank. "Laura even talked me into digging out my old high school yearbook."

Alice laughed. "You love looking at your yearbook, Mom. Admit it."

"Okay, so she didn't have to twist my arm," Sadie admitted. "I do like reminiscing every once in a while. And speaking of reminiscing about the past, will you and the kids be at the Founder's Day Picnic?"

"We wouldn't miss it. Sara and Mia are planning to dress up as pioneer girls."

Sadie sat down on the sofa as Laura and Alice each took a chair. "Are you making their costumes?"

Alice shook her head. "Not this time. Mia's grandmother, Isabel, is making both of them. She's an excellent seamstress, so I'm sure they'll look great."

Laura leaned back in her chair. "Tell me more about this Founder's Day Picnic. Is it an annual event?"

"Yes," Sadie replied. "William Tate and his wife, Antonia, settled here at the start of the silver rush in 1878. They were instrumental in building the town and making it thrive. So we celebrate every fall with a picnic to reminisce about that era and the history of the town." Then she turned to her daughter. "By the way, Jeanne Sweeting asked me to take over as the picnic director this year."

"I saw Pastor Don in passing yesterday," Alice said, "and he mentioned that Jeanne was going to be in Fort Collins for a few weeks to take care of her mother. But I had no idea she'd recruited you to take over as the director."

"Roz has agreed to help me," Sadie told her. "And really, Jeanne's done most of the work already, but I do have to find someone to provide the entertainment."

"Too bad William and Antonia aren't still around," Alice said wryly. "They could give a firsthand account of all the hard work that goes into building a town."

Sadie sat up on the sofa. "That's a great idea!"

"Mom, I was just joking."

"I know," Sadie replied, "but we could have someone do an historical reenactment."

"But who could you find to do it at this late date?" Alice asked.

"Alfred Daly." Sadie turned to Laura. "He's a professor of American History at Colorado Mountain College in Breckenridge and has been a wonderful mentor for me, as well as a dear friend." Sadie both respected and trusted Alfred, a man who loved history as much as she did. She reached into her pocket for her cell phone. "I'm going to give him a call right now."

———

The next day, Sadie knocked on Professor Daly's office door.

"Come in," he called out.

She walked through the door and saw him seated at his desk, his back to her as he typed on his computer. The sixty-year-old professor peered intently at the screen through his silver wire-rimmed glasses. Then he mumbled something under his breath as he raked a hand through his wavy white hair.

Sadie cleared her throat. "I'm here to plead my case, professor."

He twirled around in his office chair. "Sadie!" He grinned as he stood up and walked over to greet her. "Just the woman I wanted to see."

She laughed. "That's not the greeting I expected. Especially when you turned me down last night."

"Your phone call caught me off guard," he confessed, ushering her over to a padded chair next to his desk. "I'd just awoken from a nap, so my brain was a little foggy." He chuckled. "Although, my wife claims my brain is always a little foggy."

Sadie enjoyed spending time with both Alfred and his wife, Cecile. They were both bright, witty people. Alfred was one of the smartest men she knew—and one of the most entertaining. "Does that mean you've changed your mind about the reenactment?"

He pointed to his computer. "I've been researching William Tate all morning. He was a fascinating man."

"And since you're fascinating, as well, you'd be the perfect man to play him."

He held up both hands, chuckling at her enthusiasm. "No need to butter me up, Sadie. I'll do it."

She clapped her hands in delight. "Wonderful!"

"I've already gathered some good material. Is there anything specific you'd like me to focus on?"

She reached into her purse and drew out a sheaf of paper. "I put together a few scenarios last night, just in case you changed your mind."

He laughed. "You know me too well." He took the papers from her and studied them, nodding thoughtfully as his gaze moved over the pages. "Yes, I like this. I think it will fit well with the sketch I had in mind." Then he lowered the papers, his gaze fixed on Sadie. "There's only one problem."

"What's that?"

"I think we need someone to play Antonia. I considered doing a monologue, but a reenactment with both of Silver Peak's founders will not only be more authentic but more interesting for the audience."

"Everything I've read about Antonia portrays her as a very strong, equal partner with her husband," Sadie said, liking the idea. "She's the one who insisted that the town needed a church and a school before anything else."

Alfred nodded. "She sounds like a real firecracker."

"Speaking of firecrackers," Sadie said with a smile. "How about Cecile? She'd make a great Antonia."

He shook his head. "No, I've already asked her. She says her voice just isn't strong enough anymore for that type of performance."

Sadie considered other possibilities, knowing it wouldn't be easy to find someone on such short notice.

"How about you?" Alfred asked, his eyes twinkling. "You know more about the history of Silver Peak than anyone I know."

"It's tempting," she said. "But I just don't think I'll have time in addition to my director duties. But I wonder if Roz will do it."

"Roz Putnam?" He nodded in recognition, having met her a few times over the years. "She has a strong voice."

"And she used to act in several community plays when she was younger. I bet I could talk her into it."

"It's one of the things you do best." Alfred rubbed his hands together. "This should be a lot of fun."

"It will," Sadie agreed. "I'm glad I made the trip to Breckenridge to talk to you in person."

"I am too. It's been awhile since I've seen you. What's new in your life?"

"I'm not sure where to start," Sadie said. Then she told him about Edwin's arrival back in town and the discovery of the antique wedding dress.

He whistled low when she finished the long story. "Wow, it sounds like you have a real-life drama on your hands."

She smiled. "I think it falls under the category of truth is stranger than fiction. Unless it's all fiction." She reached into her purse again and pulled out the brass key she'd found with the wedding dress. "There's something I want to show you."

Sadie handed him the antique key and watched him examine it. "I found it with the dress—actually in an envelope with a letter from my grandpa Jacob to his best friend, James Marshall."

"Did the letter say anything about this key?"

"No. Grandpa Jacob asked James to keep the dress and the revolver, which was also in the box, until he returned to Silver Peak."

Alfred retrieved a ruler from his desk and measured the key. "It looks like it's meant to fit a lockbox of some sort."

"That's what I thought. There was some jewelry and several stock certificates stolen the same day my great-aunt disappeared. I suppose it's possible the key might lead to those items."

He picked up the cell phone on his desk and took a picture of the key. "Let me do some research and see what I can find out."

"Thank you," she said. "I'm not sure it will lead anywhere, but I'd like to satisfy my curiosity."

"You've got quite the mystery on your hands." He smiled, giving her back the key. "I rather envy you."

She chuckled as she placed the key in her purse. "I'll let you know how it turns out."

"Please do."

They chatted for a few more minutes before Sadie stood up to take her leave. "Thanks again, Alfred, for agreeing to perform the historical reenactment. You really saved me."

"It's my pleasure. I'll start writing the script right away." He turned back to his computer. "Shoot me an e-mail if you have any more ideas."

"I will. And we'll probably need a rehearsal or two before the performance, so I'll be in touch soon."

"I can't wait," he said, already immersed in his typing again.

Sadie smiled to herself as she walked out of his office. When Alfred committed to something, he gave one hundred and ten percent. The residents of Silver Peak were in for a treat.

Now she just had to convince Roz to play the part of Antonia.

Sadie almost called Roz on her trip back from Breckenridge, then decided to wait and have the conversation in person. Lately, Roz seemed to get so distracted on the phone that she'd sometimes lose track of the conversation. Sadie suspected Roz might be watching one of her favorite television shows during their talks, so now she preferred to discuss important subjects face-to-face.

Sadie enjoyed the scenic, twenty-minute drive from Breckenridge to Silver Peak. Located about one hundred miles west of Denver, Breckenridge was a popular ski resort. As she drove, she could see the ski trails on the pine-covered mountains with a backdrop of clear blue sky. The rushing waters of the crystal-clear creeks were a frequent destination of whitewater rafters. She passed historic towns and old gold and silver mines, and glimpsed a young moose and other wildlife along the way.

When she reached Silver Peak, Sadie decided to drive home for a quick lunch before heading to the shop for the afternoon. Hank was thrilled to see her in the middle of the day and followed her to the kitchen, where she put together a sandwich of deli ham and sliced Swiss cheese that Laura had purchased at the Market the day before. Then she took her lunch outside to eat on the front porch so Hank could frolic in the evergreen trees before she headed into town.

She set her plate on the table and sat down in an Adirondack chair as Hank scampered off the porch and onto the driveway. As she took a bite of her sandwich, Sadie noticed a plume of dust in the distance, which told her that someone was driving down the road.

A few minutes later, she saw a green Prius pull into her driveway. She didn't recognize the car and neither did Hank. He started barking, although he stayed out of the way as the Prius slowly traversed the driveway.

As it moved closer, Sadie could see a Colorado license plate on the front of the car, but that didn't mean the driver was from Colorado. Laura's rental car sported a Colorado license plate too.

The car came to a stop in front of the house and the driver, a man wearing a cowboy hat, just sat there watching her.

Sadie's first thought was that the man might be Laura's fiancé. Had he somehow tracked Laura to Sadie's house?

Or he could just be a salesman, she told herself. They often stopped out in the country, selling lightning rods or horse feed.

Hank trotted over to the Prius and stood by the driver's door. The man rolled down his window and called out to Sadie. "Does your dog bite?"

"Only when I tell him to," Sadie called back, bluffing a little. Now that she could see him more clearly, the man looked to be in his midforties and a bit on the stocky side.

A moment later, the man climbed out of the car and gave Hank a tentative pat on the head before moving toward the house. He wore a pea-green suit and tie, along with alligator-skin cowboy boots.

Sadie set down her sandwich and rose to her feet, walking across the porch to meet him at the steps.

"Howdy," he said, holding out a beefy hand. "I'm Nathaniel Green and I'm here to make your day."

Salesman.

Hank joined her on the porch and stood by her side, ready to bolt into action if the man presented any threat. Her dog was gentle, but protective.

Sadie gave him a polite smile as she reached out to shake his hand. "Hello, I'm—"

"Sadie Speers," he interjected. "You're not an easy lady to find. You weren't at the Antique Mine and I had to ask all around town before someone finally pointed me in the right direction."

Okay, not a salesman, Sadie thought to herself. At least, not the type who usually showed up at her place. "Are you an antique buyer?"

"Some people call me that, among other things." Then he reached into the pocket of his green suit and pulled out a business card, handing it to her. "I recently opened a museum and souvenir shop in Breckenridge called Secrets of the Old West."

She took his card and saw a photograph of his museum. The signage on the front of the brick building reminded her of one of those Ripley's Believe It or Not places. "So what can I do for you?"

"That's easy," he said with a grin. "I'd like to make an offer on an item that I never thought I'd see."

Sadie felt a strange feeling in the pit of her stomach that she couldn't attribute to the ham and cheese sandwich. "What item?"

"The wedding dress belonging to Rachel Wright, the most infamous runaway bride in Colorado history."

9

"You've come to the wrong place," Sadie told him.

"I don't think so." He smiled. "I'm an avid reader of all the Colorado blogs and saw the most recent item in the *Chatterbox*."

"But why do you care about Rachel Wright?" Sadie asked, still confused.

"Because her story is fascinating." He tipped up his cowboy hat. "I first heard about her when I was a teenager and saw a play called *The Treasure in the Wedding Dress*. I've been fascinated by her story ever since. Now that Rachel's wedding dress has been found, I can play up the treasure part of the legend in the display. Maybe even sell maps of the area as souvenirs so that tourists can hunt for the lost treasure!"

Sadie stared at him for a long moment, wondering if he was serious. "I've heard that play had a lot of inaccuracies in it—some might even say falsehoods."

He grinned. "Well, I don't mind if a story skates around the truth as long as it's exciting. Most stories tend to grow a little in the telling—so we might as well make them as entertaining as possible."

Sadie smiled, realizing Nathaniel was more of a huckster than a historian. But at least he seemed genuinely enthusiastic about his work. "I'm afraid I can't help you."

"But you haven't even heard my offer yet. And it's a mighty high one."

"I don't have the dress here to sell to you," she hedged. "And if I did, it wouldn't be for sale."

"Then you could just lend it to the museum for display," he said. "I'd even pay you a nice commission."

"I'm sorry, but I'm not interested," Sadie said, growing a little weary of his sales pitch. Her lunch break was almost over and she needed to get to work.

"I'm afraid the word *no* isn't in my vocabulary," he said cordially, placing his cowboy hat back on his head. "Let's consider this the first step in our negotiation."

"I won't change my mind, so please don't make another trip to Silver Peak on my account."

He slowly walked backward to his car, his gaze fixed on her. "Changing minds is what my job's all about," he said, finally turning to open his car door. "Now, keep that business card of mine handy. You can call me day or night."

"Really, Mr. Green," Sadie began as he climbed into his car and started the engine, "I'm not going to change my mind."

"Call me Nathaniel," he called through the open window. "After all, we'll soon be doing business together." Then he gave her a jaunty wave before he turned his car around in the driveway and made his way toward the country road.

Sadie looked at Hank. "Well, he's quite a character, isn't he?"

Hank nudged his nose under her hand and she began petting him. First, Wade approached her wanting the wedding dress, and now Nathaniel Green. And she couldn't discount Laura's potential role in all of this. Laura had mentioned the wedding dress twice now without prompting, and the treasure connected to it, as well. Since Laura had been researching Silver Peak and her genealogy, she could have found the *Chatterbox* blog online and read about the discovery of Rachel Wright's wedding dress. Sadie didn't even have any proof that she'd attended that genealogy workshop in Breckenridge. Laura might have taken a plane from Massachusetts to Colorado the same day that she'd read the blog.

"I've got to get to work," she told Hank. She headed back to the porch and picked up her lunch plate. The visit from Nathaniel and the perplexing intrigue surrounding the wedding dress had curbed her appetite, so she gave the rest of her sandwich to Hank, who gobbled it up in two bites.

———

Later that afternoon, Sadie and Roz sat with their heads together in the Antique Mine, going over Jeanne's notes for the picnic.

"Wow, she really is organized," Roz said, the gold bangle bracelets on each arm jingling as she paged through the binder. "She's even got a flow chart in here and a detailed task list for before, during, and after the picnic."

"Which only makes our jobs easier." Sadie picked up the large coffee cup that Roz had brought her from Arbuckle's and took a sip. Sadie could drink coffee all day and often did. "Why don't we divide the list of committees in half? Then we can check with each committee chair to make sure everything is going smoothly."

Roz paged back to the front of the binder. "Okay, here's the committee list. We've got the food committee, the entertainment committee, and one for setting up the picnic area with tables and chairs."

"I'm tired already," Sadie joked.

Roz chuckled as she continued reading. "There's the table service and beverages committee, the children's games and toys committee, the music committee, and the cleanup committee."

"That's seven," Sadie said. "How about if I take the first four and you can take the remaining three?"

"I can take the extra one if you want," Roz said. "I've got plenty of time on my hands while you've got plenty on your plate, with your houseguest and people lining up at your door to buy that wedding dress."

Sadie had told Roz about Nathaniel's recent visit and his offer to buy the dress. Roz had heard about the Secrets of the Old West museum and confirmed Sadie's suspicion that it sensationalized local historical events.

"Well, we're in charge of the entertainment committee," she reminded Roz, "and the good news is that I've already found the entertainment for the picnic."

Roz's eyes widened with delight. "Wonderful! Who will it be?"

"Alfred Daly has agreed to perform an historical reenactment of William Tate's founding of Silver Peak."

"He'll be perfect," Roz exclaimed. "He even resembles William from the old photos I've seen, minus the white beard down to his belt buckle, of course."

"I'll find a beard as part of his costume, but you haven't heard the best part," Sadie said. "We have an actress who will be perfect in the role of Antonia. So both the founders will be portrayed in the reenactment."

"Who's the actress?"

"She's someone you know and she has acting experience. With her buoyant personality and unique style, I know she'll be a hit with the audience."

"Enough suspense!" Roz exclaimed, laughing. "Who is it?"

"You."

Roz blinked. "What did you say?"

"You'll be perfect in the role of Antonia," Sadie said, leaning toward her. "You've definitely got the voice for it. In fact, I think you project better now than you did when you were younger."

"Oh, Sadie," Roz said, looking both shocked and pleased at the prospect. "I haven't acted in years!"

"Then it's the perfect time to come out of retirement. Alfred is putting together the script and we'll have a rehearsal before the picnic. I know you'll be great."

Roz picked up her coffee and took a long sip. "You really think I can pull it off? I'm not as starchy as Antonia was reported to be."

"Make the role your own," Sadie encouraged her, knowing that Roz would stay true to history. "Think how much fun it will be, and you just told me that you have plenty of time on your hands."

"I suppose I could do it," Roz said, her brown eyes shining with excitement.

Sadie grinned. "How do you want your name to read in the program?"

"Lady Rosalind Eugenia Putnam, if you please," Roz said with an exaggerated British accent. She rose to her feet and performed a curtsy. "At your service."

"Eugenia?" Sadie smiled at her performance. "But your middle name is Jane!"

"Please," Roz said, adding a disdainful sniff to her fake accent. "Eugenia is my stage name." Then she snorted with laughter and fell back into her chair. "Oh, you *should* list me as Rosalind Eugenia in the program just to see if anyone notices—especially Roscoe. It would be a hoot!"

Sadie loved the fact that Roz was already embracing the role. "I'll do it. And I can't imagine a better Antonia." Then she snapped her fingers together. "That reminds me—we'll need to have a costume for you, as well as someone to do your hair and makeup."

"I can't wait to see myself in one of those fabulous Victorian gowns. I suppose I'll need a petticoat too, but I draw the line at a corset. I'm too old for that kind of nonsense."

"Deal," Sadie said. "I'll contact some of those Old West photography studios in Breckenridge. Maybe we can rent a couple of their outfits."

"I'll make the call," Roz offered. "And I can ask Sally Henderson to do the hair and makeup too." Sally owned Alpine Salon and had been both Sadie and Roz's stylist for years.

"Perfect choice," Sadie said. "Sally's done stage makeup and hair for the high school plays, so she'll know what she's doing."

"Let me write this all down," Roz said, "so I don't forget it."

Sadie turned to the computer and searched for Old West photography studios in Breckenridge. "Here's the number for a studio and they do rent costumes," she said, reciting it for Roz to copy down in the binder. "Don't forget to ask them for hats too."

"What?" Roz asked, looking up at her.

"Hats," Sadie repeated. "They usually come with the costumes."

"Oh, of course," Roz said with a smile. "I guess my mind is still spinning with the fact that I'm going to be one of the performers. Wait until I tell Roscoe."

"I'm sure he'll be excited for you."

"I hope so," Roz said, her smile fading. "He's been a little growly lately."

"Problems at the hardware store?"

"No, it's been busier there than ever." She gave a slight shrug. "Maybe he's just coming down with something. I'll pick up some pastries from Arbuckle's for dessert tonight. That always puts a smile on his face."

Two customers entered the shop and started to browse. Sadie recognized them from the group of genealogy workshop attendees who had visited on Tuesday. She walked over to greet them, offering her assistance whenever they were ready. Then she returned to the front desk where Roz still sat.

"Speaking of Arbuckle's," Sadie said, leaning against the counter, "I had coffee with Edwin there yesterday. Guess who might have seen the wedding dress in his attic?"

"Who?"

"Miranda Rhodes. Edwin hired her to clean up the house before he arrived and specifically asked her to look around the attic."

"So she might have spilled the beans that led to the item in the *Chatterbox*."

Sadie nodded. "Yes, unless she's the one who writes the *Chatterbox*. You know it has to be someone living in Silver Peak."

"Interesting," Roz mused. "I don't know Miranda that well, but I suppose it could be her. Do you plan to ask her?"

Sadie shrugged. "I don't know. I doubt she'd admit to writing the *Chatterbox*. I mean, it's clear from the author's style that he or she enjoys the anonymity." Sadie gave the idea some more consideration and then shook her head. "No, I think I'll wait until the DNA results come back on the dress. If it is a fake or simply a prop from the old play, then it doesn't really matter."

"Except that you'll have a fake cousin at your house," Roz reminded her. "Are you sure it's safe with Laura staying there?"

"She's harmless," Sadie said with a smile. "Nice too, and very helpful around the house. She spends most of her days working at the library and her evenings reading the Colorado history books I have on my bookcase."

The two customers approached the front counter with their purchases. Roz wrapped them up as Sadie chatted with them and handled the transaction. A few minutes later, she and Roz were alone in the shop again.

"So tell me more about this coffee with Edwin," Roz said. "What did you two talk about besides Miranda?"

"Our families and some of the old times we shared." Sadie smiled. "He even remembered that one of my favorite pastries was cherry turnovers."

"You two always did a make a cute couple."

Sadie shook her head. "It was just coffee."

"Then why are you blushing?" Roz asked, her eyes gleaming with amusement.

"I'm not." Sadie picked up her coffee cup and took a drink, trying to collect herself. "Edwin and I are just friends. My goodness, he hasn't even been back in town a week yet."

"But who was the first person he called?" Roz asked. "Not only called, but invited you over to see him that same day."

"To see the dress," Sadie countered even as she considered Roz's words. "I'm sure he was shocked when he found it."

"Still, he could have waited until he was settled in. After all, that wedding dress hasn't been seen for over a hundred years. A few more days really wouldn't have mattered."

"It still would have appeared in the *Chatterbox*. Although, Edwin didn't even know the *Chatterbox* existed until I told him about it." She chuckled. "Imagine how bewildered I would be if Wade and Nathaniel had turned up asking for the wedding dress if I didn't even know about it!"

"You would have figured it out soon enough," Roz said knowingly. "You're good at ferreting out information. You always have been."

"About antiques, maybe," Sadie told her. "And that's because there's a story behind each one."

"Everyone has a story. We just don't always know all of it. Take Laura, for instance. You still don't really know her story."

"No, I don't," Sadie admitted. "And I have to wonder if she would have shown up in Silver Peak at all if that item about the wedding dress hadn't appeared in the *Chatterbox*."

"Do you plan to ask her about it?"

"No, not yet. I think I'll wait for the results of the test. If the wedding dress did belong to Rachel, then it rightly belongs to her granddaughter. I'll give Laura the dress and the brass key, although I still don't know where the key leads."

Another customer entered the store and approached the desk.

"Hello," said the young woman. "I'm Kayla Polmiller, Harry's great-granddaughter."

"Well, it's nice to meet you, Kayla," Sadie said warmly. "My friend Roz and I both attend church with Harry."

"Yes, he's a wonderful man," Roz said with a smile. "And the best gardener around."

Kayla nodded. "We love Grandpa Harry. I live in Pueblo, otherwise I'm sure he'd give me enough zucchini every summer to fill my freezer." Then she placed a large bag on the desk and carefully removed two antique dolls from it. "Instead, he's given me these dolls."

Roz stood up and grabbed her coffee cup. "I'll leave you two alone to talk antiques. It was nice meeting you, Kayla."

"You too," Kayla said as Roz moved toward the door.

"Give me a call later, Sadie," Roz said over her shoulder.

"I will," Sadie promised, waving good-bye to her friend. Then she turned her full attention to Kayla and the dolls in front of her. Sadie found all antique dolls interesting, although some were a little creepy. She could already tell these were something special. "Where did Harry find these dolls?"

"He found them in one of the overstuffed closets in his house. I was hoping you could tell me something about them."

"Well, they're quite lovely," Sadie said, carefully picking up the first doll and studying it. She'd learned about antique dolls from her best friend in college, who had inherited several rare dolls from her German grandmother.

She carefully held the doll as she examined it for any markings. It was dressed in a pink silk and white lace Victorian child's gown and had small pink shoes on its feet.

"This is an original Kestner bisque doll from Germany," Sadie said at last. "They were produced in the late 1800s through the early 1900s. Here is the marking," she said, lifting the doll's brown mohair wig, where letters and numbers were printed. "It's a JDK 237 doll. The wig isn't original, but the doll is otherwise in wonderful condition."

"Oh, wow," Kayla said, taking the doll from her. "I had no idea the doll was that old." Then she picked up the other doll, dressed in a white gown with the original diaper and crocheted booties, and handed it to Sadie. "How about this one?"

"This is another original Kestner doll," Sadie told her after examining it. "The marking is JDK 211. I'd say that given the condition of these dolls, their value is between five hundred and seven hundred dollars."

Kayla blinked. "Well, that's a shock, although I don't have any intention of selling them."

"So Harry really doesn't know where they came from?"

Kayla laughed. "Well, I think he does know. He told me that his aunt used to visit every summer and always brought gifts from her travels abroad. One time she even brought a pet wallaby from Australia . . ."

Sadie breathed a contented sigh as she listened to Kayla's story. This was her favorite part of her job, discovering history through family stories and folklore. The threads of the past were woven into the present, and that was never more apparent to Sadie than when she heard the tales behind precious antiques and collectibles.

Sadie's own family history had started to unravel the moment Laura showed up in her shop. She just hoped she'd be able to put it back together again.

After Sadie closed the Antique Mine for the day, she headed to the library on the corner of Main Street. She wanted to look for some books on the Tates, specifically Antonia Tate, to give to Roz.

Sadie pulled her Tahoe into an empty parking stall next to Laura's rental car. The fact that Laura insisted on working at the library every day instead of at the ranch house seemed to confirm Sadie's impression that the woman was afraid to be alone. She wondered if Laura was telling the truth about her fiancé not being physically abusive. Too many women minimized that kind of abuse in the hope of saving the relationship or mistakenly believing that they deserved it.

But the Wright women weren't among them.

Like Sadie, the Wright women prided themselves on their strength, and she knew that more than one matriarch had run the sprawling family ranch after becoming a widow. In fact, that was one part of Rachel's story that had always puzzled Sadie—the fact that she'd acted so desperately, choosing death over an unwanted marriage. That was contrary to every other Wright women in the family history.

But running off to Boston to start a new life? Yes, Sadie thought to herself, she could see a Wright woman doing just that. In fact, a big part of her wanted to believe it, since it made Rachel's story triumphant instead of tragic. But too many people knew of the legend of the runaway bride—and some of them had added their own details to the story, so Sadie didn't know anymore what was fact and what was fiction.

She walked in the front door of the library and took a moment to enjoy one of her favorite places in Silver Peak. The gorgeous, lofted, high-ceiling library was once a multi-use building that had been renovated by a generous benefactor. Sadie loved the light oak woodwork and the local artwork tastefully displayed on the cream-colored walls.

The large first floor contained all the books, both fiction and nonfiction, while the second and third floors served as public meeting rooms and media rooms.

A long, hand-woven Shoshone rug ran from the front entrance to the round circulation desk. On the left were oak bookshelves full of fiction books and on the right was the non-fiction section as well as the computer stations and periodicals. A cozy children's nook filled the back of the library behind the circulation desk.

Sadie looked around but didn't see Laura at any of the tables. She approached the circulation desk, where the head librarian, Kimama, a lovely Native American woman, was checking out books for an elderly man. Behind him stood Julie Henderson, holding her two-year-old son, Caleb.

"Hello there, cutie," Sadie said, as Caleb smiled shyly at her. "Did your mom find some books for you?"

Julie turned around. "Oh, hi, Sadie. I didn't see you there."

"I just got here," Sadie said. "Caleb is growing up so fast."

Julie smiled. "I know. He keeps me busy."

Wyatt and Julie Henderson had been married five years and lived in town, where Wyatt worked as contractor. He was the younger brother of Milo Henderson and the son of Sally Henderson.

Caleb held out one hand toward Sadie and said, "Cookie?"

"Caleb," Julie gently scolded. "You don't ask people for cookies."

"Cookie," Caleb repeated again, blinking his big blue eyes at Sadie.

"Sorry, Caleb," Sadie told him. "I don't have any cookies with me."

Julie held up a book in front of him. "We have a book about cookies, see?"

Successfully distracted, Caleb took the book from her and started looking at the cover. Then it was Julie's turn at the check-out desk.

When she was done, Sadie waved good-bye to both Julie and Caleb and then approached the desk. "Hello, Kimama. How are you?"

"Busy today," Kimama said. "Which I love. What can I help you with today?"

"I'm actually looking for someone. Her name is Laura Finch and she's been working on her laptop here for the last couple of days. Have you seen her?"

"Yes, just a few minutes ago. She was standing behind one of the nonfiction bookshelves with a man."

"A man?" Sadie asked, a queasy feeling stirring in the pit of her stomach. "Did you recognize him?"

"Nope," Kimama replied. "I've never seen him before."

10

———

After Kimama pointed out the bookcase where she'd last seen Laura, Sadie approached it with a mixture of curiosity and trepidation.

As she neared the end of the bookshelf, she could hear the hushed voices of a man and a woman, but couldn't make out the words. She hesitated a moment, wondering if she should interrupt them. Then she remembered Laura's fear that Ray would be able to talk her into leaving Colorado with him.

Squaring her shoulders, Sadie rounded the bookcase.

Edwin looked up at her. "Sadie! This is a surprise."

Laura turned around to face her. "Oh, hello!"

For a moment, Sadie couldn't speak. Edwin was the last person she'd expected to see. As far as she knew, the two of them had never met.

"Hello," Sadie greeted them, tamping down her shock with a smile. "I didn't realize you two knew each other."

"Oh, we didn't," Laura replied, glancing up at Edwin, "not until today. I saw Edwin walk into the library and I recognized him from your high school yearbook, so I walked up and introduced myself to him."

Edwin nodded. "It turns out we have a mutual acquaintance. A judge I knew in Chicago moved to Boston recently and campaigned for a judgeship there. He said that Laura Finch was instrumental in helping him win the election."

"Isn't it a small world?" Laura chimed in, glancing up at Edwin again. "I'll have to e-mail George and tell him that we ran into each other."

"Please tell him I said hello," Edwin told her. Then he moved toward Sadie. "This is perfect timing. I was hoping we might have a chance to tour your shop after hours."

"Oh." His request caught Sadie off guard, something that didn't happen often. "Yes, I guess we can."

Edwin smiled. "Wonderful!" He turned to Laura. "Would you like to join us?"

"No, thank you," Laura said. "I still have some work to finish up here." She looked over at Sadie. "I'll see you back at the house."

"Okay, do you have the spare key in case you get there before me?" Sadie asked.

Laura nodded. "It's in my purse. You take your time, though. Don't worry about me."

Edwin held his hand out to Laura. "It was so nice to meet you."

Laura clasped her hand in his. "You too, Edwin. I hope we'll have a chance to meet again before I leave Silver Peak."

He smiled. "I'm sure we will."

Sadie watch as Laura headed toward the row of library tables near the computer station. Now she saw Laura's laptop bag hanging from one of the chairs.

"Are you ready to give me a tour now or would you like to grab a bite to eat first?" Edwin asked her.

"Now is fine," Sadie replied, realizing that her reaction had been a little silly. She'd been almost certain she'd find Laura with her controlling fiancé and had braced herself for a possible confrontation. Instead, she'd found Laura with Edwin, a man who had given her butterflies in her stomach only hours before.

Concern washed over his face as he looked at her. "Are you sure this is a good time? I didn't mean to spring it on you like this."

She smiled, relaxing now that the shock had started to fade. "It's a perfect time."

They walked out to the parking lot together and then Edwin followed her, driving a silver BMW. Sadie parked her Tahoe in front of the Antique Mine and he pulled in beside her.

"We almost could have walked here," Edwin said as he met her on the sidewalk. "It's such a beautiful fall day."

"Yes, but the sun will be going down soon and it gets quite chilly."

He smiled. "I remember."

"Do you miss Chicago?" she asked as she unlocked the front door and they walked inside.

"Sometimes," he admitted. "We had a lot of friends there and I had season tickets to the Cubs' games. Of course, Colorado has a professional baseball team now too. They didn't when I left Silver Peak."

"That's right," Sadie said. "The Rockies have been here since, what, 1993? I've taken Sara and Theo to a few games in Denver. Sara even caught a fly ball once."

"Good for her." Then he chuckled. "Remember the summer we played a softball game with some of the kids from school? I was playing second base and you hit a line drive straight at me."

"And you missed," she said, wincing. "And the ball hit you square in the eye."

"It sure did. I had a shiner for two weeks. The worst part was when I had to tell my dad how it happened. Then he nicknamed you Slugger for the rest of the summer."

"I didn't hit it toward you on purpose," she said in her own defense. "And I brought you ice cream every day for a week afterward."

He smiled. "That was the best part."

The butterflies in her stomach started fluttering again, but she tried to ignore them. "Are you ready to start the tour?"

"I sure am." He turned in a slow circle, looking up at the original, pressed-tin ceiling. "This place is really something. I can't imagine how long it's taken you to gather all this inventory."

"It was a labor of love," Sadie said with a smile. "I attend a lot of estate sales and auctions, because you never know where you're going to find a special piece. Some people bring items into the shop to sell too, or to trade if I have something they want."

"Still, this is impressive." He walked over to the desk. "Even your cash register is an antique." She moved to his side as he looked at the brass register, shaped like an old-fashioned typewriter with a window at the top that showed the numbers as they were rung up. "Does it work or is it just decorative?"

"Oh, it works, all right," she told him, rounding the desk and typing in some numbers to demonstrate.

Edwin began to chuckle as the numbers popped into the register window. "Delightful."

"Do you want to try it?"

"I sure do," he said without hesitation. He joined her behind the counter and typed in some numbers of his own. "This is fun."

"You're a natural," she teased. "Much better at this than softball. Let me know if you ever want a part-time job."

"I may take you up on that offer someday," he said with a smile. "Especially with that door connecting your shop to Arbuckle's Coffee. Although I'd probably spend more time there than I would here."

"It's almost too convenient," she said with an amused sigh. "But I wouldn't have it any other way."

He leaned against the granite counter, his gaze intent on her face. "You haven't changed a bit, Sadie. Still diving into life with that sunny smile and your great sense of humor." A comfortable silence lingered between them. Then Edwin said, "I'll be honest, Sadie. I had an ulterior motive for coming to your shop tonight."

Her heart skipped a beat. "Oh?"

"I've been getting settled in at the house, but it still doesn't feel quite like home to me yet. I was hoping you could offer some decorating advice to give the place a woman's touch." He looked around the shop. "And I think some of these antiques would fit right in with the rest of my décor."

"I'd love to help you decorate," Sadie said. "And I even have a secret weapon named Julie, who works part-time here and is an interior designer."

He gave a nod of approval. "Then I definitely came to the right place. Shall we set a date and time?"

"Let me check with Julie first, and then I'll give you a call."

"Let me give you my cell phone number," Edwin said, pulling his cell phone out of his pocket. "And I'd like to have yours too."

"Of course," Sadie replied, pulling her cell phone from her bag. She gave him her number first and he punched the numbers into his phone. Then he did the same for her.

"Now let's make sure I have the right number," he said, a mischievous glint in his eyes as he tapped another button on his phone.

A second later, Sadie's phone began to ring. "Are you calling me?"

"Pick up and find out."

Sadie grinned as she answered her phone. "Hello?" she said, her gaze on Edwin, who stood only two feet away.

"Hi, Sadie. I'm hoping you'll change your mind about having dinner with me tonight." His voice was solemn but his eyes twinkled as he watched her.

"Who is this?" she teased, looking straight at him.

He laughed, placing one hand over his heart. "You really know how to wound a guy. It's Edwin Marshall, your old flame."

"Oh, *that* Edwin," she said with a smile. "I wish I could join you for dinner, Edwin, but I'd better not since I have a houseguest waiting for me at home."

Disappointment gleamed in his eyes. "I understand."

"How about a rain check?"

His smile reappeared. "You've got it." Then he ended the call with a push of a button. "Looks like I've got your number."

Sadie laughed as she ended the call on her phone as well. "And I've got yours."

He grinned. "You sure do."

For the next twenty minutes, Sadie showed Edwin around the rest of the shop, enjoying his company and more than a few laughs. By the time she returned home, she found Laura standing at the stove, stirring something in the soup kettle.

"I hope you don't mind," Laura said, "but I made some chili for us for dinner."

"Mind?" Sadie said, setting her purse on the counter and then leaning down to greet Hank. "Not at all."

"Did Edwin enjoy the tour of your shop?"

"Yes, he did. I showed him some old memorabilia from our high school days that I picked up at an auction this summer. It brought back a lot of memories."

"I'm sure it did." Laura picked up the salt shaker and added a few sprinkles to the pan, before turning to face her. "You never said why you were looking for me in the library."

"Oh," Sadie said, "it was nothing important. I just stopped in to pick up some books for a friend and thought I'd check in with you while I was there."

Laura nodded. "Well, that was nice of you." Then she turned back to the stove and stirred the chili once more. "Edwin sure is a handsome man. He reminds me of the actor Howard Keel when he appeared as the patriarch on *Dallas*. The same silver hair and blue eyes. Do you remember him?"

"Yes. In his younger days, Howard Keel was the star of one of my favorite musicals, *Seven Brides for Seven Brothers*."

"I like that one too. He was also in *Calamity Jane* with Doris Day. His singing voice was amazing." Laura breathed a wistful sigh. "I love old movies. They just don't make leading men like they used to. Men like Cary Grant and John Wayne and Clark Gable."

"Times change," Sadie said, remembering Edwin's remark that she hadn't changed at all. She knew it wasn't true, but the way he'd said it had touched her. As if she was still the girl he'd fallen for in high school.

"Sadie? Did you hear what I said?"

Sadie looked up, realizing she'd been lost in her own thoughts. "No, I'm sorry. I guess I was daydreaming."

"It happens to the best of us," Laura replied, picking up two hot pads and carrying the pot over to the table. "The chili is ready."

"Perfect." Sadie walked over to the table, which Laura had already set for the meal. Laura had made herself right at home, she thought to herself. And while she was happy that Laura felt more comfortable here, she wasn't quite as thrilled that Laura had appeared so comfortable around Edwin.

They chatted about Laura's research as they ate, with Hank seated under the table waiting for crumbs. Laura was putting together a family tree and Sadie helped her fill in a few blanks.

"I learned something interesting today," Laura said, setting down her spoon. "At the library, I overhead two women talking about the recent discovery of the runaway bride's wedding dress."

Sadie looked up from her bowl, weighing her options. She could pretend this was news to her, or tell Laura the truth and see where it led. Although she didn't fully trust Laura yet, she decided to go with the truth. "Yes, that's true. Although, I don't know yet whether it's really her dress. That's why I didn't say anything. I've already sent it to a lab for a DNA test hoping to learn if I'm related to the person who left the blood on the dress."

Laura gave a slow nod. "I can understand your concern, Sadie, and I really don't blame you for not telling me about it sooner. I'm a stranger to you, with an even stranger story about your great-aunt. I'm glad the DNA test will give you the proof you need." She picked up her spoon. "So did you find anything else with the dress?"

Sadie let the question hang in the air for a moment, debating whether to tell her about the key. "No treasure, that's for sure. I did find the revolver that Rachel used to make that bullet hole in the dress. It belonged to Grandpa Jacob. It's in the gun safe if you'd like to see it later."

Laura shook her head. "Thanks, but I don't like guns—even antique ones. So when do you expect the dress and the DNA test to come back?"

"I was told it could take a couple of weeks and I sent it off the day before you arrived in Silver Peak."

"Well, I can't wait to see the results. And to finally see the wedding dress Nana wore."

Sadie steered the conversation to questions about Laura's grandmother, wanting to learn more about the woman and talk less about the wedding dress and what else she'd found with it.

When dinner was over, Sadie pushed her chair back with a contented sigh. "Thanks for the chili. It was delicious."

"You're welcome." Laura stood up and started to gather the dinner dishes.

"Just relax," Sadie told her. "I'll clean the dishes tonight since you did the cooking."

"Are you sure?"

"Positive," Sadie replied just as the telephone rang. She walked over to the cordless phone on the kitchen counter and picked up the receiver. "Hello?"

There was silence on the other end of the line and then a *click*.

Sadie hung up. "Must have been the wrong number." She walked back to the table and started picking up the bowls and silverware when the telephone rang again.

"Do you want me to get it?" Laura asked her.

"No, I'm already up," Sadie said, walking over to the phone again. She set down the dishes in her hands and picked up the receiver. "Hello."

There was silence again, but this time she thought she heard someone breathing on the other end of the line.

"Hello?" Sadie said again, a little louder this time.

Click.

Sadie hung up the phone, a little irritated this time. The least people could do if they dialed a wrong number was apologize—especially if they did it twice.

Laura rose from the table. "I'm going to run up to my room for a bit."

"Okay," Sadie said, watching her leave the kitchen. Laura's sudden departure seemed a little strange to her. She carried the dishes over to the sink, wondering what Laura was doing. Then she turned on the tap to rinse them off before placing them in the dishwasher. It didn't take her long to clean up and wipe down the stove and the kitchen table.

When she walked out of the kitchen, there was no sign of Laura, but she saw Hank curled up on the living room rug. "Are you ready to go for a walk?"

Hank sprang up and bounded toward the back of the house, his exuberance making her laugh.

"I need to change my shoes," she told him. "Then I'll be ready to go."

Hank waited by the mudroom door while Sadie hurried up the stairs to her bedroom. When she passed Laura's room, she thought she heard someone talking. She paused, listening for a moment.

Although it was muffled, Sadie could hear Laura talking. Her tone sounded low and furtive, and the pauses told Sadie that she was talking to someone on her cell phone. She stood there a moment longer, unable to make out the words, then continued down the hallway and into her bedroom. She closed the door and leaned against it, wondering if she should have kept eavesdropping.

Was it possible those two hang-up calls were some kind of signal? Laura had gone up to her room almost immediately afterward. Sadie pondered that possibility as she retrieved her hiking shoes and sat down to put them on. *But why signal with the landline?* she wondered. *Why not call Laura's cell phone directly?*

Then she remembered that Laura usually charged her cell phone in her bedroom after returning from the library, so she would have missed a call or text that had come in during their dinner.

Or it simply could have been someone dialing a wrong number, she told herself, trying not to jump to conclusions. After all, she knew Laura had clients in Boston. One of them might be calling to talk business.

She grabbed a jacket from her closet and then walked out of her room. Laura was still in her bedroom with the door closed, so Sadie headed downstairs where Hank awaited her. He paced back and forth in front of the back door, his tail wagging furiously behind him.

"Ready, boy?" she asked, opening the door.

He raced out ahead of her and headed straight for the nearest fir tree. A rabbit ran out and Hank started giving chase, but he was no match for the bounding rabbit.

Sadie walked along the trail, watching the action, but her mind was filled with thoughts of Edwin and hang-up calls. Then she took a deep, cleansing breath and cleared her mind. The magnificent sunset cast purple, green, and blue rays between the mountain peaks, lighting the tree-filled valleys with a rainbow glow. The air was fresh and bracing and just a touch on the cool side. She picked up her pace, knowing a brisk walk would keep her warm.

Hank ran in a zigzag pattern in front of her, diving underneath the trees on both sides of the trail, still in search of the elusive rabbit.

Each step along the trail brought a relaxing peace to her mind, heart, and soul. A time when God felt so close that she spoke to Him out loud. "Heavenly Father," she said, "thank You for the blessings of this day. Especially for bringing Edwin back into my life so we can renew our friendship."

Sadie continued to pray as she walked along the trail with Hank. She prayed for Alice and Theo and Sara, as well as other friends and family members. She also prayed for Laura, asking the Lord for guidance and an open heart.

Near the end of their hike, Sadie bent down to pick one of the last wildflowers of the season, its pink bloom leaving a smile on her face. She couldn't wait to see what tomorrow would bring.

Sadie and Laura spent the rest of the evening watching a documentary about the Colorado silver and gold rushes in the second half of the nineteenth century. It was a DVD that Sadie owned and had watched before, but she thought Laura would enjoy the historical aspects of it.

The landline phone didn't ring for the rest of the night and Laura didn't mention anything about the phone call in her room. Sadie knew she couldn't bring it up without confessing to eavesdropping, but she was still very curious about who had been on the other end of that call.

Early Friday morning, Sadie awoke to the sound of Hank's frantic barking. She sat up in bed, trying to orient herself. Then a loud knocking sounded on her bedroom door.

"Sadie!" Laura cried out, her voice laced with panic. "Someone's outside! I can see him through my window."

Sadie threw back her covers and climbed out of bed. She grabbed her long bathrobe and slipped it on, cinching it snugly around her waist. Then she opened the door to find Laura clutching her robe around her neck, her eyes wide with fear.

"Do you have any idea who's out there?" Sadie asked.

"No," Laura said, shivering a little.

Sadie hurried downstairs where Hank was still barking and growling near the front door. She headed to the window and parted the curtain. The rising sun cast just enough light for her to see a dark figure running in front of the house.

Laura stood behind her, her hand tightly clutching Sadie's shoulder. "What's going on out there?"

"I don't know," Sadie said, trying to keep her eye on the dark figure. "Call 911."

11

LAURA RAN FOR THE PHONE WHILE SADIE KEPT HER EYE ON THE driveway. She couldn't see the dark figure now and hoped he wasn't circling his way around to the back of the house.

Hank kept barking and growling, his teeth bared as he stared intently at the front door.

Then Sadie heard the roar of an engine and the sound of tires spitting up gravel as the car tore out of the driveway. She hurried to the door and unlocked it, running out onto the porch to see if she could catch a glimpse of the car. But by the time she made it down the steps and out into the driveway, the car was gone.

Laura appeared in the threshold. "Sadie, what are you doing out here. It's not safe!"

"He left," Sadie said, turning around. That's when she saw the shards of glass on the ground near her Tahoe. The rear window had been shattered. "Looks like he left a message, though."

Sadie called Hank to her side, not wanting him to step in the broken glass. Then she loosely gripped one finger under his collar and carefully led him back toward the house. The gravel bit into her bare feet, something she hadn't even noticed when she'd run outside to try to identify the fleeing car.

"Did you call 911?" Sadie asked Laura as they entered the house and closed the front door.

"Yes. The dispatcher said they'd send someone out right away. I didn't know your address, though."

Sadie looked up at her. "But you told them it was Sadie Speers's house?"

"Yes." Then tears filled Laura's eyes. "I'm so sorry. This is my fault. If I hadn't come here . . ."

"You're not the one who broke out my window," Sadie said gently. Then she sat down near Hank and gently lifted each one of his paws to check for any embedded glass. "It looks like he's not cut anywhere."

"How about you?" Laura asked as she took the chair next to Sadie, her hands visibly trembling. "You ran out there barefoot."

"I know," Sadie said wryly, her feet still a little sore. She checked them, gently pressing on the sole of each foot, but there was no sign of any blood or glass. "I'm fine, there's no glass or cuts." Then she sighed. "I wish I could say the same for my car."

Then she stood up. "Why don't we get dressed while we wait for the sheriff? He should be here soon."

"Good idea," Laura said, as she followed Sadie to the stairs. Hank stayed behind on the first floor, silently patrolling the front door.

"I still can't believe it," Laura breathed when they reached the upstairs landing. "Thank God Hank let us know that man was out there."

Sadie nodded, breathing a silent prayer of gratitude that none of them had been hurt. She walked into her bedroom and dressed quickly, throwing on a pair of jeans and a green knit turtleneck sweater. She heard a siren in the distance as she slipped into a pair of loafers. Her pulse raced as she headed back downstairs, grabbing her North Face jacket off the coatrack and opening the front door just as the sheriff's patrol car pulled into the driveway.

She stepped onto the porch, keeping Hank next to her as Sheriff Mac Slattery climbed out of his car and placed the brown felt campaign hat on his head. He was in his late fifties, with a stocky build and dark gray hair shorn into a crew cut. His sheriff's uniform consisted of a brown shirt and beige khaki pants that bulged at the waist along with a matching beige tie. The gold star on his chest gleamed under the light of the morning sun that had just peeked over the horizon.

Laura appeared on the porch next to Sadie, both of them watching as the sheriff made a wide circle around Sadie's SUV. Then he pulled his flashlight from his belt and stepped near the broken window, glass crunching under his feet. He shone the light in the backseat for several seconds before finally switching it off.

"Is there any damage inside?" Sadie called out to him.

"No," the sheriff said, walking toward the porch. He had a gruffness about him and a world-weary attitude. She wondered if career burnout was part of the reason that he and Anita had left Denver and moved to Silver Peak.

"What happened out here, Sadie?" he asked.

"Hank started barking up a storm and Laura looked through her bedroom window and saw someone outside." She pointed to the woman beside her. "This is Laura Finch. She's a guest from Boston."

"Hello," Laura said. "I didn't see a face. The man was dressed in all black."

Sheriff Slattery pulled a notepad and stubby pencil out of his shirt pocket. "You're sure it was a man?"

"It looked like one to me," Laura said, turning to Sadie. "He had a man's build," Sadie added.

"Anything else you can tell me about him?" the sheriff asked.

"He wore a black hooded sweatshirt," Sadie said, "with the hood pulled low over his face. Black pants and gloves too."

The panic at finding a stranger skulking around her property had faded and a strange numbness had taken its place. Nothing like this had ever happened to Sadie before. Half the time, she didn't lock the doors to her Tahoe when it was parked in the driveway, although she'd done so last night.

The temperature had dropped below forty during the night and a chill washed over Sadie as a brisk north wind breezed through the trees. She wondered how long the man had been skulking outside her house in this weather and what had brought him here in the first place.

"I need you to both check your cars," the sheriff said, "to make sure nothing is missing. Just watch out for the glass."

"Don't you need to take fingerprints first or test the crime scene?" Laura asked him.

He turned his baleful gaze on her. "Sadie just told me the suspect was wearing gloves, so there won't be any prints. And we don't have any crime technicians in Silver Peak. Usually don't need them."

Sadie ushered Hank into the house so he wouldn't follow her, then she and the sheriff made their way to the Tahoe. She tried to avoid as much of the glass as she could, but soon it was crunching under her shoes. She looked in the backseat and then checked the front. "Everything looks the same to me."

The sheriff turned around and called out to Laura, who was peering inside her rental sedan. "How about your car?"

"It's fine," Laura called back to him.

They returned to the front porch, where Sheriff Slattery jotted some more notes in his notebook. "No theft or interior damage to either car. Smashed rear window on the Chevy Tahoe." He looked over at Sadie. "Any idea who would do something like this?"

She wasn't sure where to start. "Do you read the *Chatterbox*?"

He scowled playfully. "I refuse."

"Well, there was an item in there about an antique wedding dress that might have belonged to Rachel Wright. Also known as Silver Peak's runaway bride."

He gave a slow nod. "I think I've heard something about her. I thought she was a fictional character."

"No, she was a real person," Laura said. "My grandmother, in fact."

Sadie glanced over at her, wondering if Laura had told anyone else about her connection to Rachel and the Wright family.

"Anyway," Sadie continued, "the author of the blog mentioned my carrying a dress box out to my car. It's possible someone thought the box with the wedding dress was still in the Tahoe and that's why he broke the window."

"For a dress?" the sheriff asked, his tone skeptical.

Laura took a step toward him. "That wedding dress is quite valuable, and not only for sentimental reasons. It's believed by some people that there's a treasure connected to it."

Sheriff Slattery's blue eyes narrowed on Sadie. "Any idea who might want that wedding dress or the so-called treasure?"

Sadie didn't want to start accusing people, but her broken car window made it impossible to keep silent. "Wade Marley showed up at the Antique Mine a couple of days ago. He wanted the wedding dress and wasn't very pleasant about it. Right before he left, Wade told me that he wasn't going to back down."

The sheriff tipped up the brim of his hat. "Why would Wade want an old wedding dress?"

Sadie swallowed a sigh, hoping Sheriff Slattery's patience wouldn't run out while she told him the story of the runaway bride. She left out some of the finer details, but made it clear that the Marleys and the Wrights had feuded since that ill-fated wedding day and that the Marleys had always believed they were due restitution.

"And this is all true?" the sheriff asked, looking skeptical again.

"Yes," Laura told him. "Except Rachel didn't drown in the creek. She escaped to Boston."

"But we're keeping that quiet for now," Sadie told him, hoping Laura didn't mind. "Laura and I are still conducting some research so we can figure out exactly what happened."

"That's right," Laura said. "That research is why I came to Colorado."

The sheriff studied Laura for a long moment before turning his attention back to Sadie. "Anyone else you suspect might have done this?"

"Well, another man showed up here yesterday. He came from Breckenridge and wanted to buy the wedding dress from me. He insisted that he wouldn't take no for an answer."

"His name?" the sheriff asked, the pencil poised above the notepad to write it down.

"Nathaniel Green. He owns some type of museum in Breckenridge called Secrets of the Old West. He told me he wanted to put the wedding dress on a display featuring the legend of the runaway bride."

"Does he know about the treasure?" Laura asked her.

Sadie nodded. "Mr. Green told me he's been fascinated with Rachel's story ever since he saw the play about her when he was younger. He seemed friendly enough, but he made it clear that he wanted the dress."

"And he obviously knew where to find you," Sheriff Slattery added.

Sadie just couldn't picture Nathaniel Green or even Wade sneaking around the house and breaking her window. Maybe there was some other explanation. "Have there been any other cases of vandalism around Silver Peak lately?" Sadie asked the sheriff.

"Nope," he said. "This is the first one in a long while. Usually it's kids throwing eggs or decorating trees with toilet paper." Then he turned to Laura. "How about you, Ms. Finch? Anyone have a beef with you lately?"

"Me?" Her gaze dropped to the ground. "No, I can't think of anyone."

"You sure about that?" the sheriff asked her.

Sadie opened her mouth to tell him about Laura's fiancé, but Laura spoke first. "I've been having second thoughts about marrying my fiancé, but as far as I know he's still in Boston. He talked about coming out here, but I haven't seen him and I have no reason to believe he knows where Sadie lives."

"That Green fellow tracked her down, so your fiancé might have done the same."

Laura finally looked up at the sheriff. "I'm sure it wasn't Ray. The guy I saw from the window looked much taller."

"All right," he said, slipping the notepad back in his shirt pocket before turning to Sadie. "I'll see what I can find out, but it's going to be hard to discover who did this damage without any description to go on."

"I figured as much," Sadie replied. "But I thought we should report it anyway."

He nodded. "Give the station a call if you think of anything else or have any more trouble."

Sadie breathed another silent prayer that the trouble was over. "I will, Sheriff. Thanks for coming out here so early."

"No problem."

Sadie and Laura watched him leave, the sun now rising above the treetops. The light of day burned away the last remnants of fear and unease stirring inside of Sadie. She placed her hands on her hips as she surveyed the broken glass around her Tahoe. "I guess it's time to clean up this mess."

"How are you going to do that?" Laura asked. "You can't really sweep a gravel driveway, can you?"

"No, but you can vacuum it up if you have the right machine. I have one in the garage that's an inside/outside model and made to vacuum up water and debris. Carpenters use it all the time."

"Can I help?" Laura asked her.

Sadie walked toward the house. "No, I can manage. It shouldn't take too long."

Laura followed her. "Well, the least I can do is give you a ride into town until you get that window fixed."

Sadie considered her options, knowing she'd need to make an appointment to get her car window fixed and it was likely that the repair shop would need to order a windshield to fit her Tahoe. "Thanks for the offer," she said with a smile, "but I have another way to get into town."

An hour later, Sadie cruised into town in T.R.'s 1960 Cadillac convertible. The classic light blue car drove like a dream and Sadie would occasionally take it out for drives during the summer. Theo loved the car as much as Sadie did, and had dropped plenty of hints that he'd like to own it someday.

Sadie had left the top up, the autumn weather too cool to enjoy the wind blowing through her hair. She'd called Julie earlier and explained the situation, asking if she might be able to work this morning. Julie had come through, just as she usually did, and offered to work at the Antique Mine as long as Sadie needed her.

That gave Sadie the opportunity to move her investigation into the wedding dress mystery into high gear. Before the broken car window, the discovery of the wedding dress had been a curiosity and a glimpse into her family's history. But now some-one had crossed the line, and Sadie didn't have much confidence that the sheriff would be able to find the culprit with so little to go on.

That meant she'd need to track him down herself. And to do that, she needed to learn everything she could about the legend of the runaway bride, because maybe the part about the stolen treasure *was* more fact than fiction.

Sadie drove straight to the office of the *Silver Peak Sentinel,* the town's small daily newspaper. The editor was a young man named Troy Haggerty, fresh out of journalism school and full of enthusiasm for his craft. He was sitting in front of a computer, typing furiously on the keyboard, when Sadie walked into the office.

She waited by the entrance, not wanting to disrupt his train of thought. She smiled as she watched him, thinking all he needed was a green eyeshade and a cigar dangling from his mouth to look like a gritty reporter straight out of a movie like *The Front Page.*

At last, Troy looked up from his computer screen and noticed her standing there. "Hey, Sadie. When did you get here?"

"Just a couple of minutes ago. I don't want to interrupt you."

"I'm just writing an article about the upcoming mayor's race. Mayor George Frink just announced that he won't be running for another term, so that means the field will be wide open."

"Well, that is interesting news."

He jumped up from his chair. "What can I do for you?"

"I'd like to take a look at the newspaper archives."

"In the morgue?" he asked, using journalist jargon for the storage space for old newspapers.

She smiled. "Yes, the morgue. Can you point me in the right direction?"

"Sure. Follow me." He led her to a back room. "You're in luck," he said. "We've recently digitized all the old editions, so you can do computer searches for specific articles and topics."

They walked into a small room with moss-green walls and a cement floor. A single computer sat on a small table. Metal shelves lined the walls, all of them stacked with newspapers. The morgue lived up to its name just by the temperature in the room. It was a good ten degrees cooler than the rest of the newspaper office.

"It gets a bit chilly in here," Troy said. He pointed toward a red fleece blanket folded neatly on one of the shelves. "My mom made a blanket for me to use when I have to work back here." He smiled. "I guess she still thinks I'm ten."

"Moms never stop worrying about their kids," Sadie told him. "So you might as well enjoy the perks."

"Okay, I will," he said with a chuckle. "Let me know if you need anything."

"Thanks, Troy."

After he left her in the morgue, Sadie switched on the computer and waited for it to warm up. Needing to warm up herself, Sadie grabbed the blanket off the shelf and wrapped it around her.

Once the computer was ready, Sadie typed in the name *Rachel Wright* and then waited a moment as several articles popped up. Then she clicked on the first link and started to read. Two hours later, she'd learned little new about Rachel, although she had been shocked at the vitriol spewed by Hester Marley Wright in an 1897 newspaper article about her missing stepdaughter. According to that article, Hester never believed Rachel died in the creek.

"Interesting," Sadie murmured to herself.

Then Sadie typed in Grandpa Jacob's name. A few articles popped up, but nothing out of the ordinary—except one. It was from the year 1897, the same year as Rachel's purported death.

According to the article, Jacob Wright started a street brawl in a nearby town and was jailed on June 15—three days before Rachel's wedding to Wallace Marley was supposed to take place. Her gaze scanned the article and she read that Jacob had been released from jail one week later—four days after Rachel's death.

"He wasn't there," Sadie breathed, suddenly understanding that her grandpa's reluctance to talk about Rachel's death probably stemmed as much from guilt as grief.

Jacob hadn't been there when his little sister had needed his help.

12

_____

WHEN SADIE RETURNED TO THE SHOP, JULIE LEFT TO RUN AN errand while Sadie resumed her work on the rocking horse. She sanded down some of the rough spots in the wood to get it ready for staining. But before she started that process, she wanted to figure out what to do with the snarled wool mane, fearing she might have to replace it.

Then she got an idea.

Sadie walked out of the backroom and looked around the shop for the basket of vintage livestock grooming supplies. She found it next to an old butter churn. She'd purchased both the churn and the grooming tools at an estate auction in Colorado Springs last spring.

Sadie carefully sorted through the basket, pulling out three pairs of hoof trimmers and several leather reins before finding the rustic sheep carding brush near the bottom.

A carding brush was used by farmers to comb out the wool of a sheep, often in preparation for a livestock show. The wooden paddle brush measured about eight inches long and five inches wide. Tiny metal teeth were angled on one side of the paddle, allowing it to pick up the wool and slide it through the teeth as the groomer gently flicked the card over the sheep.

Sadie carried the carding brush into the back room and tried it on the mane. It got stuck in the wool the first time she attempted to use it, but soon the wool fibers began to separate, smoothing out. The mane was so thick and matted that she could only work on a few inches of the wool at a time, slowly working her way to the base of the mane. Once she worked all the knots out, Sadie intended to wash away the dirt with a special shampoo.

As she carded the mane, a soulful Patsy Cline song played over the stereo speakers. Sadie had just started to sing along when the front door of the shop opened and a man walked inside.

Sadie set down the carding brush and exited the back room in case he wanted assistance.

He appeared to be in his midfifties, with salt-and-pepper hair and Paul Newman–blue eyes. A dimple popped in his right cheek when he smiled. "Hello, there. Are you Sadie Speers?"

"Yes, I am." She wiped her hands on a towel. "May I help you?"

"I'm Lance Ely," he said, walking toward her with his hand outstretched. A black leather briefcase was slung over one shoulder.

Sadie shook it, recognizing the name. "You're the travel writer."

He chuckled. "That's right."

"I heard you're planning to write an article about Silver Peak."

He nodded. "I'm still in the research phase and that's why I wanted to talk to you. I hear you're known as the Antique Lady around town, so I wanted to get your take on local history." He set his briefcase on the desktop. "Is now a good time?"

"Sure." She closed the door to the back room and then turned to face him. She didn't love the double meaning of the phrase—in her heart, she was anything but antique—but she appreciated the term of endearment for what it was. "What do you want to know?"

He unzipped his briefcase and pulled out a notepad and pen. "Tell me, how would you describe Silver Peak?"

"Well, it's my home, so I'm a little biased."

"Everybody has some kind of bias. This is an old mining town with a long, interesting history. What makes it home to you?"

She hesitated, trying to find the right words. "A sense of community," she said at last. "I could knock on any door in Silver Peak if I needed help and someone would be there for me. We all share some kind of connection, either through friends or family or church fellowship. This town has a heart and a pulse and a sense of history. Many of the houses and buildings have served generations of families, going back to the silver rush days."

She stopped, hoping she hadn't taken her description too far. But she could see Lance copying down every word on the ash-gray notepaper, using a combination of print and cursive, sometimes in a single word.

"That's great," he said, finally looking up at her. "I've only been here a couple of weeks, but I can easily imagine these streets filled with horses and buggies, prospectors and cowboys."

She smiled. "We still have some cowboys walking the streets," she said. "Ranching is big business around here and some of the mines are still active."

"I've been learning a lot about mining recently and spending most of my time at the American Mining Museum here in town. The exhibits are fascinating."

"It brings in a lot of tourists," Sadie told him, thinking of the grand, brick building that housed the museum. "Did you know that museum was once a Victorian schoolhouse?"

"No," he said, jotting down that fact in his notepad. "Fascinating." Then he looked up at her. "Tourism seems to be another boon for the local economy."

"I enjoy all the tourists who come to town," Sadie said with a smile, "and not only because they're potential customers."

He smiled. "Although I'm sure that helps. What do you think brings them here?"

"Well, not only do we have a wonderful town with lots of history, but Silver Peak has one of the best scenic views in the country. I've grown up with these mountains and see them every day, but they can still take my breath away."

"That happened to me," he said wryly. "I've had a few problems with the altitude."

"It takes a little while to get used to it. Make sure you're drinking plenty of water, because that will help."

His blue eyes widened in appreciation. "Thanks, I will." Then he cleared his throat. "So I've heard that you're not only the Antique Lady, but a relative to a legendary runaway bride from Silver Peak."

Sadie arched a brow. "How did you hear about that?"

He smiled. "Much like miners, I know how to keep digging when I find a nugget. Someone directed me to the *Chatterbox* blog and I read about Rachel Wright's wedding dress. Once I started asking questions and read that item in the *Chatterbox*, it eventually led me to you."

Sadie shifted uncomfortably in her chair. She couldn't stop him from publishing Great-aunt Rachel's story in a national magazine or newspaper article, but she also didn't have to contribute. "It's not something that my family likes to talk about."

"So it's still a sore subject even after all these years?"

"There are so many versions of the legend," she explained, "that no one really knows what actually happened. That may change someday, but until then I'd rather not speculate."

He gave a slow nod. "So tell me about this Founder's Day Picnic? I hear you're in charge. Is it worth going to?"

That was a question that Sadie could happily answer and she spent the next ten minutes telling him about the history of the picnic and how it brought the townspeople together every year. By the time she was done, Lance had filled up five pages in his notepad.

"This has been great," Lance said, flipping the cover closed on his notepad and sticking it inside his laptop case. "Thanks so much for your help."

"You're welcome," she said with a smile. "As you can tell, I love to talk about my hometown."

"I can see why. It's a lovely place."

"I hope you make it to the Founder's Day Picnic," Sadie said. "I know you won't be sorry."

"I'll do my best."

After he left, Sadie resumed the painstaking work of combing out the rocking horse mane until Julie arrived to relieve her for lunch. Then Sadie donned her jacket and made her way outside.

After the disturbance at her ranch house early this morning, Sadie hadn't found time to make a sack lunch so she made her way to the Market to pick up a deli sandwich.

As she passed Arbuckle's, Sadie saw two people through the window that made her stop in her tracks.

Edwin and Laura sat at a small table together. She watched for a long moment, then realized she was staring. Seeing them together like that bothered her more than she wanted to admit.

Had their impromptu library meeting led to a coffee date? If so, Sadie wondered why Laura hadn't mentioned anything about it earlier this morning. She supposed they could have arrived at Arbuckle's at the same time and decided to share a table.

"Sadie?"

Sadie turned around and saw Marge Ruxton approaching her on the sidewalk. Marge was a year younger than Sadie and wore a long black wool coat and black high heels.

"Hello, Marge," Sadie greeted her, moving out of sight of Arbuckle's window. The last thing she wanted was for Edwin or Laura to see her there.

"I was just coming to your shop to check on the rocking horse. Is it ready?"

"Not yet," Sadie told her, still feeling a little rattled. "I'll need a few more days."

"Oh dear," Marge said. "That's not what I wanted to hear. I need a picture of it for the silent auction brochure."

"You're selling it?" Sadie asked.

Marge flashed a smile. "I'm donating it for the silent auction at the Founder's Day Picnic."

Sadie wondered if she'd missed something in Jeanne's binder. "There is no silent auction at the picnic."

"There is now. I'm on the fundraising committee and decided that we needed more than the cake walk and bake sale to raise money. So I'm spearheading the silent auction. I've already accumulated quite a few donations."

Sadie gritted her teeth, used to Marge's habit of taking over a project or committee to fit her own agenda. Marge's husband, Lanford, was much the same.

Sadie breathed a silent prayer. *Lord, give me patience.* "Well, I should have the rocking horse done before the picnic."

"I hope so," Marge said, stuffing her hands inside her coat pockets. "I'll be quite busy that day. Why don't you just bring it to the park?"

"I suppose I can do that," Sadie said, determined to be gracious.

Marge beamed. "Wonderful. And as a member of the fundraising committee, I'd like to personally thank you for donating your time and talents to the restoration of the rocking horse."

Before Sadie could respond, Marge continued her way down the sidewalk. She stared after the woman, wondering why she was surprised at Marge's audacity after all these years. Sadie knew she had a good case for collecting her fee after putting so much work into the restoration. But, truth be told, it had been a labor of love, and it pleased her to know that it would be going to someone *other* than Marge Ruxton.

She took one last peek in Arbuckle's window and saw that Edwin and Laura were still there. Sadie turned on her heel and continued her trek to the Market, trying to convince herself that the gnawing feeling in the pit of her stomach simply meant that it was time for lunch.

Sadie passed by the historic brick buildings on her way, waving to people she knew. Her step lightened as she walked, the mountain air filling her lungs and the clear blue sky filling her spirit. She saw Josh standing on the other side of the street, talking with Jerry Remington, who owned Silver Peak Bed-and-Breakfast, and waved to them both.

Her gaze moved over the street. She loved the way the silhouettes of the storefronts were framed against the towering Rocky Mountains. It reminded her of a picture postcard, so perfect that it almost took her breath away. Even after sixty-two years, Sadie thanked God every day for the blessing of living in Silver Peak.

———

Thirty minutes later, Sadie returned to the Antique Mine, surprised to find it full of customers. Julie stood behind the cash register and gave her a frazzled wave.

For the moment, Sadie pushed thoughts of Edwin and Laura out of her mind and concentrated on assisting customers. Most of them were senior citizens on a bus tour. All of them seemed glad to find themselves in Silver Peak and bought small vintage linens or knickknacks to take back with them as souvenirs of their journey.

After most of the afternoon had passed, Sadie and Julie finally got a break.

"Wow," Julie said, leaning against the desk. "That got wild there for a while. I was so relieved to see you walk through the door."

"You should have called me," Sadie told her, straightening some of the linens. "I would have come right back."

Julie smiled. "I didn't mind. The time really flies when we're busy." She glanced at her watch. "In fact, it's probably time for me to go pick up the boys, if you don't mind."

"Go right ahead," Sadie told her. "I can handle it from here."

Julie gathered her things and headed for the door. "See you later."

"Oh, wait," Sadie said. "I wanted to ask you about offering some decorating advice to my friend, Edwin. He just moved back to town and lives in a gorgeous, old Victorian."

"I'd love to," Julie replied. "Does he have a day in mind?"

"What day works best for you?"

Julie lifted her shoulders in a small shrug. "Any day, really. I'm free all next week."

"Great," Sadie told her. "I'll talk to Edwin and let you know."

After Julie left, Sadie walked around the shop, taking care of odds and ends. She finished refolding the linens and straightened items here and there and, as always, kept an eye out for her wedding ring. She still believed it would turn up someday soon, although her left ring finger didn't look as bare as it had when she'd first lost it.

Maybe Edwin had something to do with that, she thought to herself. Then her gaze moved to the open doorway between Arbuckle's and her shop. She wondered if he and Laura were still there together and briefly considered heading over for coffee to see for herself before thinking better of it.

Now that she was alone with her thoughts, Sadie tried to look at the situation objectively. This was the second time she'd found the two of them together. Try as she might, she couldn't deny the tiny niggle of suspicion inside of her. For someone so afraid of her controlling fiancé, Laura certainly didn't seem too concerned about appearing in public with another man.

Unless Edwin was her fiancé.

That thought came unbidden to her mind, but once it was planted there she couldn't just ignore it. Laura had referred to her fiancé as Ray, but that didn't necessarily mean that was his real name. And she'd told the sheriff he was in Boston, but the way she had been so constantly jumpy might have suggested otherwise. Sadie took a deep breath, gathering herself as she considered the situation.

Edwin's sudden return to town had caught most people by surprise. He'd found the wedding dress and called her over to his house—possibly to authenticate it. Yet, he'd also let her take the dress, Sadie thought to herself. Why would he do that if he thought there might be a treasure connected to it?

It didn't take her long to realize that he might want her to lead him to the treasure. After all, she'd told him about the DNA test and would have probably told him about everything she discovered surrounding the wedding dress mystery.

Sadie hated having doubts about one of her oldest friends. But despite her fondness for him, she couldn't help being suspicious. She closed her eyes, sick at the thought that Edwin might have been involved with the smashing of her car window. And yet, if he *was* Laura's fiancé and capable of that kind of deception, then she couldn't put anything past him.

Sadie hurried over to her computer and typed Edwin's full name into the search box. The Edwin Marshall she'd known would have never been involved in such a ruse, but it had been years, decades actually, since she'd seen or talked to him. He might have changed.

Sadie watched the links with Edwin's name appear and most of them referenced his work as a circuit court judge in Chicago. That much was true, at least. She found his wife's obituary, listing Edwin and his daughter, Noelle, along with Noelle's husband and son in the list of family members. There were no computer links to indicate any type of nefarious activity or anything that included Laura's name.

"This is ridiculous," she said out loud, telling herself that Edwin couldn't be involved with Laura. *And yet . . .*

They'd been concealed behind a bookcase at the library and had looked very cozy at their table in Arbuckle's. They even had a mutual acquaintance now living in Boston. That might be just a coincidence, but what if it was something more?

The shop door opened, breaking Sadie's reverie. She looked up to see Roscoe Putnam, Roz's husband of forty years, walk inside. Heavyset and balding, he owned the hardware store next door and was a handy neighbor. Anytime Sadie needed a repair, he was right there and able to fix just about anything. Today he wore a pair of blue denim overalls with a short-sleeved, purple paisley shirt underneath that Sadie was certain Roz had picked out for him.

Sadie had always found Roscoe to be a perfect match for her best friend. They were both calm and collected, especially in a crisis, and had raised two fine sons, Randy and Raleigh, who both now resided in different states.

"Did you survive the bus tour?" Roscoe asked, walking toward the desk.

Sadie stood up to greet him. "We had quite a crush in here for a while, but I loved every minute of it. How about you?"

"We had a few customers, mostly men, and rang up a few sales too."

"Well, that's good to hear."

Roscoe loved his work and treated his hardware shop like a second home. Roz often joked that he'd sleep there if he could fit a cot amidst all the tools and lumber. In Sadie's mind, that gave sawing logs a whole new meaning.

"Got any antiques that you need me to repair?" Roscoe asked her.

"Not today," Sadie said with a smile. "But thanks for asking."

Roscoe was one of the most generous men she knew. He'd grown up poor on a farm in Kansas, the oldest of eight children, and had quit school at sixteen to work for the railroad so he could help provide for the family. Despite his lack of a high school diploma, Roscoe could hold his own in a debate and was an avid reader. He was also a skilled carpenter and often made minor repairs on items that Sadie unearthed at estate sales or the hidden treasures that could be found at secondhand stores.

He started tapping his fingers on the counter. Sadie had known him long enough to recognize this as a telltale sign that the man had something on his mind. She waited, knowing that he'd tell her when he was ready.

"Notice anything different about Roz lately?" Roscoe finally asked her.

"Roz?" Sadie echoed, the question surprising her. "No. Why?"

He gave a slight shrug. "I'm a little worried about her. She seems distracted. Sometimes she even ignores me."

"That doesn't sound like Roz."

"I know." He shook his head. "I've tried to talk to her about it, but she just brushes it off. I thought maybe she'd confided in you."

Sadie nibbled her lower lip, wondering if she'd been so caught up in her own life that she'd missed something. Roz seemed fine to her—although she had been acting a little distracted during their phone calls. "I haven't really noticed anything to be concerned about," she said honestly. "But I'll pay more attention the next time I see her."

"Maybe I'm just imagining things or looking to borrow trouble."

Roscoe wasn't the type to do either of those things, Sadie thought to herself, which gave her even more reason to worry. If he was concerned enough about Roz's behavior to come to Sadie about it, maybe there *was* something wrong.

"Has she complained about not feeling well?" Sadie asked him.

Roscoe shook his head. "No, she seems healthy enough. Still has a good appetite and goes for a walk almost every day."

"Any problems in the family?"

"None that I know about." Concern flashed in his blue eyes. "Maybe she's mad at me. She keeps the television cranked loud to keep us from talking much. And you know we like to square dance with that club in Breckenridge, but she hasn't wanted to go for months."

"I didn't know that." Sadie wondered what else her friend might be keeping from her. "Roz loves to square dance."

"Not anymore," he replied. "Not with me, anyway."

"I'll talk to her," she promised him. "We'll get this figured out."

"Thanks, Sadie. If anyone can get through to her, I know you can."

She appreciated his confidence in her and just hoped he was right. After he left the shop, she prayed for Roz and Roscoe, asking God's guidance and blessing for both of them. "Please, Lord," she whispered out loud, "watch over my friends. I love them so much."

———

The next day, Sadie yawned as she walked into the Antique Mine. She'd spent a restless night in bed, tossing and turning, her thoughts bouncing from Roz to Edwin to Laura. Now she found herself dragging, so she headed through the open doorway into Arbuckle's, hoping a cup of coffee would help her wake up.

Hector manned the counter and greeted her with a wide smile. "Good morning, Sadie. This is a double chocolate muffin kind of morning. We have some fresh from the oven if you'd like to have one."

"Sold," she said, his sales pitch making her smile. Chocolate had some caffeine, she told herself, and went so well with coffee.

Hector rang up her order and soon Sadie was back in her shop with a tall cup of hot coffee and a warm chocolate muffin filled with tiny chocolate chips. She took a bite of the muffin, letting the chocolate chips melt in her mouth. Hector was a genius, she thought to herself, taking a sip of his delicious coffee. The chocolate muffin was just what she needed.

When she finished the muffin, she licked the last smudge of chocolate off her thumb. That was when her daughter, Alice, and fourteen-year-old granddaughter, Sara, walked through the door.

"We made it just in time," Alice said, setting her purse on the desk. "Sara wanted to help out in the shop today."

"That's wonderful," Sadie said, as Sara rounded the desk to give her a hug.

"Hi, Grandma," Sara said. "I needed a break from studying. School just started and I already have to write three essays."

"Well, you have my condolences." Sadie kissed the top of her strawberry blonde head. "But I know you'll do great."

"I hope you're right," Sara said with a weary sigh. "At least Mia and I have five classes together this year."

"So you have someone to share your misery," Sadie said with a smile. "That always helps."

"I suppose so," Sara conceded. "I went for a hike yesterday with Mia, Lauren, and Nicole, and we found a wounded bird on the trail."

"You did?" Sadie replied. "Are you nursing it back to health?"

"Of course," Sara told her. "I took it to Dr. Armstead and he told me what to do. The little bird is so cute. I named him Oscar."

Sadie loved that her granddaughter's idea of fun was nursing a wounded animal back to health. And Dr. Armstead, the town veterinarian, was kind enough to offer his services and advice to Sara for free.

Alice had even let Sara convert part of the backyard into a makeshift wildlife sanctuary, where the wounded animals Sara collected were kept in various stages of recovery.

Sadie turned to her daughter. "And how are you?"

"Busy," Alice replied, giving Sadie a warm hug. "But I'm more worried about you, Mom. Any more strangers lurking around your house?"

Sadie gave her a reassuring smile. "No, I'm fine. Hank will let me know if there's any trouble. He's a great watchdog."

"He's the best kind," Sara said, "both cuddly and protective."

Sadie chuckled. "I couldn't have said it better myself." Then she turned back to Alice. "I think I'll run out for a bit this morning. I need to check in with the picnic committees and make sure everything is running smoothly."

"That's fine," Alice said. "Sara and I can handle things here. You take all the time you need."

"You're a sweetie," Sadie said.

"And Mom's cuddly and protective too," Sara said wryly. "Sometimes too protective for me and too cuddly for Theo."

Alice laughed. "So that's why he spends so much time in his room? He's getting tired of my bear hugs?"

"They must be unbearable," Sadie joked as Sara emitted an amused groan.

Sadie was still smiling as she made her way out of the shop, feeling much more cheerful than she had when she'd awakened this morning. It was time to spread that cheer a little, so she planned to make her first stop at Roz's house.

But Sadie didn't even make it as far as Roz's street. She called Roz's cell phone on her way, just to let her know that she was dropping by, but when Roz answered, sounding cheerful and upbeat, she told Sadie that she and Roscoe had decided to make an impromptu weekend trip to Denver.

Their chatty phone conversation made Sadie feel so much better. After they ended the call, she started humming "Joyful, Joyful," one of her favorite hymns, and turned the Cadillac toward the Vidals' house. She'd check in with Luz, who chaired the food committee, and then touch base with the other committee chairs on her list.

As she drove, the Rocky Mountains rose up in front of her, the sun shining in the clear blue sky. She gave her worries to God, letting His love fill her, and sang the final lines of the song out loud. *"Ever singing, march we onward, victors in the midst of strife; joyful music leads us sunward, in the triumph song of life."*

13

———

ON SUNDAY MORNING, SADIE INVITED LAURA TO ATTEND CHURCH with her. Laura happily agreed and they made their way to Campfire Chapel.

Sadie drove her Tahoe, which had been repaired and ready to pick up yesterday afternoon. She'd washed and dried the Cadillac convertible, trying to put as much care into it as T.R. had always done. Then she'd put the Cadillac back in the garage, where it would stay during the winter months.

"So tell me about your church," Laura said, as Sadie drove into town.

"Well, it was founded by our pastor, Don Sweeting, when he and his wife, Jeanne, moved to Silver Peak. We first started meeting in the high school gym, but then we purchased an old church on the edge of town that was scheduled for demolition. We restored it, trying to keep as much of the original framework and charm of the building as possible."

"Wow," Laura said, gazing at it through the front windshield. "It's like a picture from a postcard."

Sadie loved her church, both the lovely building and the people in it. "You'll get to meet my grandkids this morning. Alice told me they'd be in church today."

"Wonderful." Laura folded her hands in her lap. "It's so strange to think that they're my family too."

Sadie nodded, not ready to voice her suspicions. She'd waited for Laura to mention having coffee with Edwin yesterday, but she hadn't said a word about it. Sadie had thought about bringing the subject up herself, but she knew that if Laura was deceiving her about their relationship, she'd simply create some plausible-sounding story to explain away the meeting.

No, Sadie thought to herself as she neared the church, it was better for her to watch and wait. If either Laura or Edwin knew she harbored suspicions about them, they'd be even more careful to cover their tracks. Better to lie low and see what other clues she could gather.

She pulled into the church parking lot, which was already half-full. As she and Laura climbed out of the car, Sadie waved to Julie and Wyatt Henderson, who were walking toward the church. Little Caleb, who sat in Wyatt's arms, performed a cute little wave with his small hand.

"Those are the Hendersons," Sadie told Laura. "Wyatt's brother, Milo, boards horses, including mine and Alice's and the kids."

"I'd love to see your horse before I leave," Laura told her.

"Maybe we can go to his ranch this afternoon. It's such a beautiful day. Do you ride?"

"I haven't for years," Laura said with a smile. "And when I did, they were simple trail rides in single file, with a guide leading the way."

Sadie and Laura approached the church doors, which stood wide open. "I love riding," Sadie said, "especially on the mountain trails that are too far from home for me to walk. And just spending time with my horse, Scout, is so . . . soothing." She smiled. "It's difficult to put into words."

Laura followed Sadie into the church. "It sounds wonderful."

The original church pews had all been refinished, the intricate scrollwork on each end gleaming in the sunlight that set the stained-glass windows aglow. Sadie led Laura to a middle pew and allowed her to walk in first. They sat down, leaving plenty of room on either side for other congregation members.

As everyone waited for the service to start, church members chatted comfortably with one another. Sadie leaned close to Laura and began pointing out different friends and acquaintances.

"That's Rita Dodd," Sadie said in a low voice. "She's a good friend and works at my doctor's office. And on the other side of the aisle is Milo Henderson, sitting with his mother, Sally, who is a hairdresser."

"He's a big man," Laura said softly.

"Yes, and a big teddy bear." Sadie smiled as she looked over at Milo. With his dark hair and bushy beard, he looked like a gentle giant seated next to his petite mother. "In the row behind them is Troy Haggerty, who is the editor of the town newspaper, and seated next to Troy is Spike Harris."

Laura's gaze moved from clean-cut Troy to Spike, a tall, spare, gangly man who sported longish salt-and-pepper hair and looked a little weather-beaten for his forty-four years.

Sadie was pleasantly surprised to see Spike in church this morning since he wasn't a member and rarely attended. Then she checked the church bulletin and saw that he was listed to perform a song during the service. His friendship with the Sweetings had led to Spike agreeing to perform on occasion despite his own skepticism toward faith.

"Spike plays the fiddle and guitar," Sadie told Laura, "and writes his own music. He's quite talented."

"You have a nice mix of generations here," Laura observed, looking around at the congregation. "From the very young to the very old and everything in between."

Sadie smiled, nodding toward the elderly man seated a few rows ahead of them. "Our oldest member is Harry Polmiller. He's ninety-four and has one of the biggest vegetable gardens in town."

The church was filling up fast and a young family walked down the side aisle and sat down on the other side of Laura.

"And there are Alice and the kids," Sadie said, pointing them out as the three of them filed into the row ahead of Harry.

Sadie felt a light tap on her shoulder and turned around to see Edwin standing beside her.

"Do you have room for one more?" he asked.

Sadie hesitated for a moment, surprised to see him there. Edwin and his family had always attended a church in town with a much more formal service. "Of course," she said, not wanting to appear rude. Both she and Laura slid over on the pew to make room for him.

Edwin smiled as he sat down next to her and unbuttoned his black suit coat. She liked the subtle aroma of his aftershave and the way his blue dress shirt matched his eyes. But she hated the seeds of doubt that kept lingering in her mind, not wanting to believe the possibility that Edwin could by lying to her.

And yet, here he was—in her church. For a brief moment, she wondered if he'd followed them here. Or maybe Laura had contacted him before they'd left the house to tell him of their plans for the morning.

"This is a nice surprise," Sadie said. "I thought you attended Coventry Church."

"I met Pastor Don at the Market the other day," Edwin said. "He offered me a piece of cherry licorice and invited me to the worship service. How could I resist a man who carried licorice in his pocket?" His gaze moved around the sanctuary, taking in the solid oak floor and the exposed oak beams that braced the high peaked ceiling. "Besides, I've always loved this old church. Even though it doesn't look so old anymore with the wonderful restoration work that's been done."

The organist began to play the prelude, quieting the congregation as Pastor Don approached the pulpit. As the organ piped out the last note, Pastor Don raised his arms in the air. "This is the day that the Lord has made. Let us rejoice and be glad in it."

Edwin leaned toward Sadie and whispered, "He's got a great voice. Perfect for a pastor."

Sadie nodded, liking Edwin's nearness more than she wanted to admit. She squared her shoulders and kept her gaze on Pastor Don, who dressed in a suit and tie for Sunday services. He was in his late fifties, but there wasn't any gray in his short, black hair.

Pastor Don read passages of Scripture from Proverbs and from the Book of Matthew. Then he called the children up to the front for the children's sermon.

Pastor Don had a natural warmth and a way of relating to everyone he met. A tall, wiry African American and former rodeo star, he often joked that he'd honed the practice of prayer every time he saw a cowboy try to ride a wild bull. He'd eventually traded his rodeo career for a stint in the Denver Police Force before answering a call to the ministry.

After the children's sermon, Spike walked to the front of the sanctuary. He played his guitar as he sang "Amazing Grace," his voice strong and engaging, capturing the attention of everyone in the church.

Edwin shifted next to her and Sadie briefly wondered if he would have preferred sitting next to Laura. Doubts began to assail her again, but as Spike finished his musical performance and Pastor Don embarked on an inspirational message taken from the parable of the mustard seed, Sadie gave him her full attention, taking in every word.

Before she knew it, the congregation was rising to sing the closing hymn. She and Edwin stood side by side, each holding a hymnal as they sang "Rock of Ages." Edwin's deep, resonant voice blended well with the congregation and Sadie enjoyed listening to him. He'd sung in the choir in high school and had even starred in the senior play, *The Music Man*, excelling in the role of Harold Hill. *A man who had bamboozled an entire town*, Sadie thought to herself as the congregation sang the last refrain. Although, she reminded herself, Harold Hill had been redeemed by love in the end.

After Pastor Don gave the benediction, people began to slowly file out of the pews. Edwin turned to Sadie. "I'm so glad I came today. I really enjoyed his sermon."

"He certainly has a way with words," Laura interjected. "He's plain-spoken, but his compassion and conviction shine through in his message."

"Yes, we're very blessed to have him," Sadie said, as they moved into the center aisle. It quickly filled with people, many of whom came up to greet Sadie, as well as to welcome Laura and Edwin. Soon the three of them became separated. Sadie slowly made her way out of the sanctuary to greet the pastor, then walked through the doors of the church to the front lawn.

Small clusters of church members chatted outside, as birds chirped in the trees and six-year-old Lacie Armstead skipped around the lawn singing "Jesus Loves Me."

"There you are," Laura said, approaching Sadie. "I lost you in the crowd. Everyone here is so friendly."

Sara ran up to them, leaving Alice and Theo not far behind. "Grandma, do you want to go riding with us this afternoon?"

Sadie looked at Laura. "Well, we were talking about going to the stable. What do you say, Laura? Shall we go riding with Alice and the kids?"

Laura hesitated. "Do I need to rent a horse? I'm not sure how it works."

"No," Theo replied. A strapping young man of seventeen, Theo had his father's dark hair and his mother's eyes. To Sadie's delight, her grandson had T.R.'s smile and her heart always melted a little when he directed it toward her.

"Milo will just let you ride one of his horses," Theo continued. "He likes for them to get as much exercise as possible."

Laura smiled "Well, okay then! Let's go for a ride." Then she turned to Sadie. "I'd love to see the old family silver mine too. Is that nearby?"

Sadie nodded. "Yes, it's fairly easy to get there by horseback. Shall we leave after lunch?"

"That sounds good," Alice said as the children nodded their approval.

Edwin walked up to their little group and Laura turned to him and said, "We're going horseback riding this afternoon."

He smiled. "How fun! I haven't ridden for years."

Sara leaned over to whisper to her mom. "Is that Grandma's old boyfriend?" Only her whisper was loud enough for the rest of the group to hear.

Edwin chuckled. "Guilty," he said, glancing over at Sadie as everyone laughed.

His familiar smile warmed Sadie's heart. Her doubts about him were fueled by conjecture rather than fact. Maybe if they all spent some time together, Sadie could better understand the relationship between Edwin and Laura.

"Why don't you come riding with us too?" Sadie said to Edwin.

Edwin hesitated. "I don't want to intrude."

Alice smiled at him. "You won't be intruding. And that way Theo won't feel outnumbered."

Theo nodded. "Yeah, you should come with us."

"Then you can tell us what Grandma was like in the olden days," Sara added.

Sadie groaned, reaching out to give Sara's shoulders a warm squeeze. "The *olden* days? I'm not that ancient, you know."

"Yeah, Grandma is cool," Theo said and then turned to Alice. "We'd better go so we have plenty of time to ride this afternoon."

"Okay," Alice said. "Shall we all plan to meet at Milo's at one?"

"That sounds fine with me," Sadie replied as Laura and Edwin both nodded in agreement. Then they all headed for the parking lot.

"Shotgun," Sara called out, racing ahead of her brother to claim the front passenger seat of their Jeep Cherokee.

Theo shook his head. "Whatever." Then he turned to Alice. "This is why I want to drive myself to church."

"I think you'll survive riding in the backseat," Alice said, as she and Theo headed toward the Cherokee.

Then Edwin gave them a wave as he veered off toward his BMW and said, "See you at one."

———

"This should be fun," Laura told Sadie as they turned into Milo's long driveway later that afternoon. "I just hope I don't fall off my horse."

"Don't worry. Milo will make sure you get a gentle one."

The Henderson ranch sprawled over twenty acres, most of it pasture grass for the horses to graze. Milo had recently built a state-of-the-art horse barn, complete with twenty horse stalls, two grooming stalls, and two wash stalls. The barn also featured a video surveillance system and a fire alarm and sprinkler system. The horse barn was bigger, newer, and much fancier than the cozy, two-bedroom bungalow that Milo called home.

When they reached the barn, Sadie saw that Edwin, Alice, and the kids had already arrived. Five horses stood saddled near the white fence, their reins wrapped loosely around the top metal bar.

"They look so big," Laura said, her eyes wide as she opened the car door.

As Sadie climbed out of the Tahoe, she saw Milo leading her beautiful chestnut gelding, Scout, out of the barn. The five-year-old horse whinnied when he saw her. Sadie walked over and nuzzled his velvety nose. "Hey, boy," she said gently, one hand gliding over his long neck. "How are you?"

"Good as gold," Milo answered for him. He checked the stirrups and then handed the reins to Sadie. "It's a great day for a ride."

"It is," she said, looking up at the clear blue sky. A warm breeze from the south caressed her face, and the temperature was forecast to hit the upper sixties by midafternoon.

Sadie climbed into the saddle and settled comfortably into place, watching Alice and the kids do the same.

"I've got Opie for you, Mr. Marshall," Milo said, untying the tall pinto from the railing. "Do you need any help mounting him?"

"No, thanks. I think I remember," he said. "And please call me Edwin."

Milo smiled. "Okay, Edwin."

Edwin mounted the horse like a pro, sitting tall in the saddle. Opie snorted and pawed the ground until Edwin reached out and patted his neck. "Easy, boy." The horse instantly settled down at the sound of his voice.

Milo helped Laura mount her horse, a small white mare named Sunflower. "She'll be as gentle as a lamb for you," Milo said, as Laura tightly clutched the reins in her hands. "Just give her a nudge with the heels of your shoes when you want her to go faster and gently pull back on the reins when you want to slow up."

"Okay," Laura said, taking a deep breath as she shifted uneasily in the saddle.

Theo prodded Bronco, his black gelding, forward. "I'll take the lead."

"Are you sure you remember the trail?" Alice asked him, following behind on Rio, her gray gelding.

"Of course," Theo said, heading out of the driveway.

Sara rolled her eyes. "Theo knows *everything*," she said to her mother. "Just ask him." Then she urged her light bay filly, Daisy, forward to keep pace with Alice's horse.

Sadie, Edwin, and Laura brought up the rear, with Laura taking the center spot atop her mare. Sadie gave her advice along the way, helping her ease into the rudiments of riding a horse. Sunflower made it easy, lopping along the trail at a gentle pace and responding well to Laura's awkward use of the reins.

As they rode, Sadie found her cares falling away as she breathed in the crisp, pine-scented air and watched a hawk fly overhead. The beauty of the day and spending time with her family made it all the more special. Edwin seemed to enjoy the ride along the trail as much as she did, reminiscing about a horse he'd once had as a child. Soon even Laura relaxed enough to laugh and joke as they made their way to the old family silver mine.

An hour later, Theo turned around in his saddle. "We're almost there."

Sadie could hear the creek water bubbling over the rocks as Theo led them off the main trail and onto a smaller one surrounded by more rocky terrain. The horses fell into single file until they reached the silver mine.

"Here it is," Sadie said, climbing off of Scout. She led her horse over to the creek to drink the water, soon followed by the others. Theo and Sara began to splash each other in the water while Alice wandered along the grassy trail and gathered some of the golden leaves that had fallen from the aspen trees.

"So is that the silver mine?" Laura said, pointing toward it.

"Yes," Sadie replied, as they approached the dark mouth of the mine.

The opening of the silver mine spanned about six feet wide and six feet high and was braced by thick beams of old wood. Two large flat gray stones bordered the mine opening, like small stools where the prospectors could rest and count their silver nuggets. Sadie's great-great-grandfather had been one of those prospectors, along with his brother. The silver they'd found had provided enough money to buy the Wright family ranch.

Alice and the kids were now seated by the creek, chatting together as the horses munched lazily on clumps of grass.

"So this place was Nana's destination when she ran away from her wedding," Laura mused, turning in a slow circle.

"Her wedding dress was found on the edge of the creek," Sadie said as they all turned toward the rushing water. "The search party reported that some of those boulders in the creek had blood on them, which made everyone believe that Rachel had waded into the creek, either to wash the blood from her wound or to drown herself."

"Or to make it look like she did," Laura said. "Nana must have had a plan all worked out. She probably hid some clothes up here beforehand. Maybe she even had someone helping her hide the treasure."

Then Laura looked over at Edwin. "Where should we start digging?"

14

―――――

"DIGGING?" EDWIN SAID, STARING AT LAURA.

Laura laughed. "Sorry. Bad joke." She turned to Sadie. "But I wish it was as simple as digging to find some answers. I still don't understand how Nana could have let her brother and the rest of her family in Silver Peak believe she had died—especially in such a tragic way."

"I know." Sadie's heart still ached at the thought that Rachel might have been alive all those years in Boston while Jacob mourned for his sister. Had Rachel been afraid to contact him? Or upset that he hadn't helped her escape? It occurred to Sadie that Rachel might never have known that Jacob had been jailed in another town on the day of her wedding.

Tears shimmered in Laura's eyes. "I remember my nana's ninetieth birthday party. There were so many people there. She'd been an active volunteer in the community her entire adult life."

Edwin took a step closer to Sadie. "Is there any way I can help you find some of those answers? I'm pretty resourceful when I put my mind to it."

She smiled, grateful for his offer of help. "Thanks, I'll keep that in mind."

Laura started wandering around the front of the mine, taking pictures from different angles with the camera on her cell phone. Then Laura moved toward the creek, where Alice and the kids were still sitting by the water. She took some photographs of them and then of the creek itself.

Edwin stepped closer to Sadie. "What do you think? Is she your cousin?"

Sadie yearned to confide in him, but those lingering doubts made her cautious. "I'm not sure yet," she said at last. "You've had a chance to talk with her, what do you think?" She waited, wondering if he'd mention having coffee with Laura.

"The jury is still out," he replied. "She seems nice and sincere. Her interest in Silver Peak and its history certainly isn't fake."

"No, it's not." Sadie watched Laura chatting and laughing with Alice. "I like her. We have a lot in common and the way she talks about her nana rings true. But . . ."

"But you can't be sure," Edwin said with a nod of understanding. "Give it some more time, I guess. Laura doesn't seem to be in any hurry to leave."

"I know." Sadie looked up at him, carefully studying his handsome face. "It makes me wonder if she's waiting for the alleged treasure to surface."

"She and half the town. I've heard more talk about the legend of the runaway bride this week then I can ever remember." He met her gaze. "Do *you* believe there's a treasure to find?"

Sadie gave a slight shrug, thinking about the antique brass key that was still in her purse—the key she'd kept secret from Edwin.

There had to be a reason it had been included with that letter. "I don't know," she said at last.

"Hey, Sadie," Laura called over to them. "You two need to join us. It's picture time."

"Come on, Mom," Alice said. "I want a picture with you and the kids."

Sadie and Edwin joined them by the creek. For the next twenty minutes, they took several photographs.

"This is great," Laura said. "I'll have wonderful pictures to take back to the family in Boston." Then tears shimmered in her eyes. "Nana always insisted on taking lots of pictures at family get-togethers." She sucked in a deep breath. "I miss her so much."

Sadie and Edwin exchanged glances. Then he walked up to Laura and placed a hand on her shoulder. "It sounds like she was a wonderful woman."

"She was," Laura said, wiping a lone tear from her eye. "She was so loving to everyone around her. And always so cheerful, which I found a little puzzling given the circumstances that had brought her to Boston."

"So she was happy?" Alice asked, her voice wistful.

Laura nodded. "Yes. She often said a cheerful heart was good medicine."

"That's from Proverbs," Sadie said, her mind drifting to an embroidered pillow that had been in Grandpa Jacob's house with the same verse on it. She'd never thought much about it at the time, but now she wondered if that verse had special meaning to her grandpa. Despite his silence about his sister, Grandpa Jacob had been a cheerful man, always making jokes and telling funny stories.

"We probably should start heading back before the sun goes down," Alice said. "Is everyone ready?"

"Yeah," Sara said, moving toward the horses. "I have homework to do."

Sadie took one last look at the old silver mine and the creek running beside it, wondering what answers they held that she hadn't yet discovered. Maybe Laura was right—it was time to do some digging.

———

On Monday, Sadie made a visit to Judith Marley, the matriarch of the Marley family. A former high school English teacher, the seventy-seven-year-old woman was one of the few Marleys who seemed to have no grudge against the Wright family.

Sadie walked up to the front door and knocked, hoping she wasn't on a fool's errand. The legend of the runaway bride had been so seldom spoken about in her own family, she hoped Judith might be able to shine some new light on the story.

A few minutes later, Judith answered the door. If she was surprised to see Sadie standing on her front porch, she didn't show it. Judith had never married, devoting herself to a career as an educator and serving as a mentor for her many nieces and nephews. She prided herself on her appearance, with a standing weekly appointment at the hair salon and impeccable taste in clothes.

"Hello, Judith," Sadie greeted her. "How are you?"

"I'm fine." Judith wore a pair of black slacks and a white silk blouse, with a string of pearls circling her neck. "How are you?"

"Good. I'm hoping you have a few minutes to talk."

"Of course." Judith stepped back from the doorway and ushered Sadie inside. "I assume you're here about the wedding dress."

"So you've heard about it?" Sadie asked as she walked into the well-appointed parlor, filled with family heirlooms and a few antiques that Judith had purchased from the Antique Mine.

"Yes, I've had a few visits from family members wanting to plan strategy." Judith waved one manicured hand toward the vintage wingback chair. "Please have a seat, Sadie. Would you like to join me for tea?"

"That would be lovely, thank you." Sadie took a seat as Judith disappeared into the next room. Judith had never exuded much warmth, but she was honest, in Sadie's experience, even though her comments were sometimes very blunt.

A short time later, Judith returned to the parlor carrying a tray with a white ceramic teapot and two matching cups and saucers. She poured a cup for Sadie and handed it to her. "Milk or sugar?"

"No, thank you," Sadie said, carefully taking the cup and saucer from her. Then she watched Judith measure out a precise teaspoon of sugar and add it to her steaming tea. She used a silver spoon to give it three quick stirs and then sat down on the curved, gold velvet sofa opposite Sadie.

"As you know, I think the feud between the Marley and Wright families is quite silly," Judith said. "I apologize for Wade's recent behavior, which he made the mistake of sharing with me. He inherited a stubborn streak from his father and grandfather, which can be difficult to manage."

"You mentioned the word *strategy* earlier," Sadie said. "What did you mean?"

Judith took a small sip of her tea, then set it on the table in front of her. "Only that several members of my family believe that we deserve to take ownership of the wedding dress. But I believe any rights the Marleys had with the dress reached an expiration date long ago."

"So you don't agree with them?"

"Of course not. When someone remains stuck in the past, it becomes impossible for them to move forward in the future. Wade has done fairly well for himself, but this matter has him all tied up in knots. I have to wonder how much his business suffers when he doesn't give it his full attention."

Sadie took a sip of the hot tea, recognizing the flavor as Earl Grey, one of her favorites. She wondered if Wade had run into financial difficulties, which wasn't unusual in the property business. Perhaps he saw the treasure as a way out of possible financial troubles.

"Is there anything I can say to him so he'll let this go?" Sadie asked her.

"I'm afraid not. Wade is determined to take that wedding dress away from you—one way or another."

She thought about her broken car window. *How far would he actually go?*

"What's the real reason you're here today, Sadie?" Judith asked, tilting her head slightly. "You've known about the feud between our two families since you were a tot. Certainly it's no surprise to you that some of the Marleys would want the wedding dress and anything connected to it."

"No, it's not a surprise," Sadie said, deciding to match the woman's bluntness. "I came here to ask you about Marley Hopkins."

Judith arched a thin, white eyebrow. "That's a name I haven't heard in a very long time."

"So you recognize the name."

Judith scowled. "Of course, he was family. Marley was the son of Lavinia Marley Hopkins, the only sister of Wallace Marley."

"And Wallace was Rachel's fiancé."

Judith nodded as she reached for her tea once more. "What do *you* know about Marley Hopkins?"

"Only that he was involved in a street brawl in a nearby town with my grandpa Jacob. Both men spent a week in jail." Sadie tipped up her chin. "I believe that Marley Hopkins probably instigated that fight to keep Jacob away from Rachel in the wedding. Wallace or Hester might have sensed that Rachel was getting cold feet."

"You are correct," Judith told her. "Marley Hopkins didn't do much in his life to make his family proud, but he was quite good at brawling. His mother asked him to find a way to keep Jacob Wright away from the wedding and he used his fists to make it happen."

"And it worked," Sadie mused. "Jacob missed the wedding. And he never saw his sister again."

Judith frowned. "It's a piece of my family history that I'm not proud of, Sadie. But none of us are responsible for the actions of our ancestors. That's something I've tried to drill into Wade's head, but his pride blinds him."

Sadie wished all the Marleys could be more like Judith. Although her formality and stiff manner was off-putting to many people in Silver Peak, Sadie appreciated her candor. Now she decided to return the favor with some candor of her own.

"Wade is a suspect in an act of vandalism. Someone broke my car window."

"In Silver Peak?" Judith asked, perplexed.

"At my home, actually. I couldn't see a face, but Wade had made it clear he wasn't going to back down."

"I'll talk to him," Judith told her. "If he broke your window, I'll make sure that *he's* the one paying restitution."

"Thank you," Sadie replied, drinking the last of her Earl Grey and then setting it on the table. "I appreciate your taking the time to talk with me."

"You should have come sooner. The best way to stop this kind of nonsense is to nip it in the bud immediately."

"I'll remember that," Sadie said with a smile. Then Judith walked her to the door and they said their good-byes.

Sadie walked to her car, the picture of the past now a little clearer in her mind. Grandpa Jacob had been lured into a fistfight to keep him from his sister's wedding—or more likely, to prevent him from helping Rachel escape. But Rachel had found a way to escape on her own—all the way to the old silver mine. As for the rest . . .

Her cell phone rang, interrupting her reverie. She answered it as she climbed into her Tahoe. "Hello?"

"Sadie, this is Dr. Conroy. I've got those test results you wanted."

Her heart skipped a beat. "I'll be right there."

———

Sadie sat down in the waiting room of Dr. Conroy's medical office and leafed through the magazines sitting on the table. Several patients came and went as Sadie waited and she tried not to grow impatient, aware that an illness took precedence over a DNA test result.

Then Rita called her up to the front desk.

"Doc will be ready for you soon," Rita told her. "You can head back to exam room one."

"Thanks." Sadie walked down the narrow hallway, hearing the cry of a baby behind one of the closed doors and inhaling a quick, unpleasant sniff of iodine. Sadie reached the door to exam room one at the same time as the doctor.

"Well, this is what I call perfect timing," Doc said, opening the door and waving her inside. "How are you today?"

"Fine, but a little nervous."

"Well, that's to be expected, given the circumstances." He sat down and opened the file in his hand.

"So as I'm sure you're aware," he began, "the DNA tests on the blood on the wedding dress as well as the cheek swab sample you provided are in."

"And?"

"And it's a match." He met her gaze as he handed her the report. "You can keep this, if you'd like."

"Thank you," she breathed, feeling a little off balance. During the drive to his office, she'd almost convinced herself that the wedding dress wasn't authentic. Now she knew differently. The wedding dress Edwin had found in his attic truly did belong to Rachel Wright.

"You'll want the wedding dress back," he said, rising to his feet and moving toward the door.

"Actually, I'm not sure I do," she said, stopping him in his tracks. "Not yet, anyway. Would you mind keeping it here for me? It won't be for long."

"Sure," he said, curiosity gleaming in his eyes. "If that's what you want."

Sadie paused for a moment, then nodded. "I think that would be best for now. It's become an . . . object of interest and I'd prefer to keep it out of sight for a while."

"Understood." He smiled. "You may keep it here as long as you like, Sadie. I'll make sure it stays under lock and key."

"Thank you, Doc," she said, "for everything."

"You're welcome. Let me know if there's anything else I can do for you."

"Actually, there is one more thing and it's kind of a delicate matter. A woman named Laura Finch is staying with me. When she arrived in Silver Peak, she claimed that she was my cousin and that she was a direct descendant of Rachel Wright."

Doc whistled low, taking a seat on the stool. "And you believe her?"

"I want to believe her," Sadie said slowly, "but her story is so outlandish that I'm not sure what to think. Would it be possible to run another DNA test to match the blood on the wedding dress to some of her DNA?"

"Yes, it's possible, especially since the lab already has already retrieved the DNA from the wedding dress. I'll just need a DNA sample from her. A few strands of hair will do, if she's not able to come into the office."

"I'll bring some in."

He reached into the drawer and pulled out a couple of plastic bags. "You can put the hair into these specimen bags."

"Thanks," she said, taking the bags from him. "I really appreciate this."

"And I'm always here," Doc said, meeting her gaze. "If you ever want to talk about this . . . situation. They make pills for just about everything these days," he said with a chuckle, "but sometimes lending a listening ear is the best medicine."

"You're right." His words touched her heart. "I may borrow your ear one of these days." She smiled. "Maybe both of them."

He chuckled. "Take care, Sadie."

As she left his office, Sadie thought about the night ahead and wondered if there was a pill to ease a guilty conscience.

15

THAT EVENING, SADIE BIDED HER TIME, WAITING FOR AN opportunity to obtain a DNA sample from Laura. She didn't like deceiving a woman she'd come to know and like, but it was the only way she could think of to prove once and for all that Laura was a direct descendant of Rachel Wright, and truly Sadie's cousin.

It occurred to her that Laura rarely talked about her fear of her fiancé anymore. Sadie wondered if distance had made her feel more in control of her own life, or had it just been a ruse? Had Laura exaggerated or even faked her fears to get closer to Sadie?

If so, it had worked. Those niggling doubts assailed Sadie more each day, making Sadie want to know the truth.

"Are you feeling all right?" Laura asked, one of the family photo albums propped open in her lap. "You're awfully quiet tonight."

"I just have a lot on my mind."

Laura nodded. "The Founder's Day Picnic is coming up fast, isn't it? Is there anything I can do to help?"

A tiny stab of guilt pricked Sadie's heart. "Thanks for the offer, but I think we have everything under control right now."

"Well, the offer is open. Just let me know if you need anything."

"Thanks, I will." Sadie reached over to pet Hank, who lay snuggled next to her on the sofa, his head resting on her leg.

"How is the genealogy work coming along?" Sadie asked her. "Have you learned anything new about our family?" The *our* just slipped out, but Sadie didn't correct herself.

"Just fine," Laura said with a smile. "The library has wonderful books on local history, so I'm picking up tidbits about the family as I'm reading how Silver Peak was built. I've got pages and pages of notes. I'll let you read them someday after I get them all organized."

"I'd like that," Sadie said. A large part of her wanted Laura's story to be true—that Rachel had left Colorado and went on to lead a long, happy life in Boston. The way Rachel had gone about it bothered Sadie, especially not letting her own brother know that she was still alive. But times had been so different then, and it was possible that Rachel was trying to protect Jacob as much as she was trying to protect herself.

The fact that most of the Marley family still harbored ill will toward the Wright family, even after so many years, showed a glimpse of the motivation behind Rachel's secret escape act.

Sadie swallowed a sigh. In truth, there could be many different endings to the legend of the runaway bride. She simply had to find a way to verify the possibilities one by one until she found the truth. And as much as she wanted to trust Laura, she couldn't let that deter her from doing everything possible to find that truth.

"I'm excited for the picnic," Laura continued, flipping another page in the album. "I'll probably head back home after it's over, as much as I'd like to stay."

Sadie looked at her. "What about Ray? Have you decided if you want to marry him?"

"I'm not sure." Laura sighed. "It's so strange spending time away from him. He's been such a big part of my life for the last year. Part of me misses him, but I like my independence too. I didn't realize how much until I came here."

"And you aren't sure whether you can assert your independence with him?"

Laura shook her head. "I've tried before, but it's usually just easer to go along with whatever he wants." She sighed. "I do care about him, though. That's what makes this so difficult. I don't want to spend the rest of my life alone. What if I don't meet anyone else?"

Sadie could hear the apprehension in her voice and part of her could relate to it. After T.R. passed away, she'd never imagined spending time with another man. But now . . . "I think I'd rather live alone than live with the wrong person," Sadie said at last. "You have to be happy with yourself first, before you can find true happiness with someone else."

Laura smiled. "Now you sound like Nana. She had the same strength I see in you. Why did I miss out on that gene?"

"Maybe you didn't," Sadie said gently. "Maybe it's just been in hibernation."

"Maybe," Laura said, turning another page. Then she sat up in the chair, her gaze on the photo album. "Look, there are pictures of the old family silver mine."

Sadie gently nudged Hank's head off her lap and then stood up and walked over to where Laura sat. "Yes, that is the mine. It looks like it was taken forty or fifty years ago."

"There's the opening to the mine," Laura said, pointing it out with one finger, "and the two stone sentinels on each side. There isn't as much brush grown over it and you can see part of the creek here in the corner of the photograph."

"Someone probably took the picture for posterity. That photograph looks like it was taken around the same time the mine closed down."

Laura glanced up at her. "Why did it close?"

"The silver began to peter out and soon it cost more to keep it open than the revenue it generated. It had been in our family since the silver rush days, so it wasn't an easy decision by any means."

"You said the Wright family was wealthy when Nana was growing up here. I wonder if she ever knew about the hard times that befell her family."

"The thirties were hard times for just about everyone. I was born in 1952, but heard plenty of hardship stories from my parents and grandparents. Some folks in Silver Peak never recovered and had to move and start over somewhere else."

"Part of me hopes Nana didn't know," Laura said softly. "That her memories of her life on the ranch with her family kept her from missing them too much."

Sadie remembered times when Grandpa Jacob seemed to be lost in a daydream. Her grandma called it wool gathering and often teased him about it. He'd always laugh with Grandma, but never did say what—or whom—he'd been thinking about. Now Sadie wondered if Grandpa Jacob had been reliving memories of his beloved sister and their early years together on the ranch.

Laura closed the photo album and set it on the coffee table. "It's getting late. I think I'll take a nice, hot bubble bath before bed."

"That sounds relaxing."

"Good night," Laura said as she turned and moved toward the stairs.

"Good night." Sadie resumed her place on the sofa and Hank snuggled close to her once more. She wanted to give Laura enough time to draw her bath before she made her move.

Twenty minutes later, Sadie left Hank sleeping on the sofa and made her way around the house, turning off lights and double-checking to make certain the doors were locked. Then she made her way up the stairs. When she reached the hallway, she walked down it just far enough to see that the door to the guest room bathroom was closed.

Then she turned quickly and walked to Laura's room. She placed her hand on the doorknob, turning it slowly and then pushing the door open. It made a slight creaking sound and she froze, hoping Laura hadn't heard it. Logically, the sound could have come just as easily from Sadie's bedroom door, but this type of subterfuge was new to her.

Sadie supposed she could have just asked Laura for a hair sample. Laura's reaction might have told her a lot. But she thought it was also very possible that Laura truly believed Rachel Wright and her Nana had been the same woman.

After all, Sadie thought to herself, the legend of the runaway bride had been well known around the area. Another woman, perhaps one in desperate straits, might have traveled to Boston and assumed the identity of Rachel Wright. That would also explain why Laura's nana had rarely talked about her life before coming to Boston—except to claim herself as a runaway bride and that she'd left her wedding dress behind—facts easily known to most of the people in the region at the time.

Still, Sadie didn't know if she couldn't trust someone she'd only known for a week. And asking Laura for a hair sample might break the fledging friendship growing between them. Sadie suddenly realized she was standing in Laura's bedroom doorway, arguing with herself.

It was time to make a decision.

She took a step into the room, noting how clean Laura kept it. The bed was made and her toiletry items neatly laid out on the dresser. Sadie spotted a hairbrush and hurried over to the dresser, keeping one ear open for any sounds coming from the hallway.

She retrieved the plastic specimen bag that Doc had given her from her pocket, then picked up the brush.

Suddenly, the door creaked. She whirled around, her heart beating her throat.

Hank looked up at her from the open doorway, his tail wagging behind him.

She released a deep breath, her heart still pounding. Then she quickly pulled a few light brown hairs from the bristles on the brush and dropped them into the specimen bag. After sealing it, Sadie was careful to place the brush back on the dresser exactly as she'd found it. She took one last look around to make sure nothing else was disturbed, then walked quickly out of the room.

Out in the hallway, Sadie glanced quickly toward the guest bathroom, relieved that the door was still closed. Hank had followed her into the hallway, his tail still wagging as she reached out to close Laura's bedroom door.

Mission accomplished.

Now she just needed to drop off the specimen bag at Doc's office tomorrow morning. She looked down at Hank, who was gazing up at her with his soft brown eyes.

"Don't look at me like that," Sadie whispered, still feeling a little guilty.

He moved a step closer and licked her hand. Sadie took it as a sign of approval, although she knew that was probably wishful thinking on her part.

"*Show me the way, Lord,*" Sadie whispered as she walked into her bedroom, closing the door behind her. He knew her heart even better than she knew it herself. "*Show me the way.*"

————

On Tuesday, Sadie worked at the Antique Mine, dividing her time between helping the occasional customer and putting the finishing touches on the rocking horse she was restoring in the back room.

Roz walked in through the open doorway between the coffee shop and the Antique Mine, carrying two tall paper cups. "Coffee, anyone?"

"Me!" Sadie called out as she carried the rocking horse out on the floor, looking for somewhere to put it. The shop was packed full, especially since Jason had brought in two more chairs earlier this morning to display in his furniture space.

"Looks like you've got your hands full," Roz said, setting one of the cups on the counter, and then taking a seat on the stool beside it.

"I finally finished the rocking horse. It turned out even better than I expected." She placed the rocking horse near the pie safe, one hand smoothing down the wool mane. Then she stepped back for a better look. "What do you think?"

"I can't believe that's the same rocking horse Marge brought to you. It's gorgeous!"

Sadie walked over to the counter and picked up her coffee cup. "I love that rocking horse so much I almost want to keep it myself. Maybe I'll buy it at the silent auction that Marge is organizing for the picnic."

Roz chuckled. "Your house is so full you'd have to wedge it into the rafters."

Sadie laughed. "It's not quite *that* bad. I prefer to call it cozy."

"I'll have to remember that the next time Roscoe complains about a new knickknack I bring home." Then she shook her head. "Though he's been complaining so much lately, it wouldn't really matter."

Sadie looked up from her cup, her heart stirring. First, Roscoe had mentioned some concern about their marriage and now Roz was doing the same. Roz and Roscoe had been happy for so many years, she just didn't want to believe that could change. "What's going on, Roz?"

Roz sighed. "I don't know. Maybe working so much at the hardware store is finally wearing him down. He just grumbles under his breath at me all the time but never really comes out and says what he means. Then he gets huffy and walks away."

"That doesn't sound like Roscoe." She found it strange that both Roz and Roscoe were blaming each other. "Has something happened recently?"

"Not that I'm aware," Roz said before taking another sip of her coffee. "It's probably just one of those little squalls that happen in marriages from time to time. I'm just hoping it will blow over soon."

"So do I."

"Enough about me," Roz said with a wave of one hand. "What's new with you? Did the DNA test results on the wedding dress come in yet?"

Sadie didn't want to let the conversation go so easily, but she didn't want to push either. "Yesterday. And there was a match showing a family relationship between the DNA on the dress and the DNA sample from my cheek swab."

Roz's brow crinkled. "I'm confused."

"My DNA and the DNA from the blood on the wedding dress matched closely enough to prove that whoever left that blood on the dress is related to me." Sadie wrapped her palms around the warm coffee cup. "In my mind, that's enough to prove it was Rachel's dress."

Roz stared at her. "So it's the real thing? It's the wedding dress left behind by the runaway bride?"

"Yes. And, apparently, it's been in the Marshall attic for the last one hundred and seventeen years." She leaned in closer to Roz. "That means that letter from Grandpa Jacob is most likely authentic too."

"And the brass key?"

Sadie gave a small nod. "I assume so. Although, who knows if I'll ever find the lock it opens."

"Have you told Laura?"

Sadie shook her head. "I haven't told anyone else but you and Alice. She called shortly after I got the news."

Roz gazed at her for a long moment. "So were you happy or disappointed with the result?"

"Happy, I guess. Although, I'm still not sure what to do with the information. Too many people want the dress and I'm not interested in a big legal fight with Wade Marley." She smiled. "Maybe I'll just put it back in Edwin's attic and pretend it doesn't exist. Or I could add it to Marge's silent auction."

"It would bring a fortune if you did," Roz said, chuckling, "although something tells me that Marge wouldn't be happy if you took the spotlight off of her."

"Even if I wanted to auction it away, if Laura is truly Rachel's granddaughter, then it belongs to her." Then her smile faded. "And if she finds out what I've done," Sadie murmured, "she might just take it and run."

Roz scowled. "Now you're mumbling just like Roscoe."

Sadie looked at her, surprised by her remark. It didn't sound like Roz at all. "Are you all right?"

"Sorry," Roz said contritely. "I just missed what you said."

"I snuck into Laura's room last night," Sadie said clearly, "and took a hair sample from her brush. Then I dropped it off at Doc's office on my way into town this morning. He's arranging a DNA test for it as soon as possible."

"You snuck into her room?" Roz's eyes widened, her expression both shocked and amused. "Sadie! That doesn't sound like you."

"I'm the most skittish prowler you'll ever meet. Hank followed behind me and almost scared me to death! And I feel plenty guilty too."

"Why, Sadie Speers, you're not a prowler, you're trying to solve a mystery. I guess that's what happens after reading so many of those first edition Miss Marple books you picked up at that sale in Denver."

"I wish I was as smart as Miss Marple," Sadie replied, feeling a little better about it now that she'd told Roz. "Then I'd know who broke my car window, what really happened to Rachel in 1897, and how that antique brass key fits into all of this."

"It sounds like you're on the right track to me. If Laura's DNA is a match, you'll know her story is true. If not . . ."

"If not, then Laura will have some explaining to do." Sadie pondered that scenario. "She just seems so sincere . . ."

"Most con artists do," Roz said dryly. "Not that I think Laura is a con artist—but how do we know for sure? That's why I don't blame you for taking her hair for a DNA test. It's the only way to know if you can truly trust her."

Sadie nodded. "I know. But if she finds out, she probably won't ever trust *me* again." Then she picked up her coffee and took a long sip. "Now, enough about my troubles. How are you doing with the reenactment script?"

"I've got most of the lines memorized. And there are a lot of them."

Sadie winced. "And more on the way, I'm afraid. Alfred e-mailed me this morning and said he has some additional lines he wants to add to the script. I'll forward the new script to you as soon as I get it."

Concern flashed in Roz's eyes. "More lines?"

"Yes. Alfred thinks the additions really help flesh out the Tates' experiences in Silver Peak."

"Oh, Sadie," she said with a groan. "There's not time for me to learn new lines—especially if they're just added willy-nilly in the script! The picnic is less than two weeks away."

"Don't worry," Sadie assured her, sensing a smidgeon of stage fright in Roz's tone. "You'll be fine, especially after you and Alfred have a chance to rehearse. How does this Sunday evening at my house sound?"

Roz looked up at her. "That should work for me." A shaky smile curved her lips. "I guess I'm starting to panic a little."

"Perfectly normal," Sadie told her, although Roz was usually one of the calmest people she knew. And Roz loved to perform in front of an audience—although it had been a while since she'd done so. Sadie tilted her head to one side as she looked at her friend, thinking about their earlier conversation. "Are you sure you're all right?"

"Yes," Roz said, her smile widening. "I'm just tired and dealing with some minor headaches. I guess I've stayed up too late memorizing the script."

"Maybe you should make an appointment with Doc," Sadie said. "You might be coming down with something."

Roz waved off that suggestion. "Oh no. I'm right as rain. I just need a little more sleep." She climbed off the stool. "I can't wait to start rehearsing with Alfred. What time should I be at your place?"

"Seven o'clock," Sadie told her. "Alfred has a meeting that afternoon, so that should give him plenty of time to make the drive to Silver Peak."

"Seven o'clock it is." Roz picked up her coffee cup. "I'll see you then if not before."

"Thanks for the coffee," Sadie told her, "and the conversation. I'll keep you updated."

"I'm counting on it."

Sadie watched Roz walk out the door, then said a silent prayer for her. The headaches and fatigue Roz mentioned worried her, especially in light of the problems she and Roscoe seemed to be having. Then again, Roz was something of a perfectionist and probably was staying up late to memorize every word of that script. Sadie couldn't wait to see Alfred and Roz in action.

Finding herself with some time on her hands, Sadie reached for the telephone, planning to call Edwin and tell him about the DNA results on the wedding dress. Then she hesitated, still wondering if she could trust him. Her heart said she could, but her head didn't always agree.

She closed her eyes, wondering which one to follow. She didn't want to become one of those people who thought the worst of others, yet she didn't want to be gullible either. But if she had to choose one or the other, she'd rather trust the people around her—especially a man like Edwin, who had meant so much to her a long time ago. She picked up her cell phone and dialed his number.

He answered on the first ring. "Hello, Sadie. This is a nice surprise."

She smiled, remembering that he'd put her phone number in his contact list, so her name had popped up on his screen. "I'm glad to hear it. I have news about the wedding dress. It did belong to Rachel Wright."

"Really? That's wonderful . . ." Then he paused. "Isn't it?"

The question made her chuckle. "I think so. I *hope* so."

"I want to hear all about it," he said. "Let's cash in that rain check and have dinner together tonight."

Sadie winced. "I'm sorry—I can't tonight. I promised to help Alice and the kids rake leaves. They have a huge yard."

"Then how about tomorrow or Thursday?" Edwin asked.

Her cheeks warmed at his gentle persistence. "Julie and I talked about coming to your place after work on Thursday to offer decorating advice."

"That's perfect," he replied. "I can take you both out for dinner as a way of thanking you for your help."

She smiled. "You haven't heard our advice yet."

"I think I can trust you," he said, chuckling. "Let's plan on it. I hear Los Pollitos is good and I love Mexican food. Does six o'clock work for you and Julie?"

"Yes, it should, and Los Pollitos is the perfect choice."

"Good," he said. "I'll see you both on Thursday evening. I'm really looking forward to it."

"Me too." She ended the phone call and realized she was still smiling. Maybe her heart had been right after all.

16

THAT EVENING, SADIE WAS SURPRISED TO SEE SO MANY LEAVES already piled up in Alice's yard when she pulled up to her house. Alice, Theo, and Sara all stood in the front yard, each holding a rake. The sun was just starting to set in the sky, casting a pinkish glow over the yard.

Alice lived on the edge of town, just inside the city limits. Her house was a sprawling, redbrick ranch, with a double garage and a wide front porch. Four towering oak trees bordered each side of the sidewalk that led to her front door. "Looks like I'm late," Sadie called out as she stepped over the curb.

"You're just in time," Alice told her. "There's another rake on the front porch if you want to join in. Or you can just keep us company." Alice glanced at her daughter. "It's been a little quiet here."

Sara didn't look up at them, her face pinched as she gathered up the leaves in a short, quick swipes of her rake.

"She's mad so she's giving Mom the silent treatment," Theo explained, taking long strokes with his rake. Then he flashed a mischievous smile. "It's been a nice break."

Sara looked up and shot daggers at her brother, but she didn't say a word. Then she continued raking, two red spots burning in her cheeks.

Sadie retrieved the extra rake from the porch and then started raking beside Alice. "So what's the problem?" she asked, keeping her voice low.

"Sara's mad because she has dinner plans with some friends at Sophia's tonight and I'm making her rake before she goes."

"I see." Sadie knew it wasn't easy raising a teenage girl, especially one as headstrong as Sara. "Looks like we'll be done soon, though."

"Yes," Alice agreed. "Although, given her attitude, I'm having second thoughts about letting her go at all."

Sadie didn't want to get in the middle of her daughter and granddaughter, so she decided to bring up a new subject. "I just found out the wedding dress did belong to Rachel Wright."

Alice stopped raking and stared at Sadie. "That's amazing."

Theo moved closer to them. "What's amazing?"

"Remember that wedding dress I told you about? The one that Grandma had tested for DNA?"

"Yeah," Theo said, turning to Sadie. "Is it the runaway bride's dress?"

"Yes, it is. The DNA test results came back today."

"Cool."

Sarah walked over to them, her expression still sullen. "What's going on?"

Alice told her about the wedding dress and the test results. Then she said, "It's nice to hear you talking again. We'll be finished here soon, and then you can go join your friends."

"Nah," Sara said with a small shrug. "Mia just texted me. Stuff came up, so nobody's going out to eat at Sophia's tonight."

"Whoa," Theo said, holding up one hand. "Who cares about Sophia's? I want to hear more about this mystery wedding dress and what it means."

"It means that the story of the runaway bride might have a different ending than everyone believed," Sadie told him.

"Why don't you tell them the whole story," Alice suggested, setting her rake aside, "while I go order some pizza." She wrapped one arm around Sara's shoulders. "If you can't go to Sophia's, then we'll have Sophia's come to you."

———

Sadie walked through the front door that evening to the sweet aroma of cinnamon and apples. Hank was nowhere in sight, so she headed to the kitchen.

Laura stood in front of the oven with the door cracked open.

"Something smells wonderful," Sadie said as she walked into the kitchen and set her purse on the table.

"It's apple cake," Laura told her, closing the oven door. Hank stood at his food bowl, looking dolefully at his dry dog food. Then he walked over to the oven and sat in front of it.

Sadie laughed. "Looks like I'm not the only one whose mouth is watering."

"It's Nana's recipe," Laura said, walking over to the table and taking a seat. "When I saw the apples at the Market today, I knew I had to make it for you."

"If it tastes as good as it looks, then I'm in for a treat." She took a seat opposite Laura. "Have you already eaten dinner?"

Laura nodded. "I had a sandwich earlier. How about you?"

"Yes, Alice ordered a couple of take-out pizzas from Sophia's for us." Sadie chuckled. "Theo ate one entire pizza all by himself, but we girls still had plenty."

"Well, I hope you still have room for cake."

"I always make room for dessert," Sadie said, laughing as she walked over to start a pot of coffee.

They each chatted about their day. Laura had stayed at the house and done some work on her computer. She told Sadie she felt safer staying alone at the house now, aware that Hank would sound the alarm if there was any sign of trouble. She and Hank had even gone for a hike together in the afternoon.

Sadie told her about some of the customers she'd met at the Antique Mine, but she didn't mention her phone call with Edwin or their plans to meet for dinner on Thursday evening. She wasn't used to keeping secrets, especially from someone whose company she enjoyed more and more.

"You know," Laura said, leaning back in her chair. "I'm really learning to enjoy the peace and quiet out here. My life in Boston was so hectic and so . . . noisy. I didn't realize how noisy until I arrived in Silver Peak." She smiled. "Don't get me wrong, I love city life. But now I love the country too, especially the mountains."

The oven timer began to buzz. Laura stood up and walked over to the oven, grabbing an oven mitt off the counter as she pulled the door open.

Laura picked up a pot holder in her other hand and lifted the glass baking dish off the rack, placing it on the cast-iron trivet on the counter. "We'll let it cool a bit." Then she leaned against the counter. "Do you ever get lonely out here?"

Sadie smiled. "This place has been my home since I was born. I was lonely after T.R. passed away, but I think that's to be expected after a long marriage. But now, I'm used to my life out here with Hank. We keep each other company."

Laura leaned down and petted him. "He is a great dog."

"And a nice alarm system," Sadie said. "I remember hearing a story about when my great-great-grandparents, Silas and Mary, first arrived in Silver Peak. Like so many others, they'd come here during the silver rush. They suffered a lot of hardships, but persevered, relying on their love and their faith to see them through."

"From what I've read, it sounds like the boomtowns were pretty wild places."

Sadie nodded. "So wild that Silas didn't want to leave Mary alone in their tent while he was out prospecting. So he bought a big dog for two dollars—a dog that was actually half wolf and half German shepherd. It had been domesticated, but still looked— and acted—ferociously to any stranger who came near."

"So the wolf dog protected Mary?"

Sadie smiled. "Not exactly. One day, Mary heard a noise outside of their tent."

Laura rose to her feet. "Hold that thought. I sense a good story coming and I think we should enjoy the cake while you tell it."

"Good idea," Sadie said. "I'll pour us some coffee."

A few minutes later, they were back at the kitchen table. Sadie picked up her fork and took a bite of the warm apple cake, topped with a generous dollop of fresh whipped cream.

"Well?" Laura asked.

"It tastes even better than I imagined." Sadie reached for another bite, then watched Laura dig into her cake.

"Oh, good. Now—" Laura's cell phone began to buzz on the table in front of her. She looked down at it and frowned.

"Do you need to get that?"

"No." Laura switched off her phone. "Now tell me the rest of the story about the wolf dog."

Sadie took a sip of her coffee. "Well, when Mary heard the noise behind the tent, she picked up a shovel and went to investigate. That's when she saw the wolf dog, cornered by a badger. So she took the shovel and used it to shoo the badger away until it finally turned and disappeared into the woods."

"Is that really true?" Laura asked, her eyes wide. "I've heard badgers can be vicious."

"Well, as far as I know it's a true story. My father told it to me, and Grandpa Jacob told it to my father. And by all accounts, Mary was one tough cookie, so I tend to believe it."

"I don't think anyone has ever called me a tough cookie," Laura mused. "My parents were very protective of me, especially my dad. He never met a stranger he liked or trusted. I think one of the reasons I chose to go into public relations was because I just wanted to meet new people—to go outside our small circle of family and friends."

"That sounds like courage to me."

"But not the fight-a-badger kind of courage," Laura said, chuckling. "I'm so glad I came to Silver Peak. I had no idea how I'd be received, but you've been so welcoming." She smiled. "And taught me so much about our family history. I don't know how I'll ever thank you."

Sadie couldn't pretend anymore. "Laura, I'll be honest. Your story about Rachel leaving Colorado for Boston and starting a whole new life there threw me for a loop. I didn't know what to believe."

"Well, no one can blame you for that."

"I had to know the truth," Sadie continued, determined to confess before she lost *her* courage, "so last night, I walked into your room and took some hair from your brush. It's being tested for a DNA match to see if you really are a member of my family."

Laura stared at her. "I'm not—" Her next words were cut off when Hank started barking loudly and scampered out of the kitchen and toward the living room. Sadie and Laura exchanged looks and then got up and followed him.

"Should we call the sheriff?" Laura asked, her voice tight.

Sadie hurried into the living room. "Let's see what's out there first."

Hank stood near the door, still barking with a chilling intensity and reaching one paw up to scratch at the wood, something he rarely did.

The sound of glass shattering made them both jump. Sadie looked over at the window near the front door and saw shards of glass scattered on the floor.

"Laura, get behind the sofa," Sadie said, hurrying over toward the door and scooping Hank up in her arms. Then she ran behind the sofa where Laura knelt and crouched on the floor. "Hold him," Sadie ordered, handing Hank over to her.

Laura wrapped her arms around Hank, speaking soothing words to him even as her voice shook. Hank continued to growl and bark, the fur standing up on his neck. Sadie reached into her pocket and pulled out her cell phone, her finger shaking as she dialed the sheriff's emergency line.

"Silver Peak Sheriff's Office," the operator said. "What's your emergency?"

"This is Sadie Speers. There is another intruder on my property. I think he has a gun."

"Somebody will be right out, Sadie," the operator said, sounding concerned. "Can you take cover in a protected place?"

"Yes, we already have," Sadie told her. "Please tell them to hurry." Then she ended the call and looked over at Laura, who was staring at her. "Are you okay?"

"Yes," Laura said, her brow wrinkled with concern. "But you're bleeding."

———

Twenty minutes later, Sheriff Slattery and his officer finished their search of the area. "No one is out there," he said, watching Laura clean the small wound on Sadie's forearm. "Are you sure you don't need to see Dr. Conroy?"

"No, I'm fine." Sadie told him. "It's just a minor cut. A piece of glass hit my arm when the bullet went through the window."

"The shot went in low," the sheriff said, "judging by the trajectory, and lodged itself in the opposite wall. From the facts you gave me, I don't think he was aiming at anyone inside."

"It was a warning," Laura said, her face pale as she applied a bandage to Sadie's arm.

"From Ray?" Sadie asked her.

Laura kept her gaze on her task, her voice flat. "I don't know."

"Well, something is going on here," the sheriff said, "that's for sure. And this guy knows how to leave the scene without leaving much evidence behind."

Like a circuit court judge. Edwin would know the type of evidence needed to solve a crime, like fingerprints and witness identification. The thoughts came unbidden to Sadie's mind and she quickly pushed them out again.

Sheriff Slattery gave orders to his deputies as they finished collecting evidence and then he walked back over to Sadie. "I think you two should find somewhere else to stay for the next few days."

Laura turned to her. "I could get a hotel room for us," she said. "Unless you'd rather stay with Alice."

"I'll understand if you want to get a hotel room," Sadie told Laura, her voice calm and resolute, "but I'm not leaving. This is my home and I won't let someone who's too scared to show his face chase me out." She reached down and placed her hand on Hank's head. "Hank will warn me if anyone comes near the house again."

The sheriff arched a bushy brow. "Well, I can't force you to leave, but—"

"Then I'm staying too," Laura interjected, her cheeks still pale.

Sadie turned to look at her, seeing the fear on her face. "Are you sure?"

"Yes," Laura said with a nod.

The sheriff sighed. "If you two plan to stay here, then I'd suggest you board up that window."

"We will." Sadie followed the sheriff to the front door and waited for him and his deputies to leave before closing it behind them.

As soon as they were alone, Laura said, "What can I do to help?"

"You can sweep up the glass on the floor," Sadie told her. "I'll take Hank outside with me to board up the window. I have some plywood in the garage."

"Do you want me to stand guard outside with a shovel?" Laura asked.

Sadie smiled. "Thanks, but I think I'll be all right. We can finish our cake and coffee when we're done. I have a feeling it's going to be a long night."

"Sounds good," Laura said, as Sadie headed for the door. "Sadie?"

Sadie turned around. "Yes?"

"I'm not upset with you for taking my hair to test my DNA. I wish you would have asked me first, but I probably would have done the same if the situation was reversed." Laura paused for a long moment. "To be honest, I wouldn't have invited a stranger into my home in the first place. But I know you're my cousin, and soon you'll know it too."

Sadie gave her a grateful nod and then continued outside. She stood on the front porch, watching the patrol cars drive away.

She hoped Laura was right, but she couldn't ignore the fact that two incidents were preceded by calls to Laura's cell phone. The last call Laura had ignored, going so far as to shut off her phone.

She wanted to trust Laura, but she sensed her alleged cousin was keeping secrets from her—secrets that might be dangerous to both of them. And she still didn't know whether Edwin was involved.

Sadie reached into her pocket for her cell phone. Maybe it was time for her to make a call of her own. An hour later, Edwin pulled into her driveway. He drove a black Dodge Ram pickup truck, and Sadie could see a sheet of plywood in the bed of the truck.

"Thanks for coming out," Sadie said, approaching his truck as Edwin climbed out of the cab. "I hate to bother you like this."

"It's no bother at all," he said, his gaze moving to her broken window. He whistled low. "I still can't believe someone would shoot out your window." He turned to look at her. "Are you sure you're okay out here?"

"Yes," she replied. "Both Laura and I were a little shaken, of course, but things have settled down now." She watched him, trying to gauge if her mention of Laura provoked any kind of reaction in him, but Edwin's expression remained the same.

"You didn't have to bring plywood," she said, pointing to the wood in his truck. "I should have plenty in the garage."

"Well, I had a few spare pieces in my garage, as well," Edwin said with a smile. "I'd build a moat around your place if I could."

"Safe, but hardly practical," Sadie said, chuckling at the image it provoked. "Although Hank loves to swim, so he'd enjoy it."

Edwin reached into his pickup cab and retrieved a pair of leather gloves. "We should probably get started boarding up that window." He walked to the back of his truck and lowered the end gate, then he climbed into the box. "Can you grab one end?"

"Sure," Sadie said, pulling gloves from the pocket of her jacket and putting them on before gripping one end of the plywood.

Edwin pushed while she pulled until the four-by-eight sheet of wood was out of the truck. Then they carried it over to the broken window.

Sadie had already retrieved screws and her cordless screwdriver before Edwin arrived and placed them near the broken window.

"Looks like the wood will fit just right," Edwin said, lifting the plywood into place. "Now, why don't you run the screwdriver while I hold the board."

"Sounds good," Sadie said, picking up the cordless screwdriver. She screwed the first screw into the window frame and then quickly made her way around the window, setting the screws about three feet apart.

As she worked, she kept glancing in the window, wondering if Laura planned to say hello to Edwin. But she couldn't see Laura from this angle, and the front door stayed closed.

As Sadie moved to put in the last few screws, she needed to work around Edwin's tall frame. Her shoulder brushed against his arm and she could feel muscle against his shirt. "Sorry," she murmured, her face growing a little hot.

"No problem," he said, watching as she placed the last screw in the board. Then they both stepped back from the window.

"Not quite as good as new," Edwin conceded, "but it should keep the wildlife and other assorted animals out."

Sadie set down the cordless screwdriver, feeling better already. "Thank you so much for your help. I really appreciate it."

"Anytime," he said, as a cool breeze drifted across the front porch.

"Would you like to come in?" Sadie asked, figuring the least she could do was offer the man a cup of coffee.

Edwin hesitated. "I'd better not. You've already had a busy night and probably want to rest." Then he met her gaze. "Unless you're not feeling safe out here."

She smiled. "No, I think we'll be fine. Hank will warn us if there's any more trouble."

He nodded. "Then I'll be on my way."

She stayed on the front porch as he walked to his pickup truck and climbed into the cab. Then she waved good-bye as he started the engine and headed down the driveway. She stood there for several minutes, letting the breeze cool her warm cheeks and wondering why Laura hadn't come out to greet him. But she was too tired to figure it out tonight.

Turning around, Sadie picked up the cordless screwdriver and leftover screws and then covered a yawn with one hand as she walked inside the house, locking the door behind her.

———

On Wednesday, Sadie arranged to have the glass in the window replaced, hoping this was the last time that she'd have to repair damage caused by the anonymous vandal. She'd also researched some home alarm systems. Hank's instincts were excellent, but someday she might need to rely on more than her dog if these types of incidents continued.

By the time Thursday arrived, Sadie was ready for an evening out. She and Julie arrived at the Marshall home a little before six o'clock. After Sadie made the introductions, Edwin led them to every room on the main floor.

"There's so much you can do here," Julie exclaimed, her eyes gleaming with delight. "It all depends on what you want," she told Edwin. "Is there any particular style that appeals to you?"

Edwin smiled as he glanced over at Sadie. "Nothing too wild. And I'd like to keep all the old furniture."

"Excellent choice." Julie nodded. "I love the traditional Victorian style."

"Yes. *Traditional* is probably the right word for me." His smile widened. "I hope that doesn't translate into boring."

"Not at all," Julie said. "The style is just a template, like a map, to make sure we don't veer too far off course when we're picking paint colors and accessories."

"Maybe you could draw up some possible plans," Sadie suggested to Julie, hoping she wasn't overstepping. "Then Edwin can see what you have in mind."

"Yes," Edwin agreed. "And your time and work will be compensated, of course. I want to make this place as magnificent as it was when my grandparents lived here."

"I'd love to be your decorator," Julie told him, her green eyes sparkling with anticipation. "I can start on those plans right away."

Sadie suddenly remembered something she'd seen in one of her old family photo albums. "I actually have a few pictures from James Marshall's eightieth birthday that was held here. My mom was quite the shutterbug."

"Great!" Julie exclaimed. "That should spark some ideas."

They spent the next thirty minutes discussing paint colors and window treatments before Julie announced that she needed to go.

"Aren't you coming to dinner with us?" Sadie asked. Julie had been pleased about Edwin's dinner invitation when Sadie had told her about it that morning.

"I'm afraid not." Julie held up her cell phone. "My husband just sent me a text. He needs to head to the hospital and check on a patient, and our son, Logan, is home sick with a fever, so I need to get home too."

"Of course you do," Edwin said kindly. "I hope your son feels better soon."

"Thank you," Julie said. "I'll be in touch with you soon."

"I'm looking forward to it," Edwin said, walking her to the door. After Julie left, he turned to Sadie. "I guess it's just the two of us."

Twenty minutes later, they were seated at a table in Los Pollitos. The Mexican restaurant was housed in a historic brick building on the Main Street. The cozy interior featured an artfully decorated dining room with a terra-cotta tile floor and a peaceful, outdoor patio full of potted plants and a scenic view of the mountains.

Gloria Garza greeted them at the door. "Welcome to Los Pollitos," she said warmly. "Nice to see you again, Sadie." The forty-two-year-old was a classic beauty, with long, dark hair and big brown eyes. She supervised the front of the restaurant while her husband, Ramon, worked as a chef in the kitchen.

"Nice to see you too, Gloria." Sadie made the introductions. "This is an old friend of mine, Edwin Marshall. He just moved back home to Silver Peak. Edwin, this is Gloria Garza."

They shook hands as Gloria smiled up at him. "So you've come home. How wonderful!"

"I think so too," Edwin said, glancing at Sadie.

Gloria picked up two menus. "I'll give you our best table," she said, leading them into the dining room. "Our special tonight is chicken molé. It's one of my favorites."

Gloria stopped in front of a corner table near the wide, stone fireplace. A small blaze burned in the hearth, providing a cozy, golden glow. "How is this?"

"Perfect," Edwin said, holding a chair out for Sadie.

Sadie sat down and Gloria handed her a menu as Edwin took a seat on the other side of the small table.

"Elena will be with you soon," Gloria said as she handed the second menu to Edwin. "I hope you enjoy your meal."

After she left, Sadie said, "Elena is Gloria and Ramon's daughter. She's sixteen and the older sister of Sara's best friend, Mia."

"Ah, a family business," he said, opening the menu in front of him. "You don't find a lot of those around anymore."

"There's actually quite a few in Silver Peak," Sadie told him. "The Garzas own Los Pollitos, Jack Wilson owns Flap Jacks, which is the most popular breakfast restaurant in Silver Peak. And Mark Portelli owns Sophia's, if you ever have a craving for the best pizza in the west."

He nodded approvingly. "I look forward to trying them all."

A few minutes later, their waitress, Elena Garza, approached the table. She had her mother's beauty, with long, dark hair and eyes, and according to Sara, she was very popular at Silver Peak High School. "Are you ready to order?"

"I'll have the chicken molé," Sadie told the girl, "with a glass of water and a cup of coffee, please."

"And I'll have the same," Edwin said.

"Perfect," Elena said, gathering up their menus. "I'll bring your drinks out right away."

"Thank you," Sadie told the girl, and then watched her walk toward the kitchen. "Isn't she a cutie?"

"Very pretty," Edwin replied, his gaze on Sadie. "Now let's talk about you."

"Me?" Sadie shifted in her chair. "What do you want to know?"

His expression grew serious. "I'm worried about you, Sadie. I can't stop thinking about that incident at your house last Tuesday night."

"Yes," she said. "It was . . . unsettling."

He scowled. "I'd call it infuriating. Why hasn't the sheriff caught this miscreant yet?"

"Apparently, my miscreant is quite good at hiding his tracks." She smiled. "But don't worry about me. I'm fine."

"Yes," he said, his voice softer now. "You are. Which brings me to another subject. Do you have a date for the Founder's Day Picnic?"

"A date?" A blush warmed her cheeks. "No."

He smiled. "Then I hope you'll let me escort you."

Before she could reply, Elena returned to their table holding a tray. She placed their water glasses and coffee in front of them.

"Thank you," Sadie said, with Edwin echoing his thanks, as well. Sadie picked up her water and took a sip, her cheeks still hot and her mind whirling. She hadn't even thought about dating after T.R. passed away. Now a handsome old friend was asking her on a date.

A date!

Sadie suddenly realized that he was waiting for her answer. She put down her water glass. "That's very kind of you, Edwin, but I'll have my hands full with the picnic, since I'm in charge. That wouldn't be fair to you."

He smiled. "I won't mind if you tend to your duties, but you're allowed to have fun too, right?"

She hesitated, torn by the decision in front of her.

"You don't have to give me an answer tonight," Edwin finally told her. "Just take some time to think about it."

"Thank you." Sadie smiled with relief. "I will."

"Good." He leaned forward, folding his broad hands on the table. "Now tell me how the picnic plans are going. Is everything on schedule?"

"I think so," Sadie replied, trying to regain her equilibrium. "I checked in with all the committees this afternoon and everything seems to be rolling along smoothly. I'm hoping this will be one of the best picnics ever, since that travel writer, Lance Ely, plans to be there."

Edwin nodded. "Positive publicity about Silver Peak will be good for tourism and the local economy. I attended the town council meeting the other day and heard some interesting new development ideas they're considering . . ."

They chatted until their meal arrived, which Edwin declared a gourmet treat. They even shared a sopaipilla cheesecake for dessert. Sadie didn't remember when she'd had so much fun. Some of her earlier doubts about him started falling away as the evening progressed.

At last it was time to leave. Edwin paid the check and then escorted Sadie to her car. That was when she realized how late it had gotten. Main Street was practically deserted, lit only by the glow of the streetlights and the crescent moon in the dark sky.

"Thank you for a wonderful evening, Sadie," Edwin said as they stood by the driver's door of her Tahoe. "I can't remember the last time I had so much fun."

"Me too," she said, looking up at him. He stood so close to her that she was finding it a little hard to breathe.

"You look like the eighteen-year-old girl who broke my heart," he said softly.

Sadie licked her dry lips. "You're the one who left, remember?"

"I remember."

He leaned closer, and Sadie's knees felt like they might collapse. Then he gently brushed her cheek with his hand. "Good night, Sadie."

"Good night."

She watched him walk away, her knees still feeling a little wobbly. Then she climbed into the Tahoe and unspooled her seat belt, latching it into place before starting the engine. Her heartbeat slowed as she took a couple of deep, calming breaths. Maybe Edwin Marshall was a dangerous man after all.

———

When Sadie arrived home that night, Laura was already asleep in bed. She walked out on the back porch, one of T.R.'s heavy cardigans wrapped around her, and looked up at the moon. Edwin had asked her to the picnic, which meant she had a decision to make.

"Lord, what should I do?" she whispered into the night.

17

"YOU SHOULD GO WITH HIM." JULIE HELD ONE END OF A LARGE, vintage dollhouse as she and Sadie carried it across the shop and set it in the store window. "Edwin is a handsome guy and so charming."

"I know," Sadie said, adding some cute vintage teddy bears to a small wooden wagon, circa 1920, for the children's toy and game display. "I used to date him."

Julie smiled as she placed a basket of cornhusk dolls in the display window. "Even more reason to let him take you to the Founder's Day Picnic. You two already have a history."

"Ancient history," Sadie said wryly. She'd called Roz last night and told her about Edwin's invitation to escort her to the picnic. Roz's reaction had been much the same as Julie's response this morning. Roz had told Sadie that a handsome man like Edwin wouldn't remain a bachelor for long and that Sadie deserved a companion of Edwin's stature and intelligence.

Sadie stepped back to look at the display, wanting to make sure it was evenly balanced. She saw Nathaniel Green walk by on the sidewalk in front of the window. He gave her an enthusiastic thumbs-up sign.

"Who is that?" Julie asked, staring at him through the window.

"His name is Nathaniel," Sadie replied, as the door chimed and Nathaniel walked inside.

"Good morning, ladies," Nathaniel called out, a cheery smile on his face. "Great window display. I'll have to create one like it for the museum. Maybe a dollhouse display depicting various historical events in our fine state."

"We have some antique doll figurines if you'd like to look at them," Sadie suggested.

"I would," Nathaniel said. "Just point me in the right direction."

Sadie hoped he was just here to shop, but something told her that she wouldn't be that lucky. She showed him the shelf with the dollhouse furniture and figurines and then made her way to the desk where Julie was cutting up some yellow cardstock paper for shelf-talkers. They used the shelf-talkers to advertise specials or describe an interesting fact about an item on display.

"I'm going over to Arbuckle's," Julie told her. "Can I get you anything?"

"A large cup of coffee and a muffin would be great," Sadie said. Her stomach had been growling for the past hour. She'd been too nervous about Edwin's offer to escort her to the picnic night to eat breakfast that morning.

"What kind of muffin?" Julie asked.

"Blueberry, if they have it, but any kind of berry muffin will do."

"Be back soon," Julie said as she headed for the doorway between the two shops.

Sadie took over the paper-cutting, keeping an eye on Nathaniel as he moved slowly around the shop. A few minutes later he approached the desk with two dollhouse figurines and a small toy boat.

"Looks like you found something," Sadie said with a smile.

"I've got an idea for an unsinkable Molly Brown display," he said, referring to the colorful Colorado socialite and philanthropist who had survived the sinking of the *Titanic*.

"That sounds . . . unusual," Sadie said, ringing up his purchase. When she told him the total, he handed her the cash, along with a white envelope.

"What's this?" she said, looking at the envelope in her hand.

"You've been served," he said calmly.

"What?" Sadie opened the envelope and pulled out a summons. Her gaze moved quickly over it. "Wade Marley is suing me for the wedding dress?"

"Along with the box containing it and any other items in that box."

She met his gaze. "How interesting that Wade used you as his process server. Something tells me that the two of you have made some type of deal."

Nathaniel gave her a sheepish smile. "We might have come to an understanding that this lawsuit would be mutually beneficial. It's nothing personal, of course," he hurried to assure her. "I have the utmost respect for you."

Before she could reply, Julie returned from the coffee shop. "Look who I found," she said, stepping aside to make room for Lance Ely to walk through the doorway.

"Hello," Lance said, holding a coffee cup and flashing a smile at Sadie. Then his gaze moved to Nathaniel. "And we meet again."

Sadie looked between the two of them. "You two know each other?"

"Mr. Green contacted me when he heard I was in Silver Peak," Lance explained. "He was kind enough to give me a tour of his museum."

Julie handed a coffee cup and a plastic-wrapped blueberry muffin to Sadie. "Did I miss anything?"

"I'll tell you later," Sadie said in a low voice.

Nathaniel picked up the paper bag where Sadie had placed his purchases. "I'd better be on my way. Please feel free to stop by Secrets of the Past the next time you're in Breckenridge. I'll give you a great discount on the entry fee."

All three of them watched Nathaniel walk out the door and disappear down the sidewalk.

"Now, he's an interesting fellow," Lance said, setting his coffee cup on the counter as he leaned against the desk. "A little odd, but interesting. He gave me the hard sell to include his museum, and I use that term loosely, in my article. I tried to explain to him that I don't usually promote commercial enterprises, especially when they're not in the same place as the town I'm writing about."

"That makes sense," Julie said. "At least you got a free tour out of it."

"And two trips to Breckenridge," Lance said.

Sadie looked at him. "Why two?"

"Well, our first meeting was scheduled for last Friday, but when I got there, I learned that Green was in the hospital with food poisoning. I felt bad for the guy, so when he called me a couple of days later to reschedule, I reluctantly agreed."

Her car window had been smashed on Friday morning and she'd considered Nathaniel a suspect. "Do you know when he went into the hospital?"

Lance shook his head. "I can't really say. We talked more about my upcoming article than anything else."

Sadie appreciated the information, even though he didn't know the answer to her question. They chatted a while longer while she ate her blueberry muffin. Julie had read several of his articles in various travel magazines and asked him about certain interior design elements in places like Cairo and Tokyo.

Lance tipped up his cup and finished the last of his coffee. "Well, I'd better be on my way."

"It was nice to see you again," Sadie told him.

"And good luck with the article," Julie added.

"Thanks, I appreciate it. I'll see you both at the picnic, right?"

"We'll be there," Sadie promised as he headed for the door.

Sadie and Julie spent the next few hours helping customers and taking lunch breaks. As Sadie assisted a woman in selecting an antique doll quilt for her young granddaughter's birthday present, she noticed that items on the dollhouse furniture and figurines shelf had been moved around and some things even tipped over. She didn't mind, as she'd placed the shelf low enough for children to play with the items there. But the last person to the view the contents of the shelf had been an adult.

"Oh, Mr. Green," Sadie chided as she began to organize the miniaturized doll furniture. She picked up a small bed and placed it back with the rest of the bedroom furniture when something slipped out of the tiny bedsheet and landed on the shelf with a *clink*.

Her wedding ring.

Sadie gasped out loud. Then she picked up the ring, joy and relief flooding into her heart.

"Are you all right?" Julie asked, coming around a corner.

"I found it," Sadie exclaimed, a wide smile on her face. "My wedding ring!" She held out her palm to show Julie the silver wedding band.

"Where was it?"

"In a dollhouse bed, under the sheet. Some child must have seen the ring on the floor and thought it belonged there." For a moment, she wondered if Nathaniel had done it, but he'd been nowhere in sight when she'd lost the ring and wouldn't know it belonged to her. Besides, she thought to herself, she or Julie would have found it before today if it had been on the floor.

"I'm so glad you found it," Julie said, reaching out to give her a quick hug.

"Me too." Sadie stepped back and slipped the ring back on her finger, where it had belonged for so many years. "I was beginning to think I'd never find it."

"So was I," Julie admitted. Then she headed off to help a customer who was just walking through the door.

Sadie stared at the silver ring. It represented so much of her past and her marriage to T.R. They'd been best friends, and when she closed her eyes she could still see him so clearly. He'd stood almost six feet tall, with dark auburn hair and gentle green eyes. He was strong too, carrying her over the threshold of their home after their wedding as if she'd been light as a feather. She breathed a wistful sigh, so thankful that God had brought them together.

T.R. was gone from this earthly life, but he'd always remain in her heart.

And then there was Edwin, another man from her past and one who might want to be part of her future. Sadie slid the ring off her finger and then back on again. She'd have to decide soon whether she was ready to start dating again.

———

Saturday flew by as Alice and Sadie worked at the Antique Mine.

Sadie called the hospital in Breckenridge and was able to confirm that Nathaniel Green had been admitted on Thursday evening last week. Although the hospital couldn't give her any other information, that was enough for Sadie to cross him off her suspect list.

By noon, the shop was hopping, but Sadie found herself slightly distracted, still trying to decide what to tell Edwin. Alice echoed the sentiments of Roz and Julie, telling Sadie that easing into dating with a man she'd known for so long was a great idea.

On Sunday, Sadie prayed about it in church. Laura attended the worship service with her, but neither of them saw Edwin there. After a simple Sunday dinner, the two of them took a long hike with Hank.

Laura took pictures along the trail, planning to make a photo album of her trip to Silver Peak. And when they returned from their hike, Sadie gave a Hank a much-needed bath, something he usually didn't enjoy. She rewarded his good behavior by brushing out his golden coat until it was dry and silky.

That evening, Sadie began to prepare for the reenactment rehearsal. Laura had helped her move the dining room table to allow enough room for a makeshift stage. Sadie had read the script for the historical reenactment several times and was eager to see Alfred and Roz in the roles of William and Antonia Tate.

"I think I'll run into town tonight," Laura said, packing up her laptop bag. "I've got a craving for some of Arbuckle's coffee and I can get some work done there too."

"You don't have to leave on our account," Sadie told her. "I'm sure Alfred and Roz would appreciate hearing what you have to say about their performance, and Cecile is a charming woman."

Laura smiled. "I wish I could stay, but I have a client really pushing me for some material for an upcoming speech. I want to finish it tonight so I can e-mail it to him."

"I understand," Sadie said as Laura moved toward the front door. "Good luck on your project."

"Thanks," Laura said, walking out of the house and closing the door behind her.

Sadie turned to Hank, who stood near the table. "The picnic's only seven days away," she told him. "Do you think we'll be ready?"

Hank stared up at her, wagging his tail in response. Then the doorbell rang. Sadie glanced at her watch. "Somebody's early."

Hank wasn't barking or growling, but Sadie still wanted to be cautious after the two vandalism incidents at her home. She lifted the curtain to peek outside. She couldn't see who stood at the front door from this angle, but she did glimpse Alfred's red Toyota Camry in the driveway.

Sadie hurried over to the door and opened it. "Hello, Alfred."

"Hope I'm not too early," he said with a smile. "Cecile tells me that I'm unfashionably early for certain appointments, but I don't like to keep people waiting."

"Well, far be it from me to disagree with Cecile, but you always seem fashionable to me." And it was true. Alfred was an impeccable dresser. This evening he wore a gray tailored suit with a light-blue silk vest and matching tie.

"Thank you, Sadie." Then Alfred spotted Hank and clapped his hands together in delight. "Hey, boy," he said as Hank trotted over to him. "Don't you look fine this evening."

"He had a bath this afternoon."

Alfred smiled. "One of life's necessary evils."

Sadie stood at the open front door and peered outside. "I thought Cecile was coming with you."

"She planned to be here, but her sister is visiting from Colorado Springs and decided to stay another night. She said to tell you hello."

"Well, tell her I miss her, but I'm glad she gets to spend some extra time with her sister."

"I will," he promised.

"Come on in and sit down," Sadie said, leading the way into the living room. "Roz should be here soon. May I get you some coffee while we wait?"

"Only if you'll have a cup too."

Sadie nodded. "You know how much I love coffee, so that's a given."

Alfred and Hank stayed in the living room while Sadie walked into the kitchen to pour some of the coffee she'd started brewing early. The rich aroma of the dark-roasted brew filled the air. She glanced over at the platter of oatmeal raisin cookies she'd baked early, planning to serve them after their rehearsal.

Sadie looked at the stove clock, noting that Roz should arrive in about ten minutes. Then she poured two large cups of coffee and carried them into the living room.

"Here we go," she said, handing one of the cups to Alfred. Sadie sat down on the sofa across from him and took a sip of her coffee. "And how are your classes this semester?"

"Busy," he said with a smile. "Just the way I like it. I'm teaching two freshmen classes and there's always a transition period for students coming straight from high school. But we're all learning, that is what's important."

Sadie nodded, remembering her own years of teaching. She'd loved introducing her students to history and showing them how past events often influenced the present. She and Alfred began talking about some of his teaching techniques, and before she knew it, thirty minutes had flown by.

"Oh my," Sadie said, looking at her watch. "Roz should be here by now." She stood up. "I'll get us some more coffee and give her a call."

Alfred took the last sip from his cup and then handed it to Sadie. "Thank you."

She carried both cups into kitchen and set them on the counter, then picked up the cordless phone and dialed Roz's number.

"Hello?" Roz said, picking up after two rings.

"Hey, it's me," Sadie told her. "Are you on your way?"

"On my way where?"

"To my house," Sadie said, a sinking feeling in her stomach as she realized that Roz must have forgotten about the rehearsal. "Alfred is here and we're going over the script for the reenactment."

"But our rehearsal is tomorrow night," Roz cried, a note of distress in her voice.

"No, it's tonight," Sadie reminded her. "We talked about it when you were in the shop on Tuesday."

"I know when we talked about it," Roz said. "I just thought you said we'd be meeting on Monday, not Sunday. I'm so sorry. I'll be right over."

"That's fine," Sadie assured her. "And don't drive too fast. Alfred and I are having a nice conversation."

"Okay," Roz said, sounding a little calmer now. "See you soon."

Sadie ended the call and then poured them each another cup of coffee.

Roz arrived a short time later. "I'm so sorry you had to wait for me," she told Alfred.

He smiled. "Don't be sorry. It was a pleasure to catch up with Sadie. And you look wonderful, by the way."

Roz blushed, glancing down at her beaded, teal tunic top and dark brown palazzo pants. "Thanks. So do you, Alfred." Then she grinned. "Or should I call you William?"

Alfred gave a small nod. "Perhaps we should immerse in our roles, Antonia."

Sadie laughed as they all walked into the dining room and talked about movement and staging. The reenactment would take place on the bandstand at Centennial Park. Alfred had been there before, so he knew the layout of the stage.

"Shall we just start from the beginning?" Alfred asked, moving into position. "And we can work out the snags as we go along?"

"That sounds best," Roz said, taking her place beside him.

Sadie watched as they went through the lines, offering some suggestions along the way.

"You're doing a great job of projecting your voice," Sadie told Roz during a short break. "Both of you are easy to hear and have just the right tone."

As they ran though their lines a second time, Sadie noticed that Roz tilted her head toward Alfred, staring straight at him as he spoke. Sadie debated whether she should mention it, because it was subtle, but it looked a little as if she was overacting.

"Roz," she said at last, "you're doing a wonderful job with the role of Antonia, but you're a little too focused on Alfred when he's speaking. Maybe look out at the audience . . ."

"Sorry," Roz said with an apologetic smile, "I'm still feeling a little frazzled from running late."

"Maybe we should have a couple of props on stage," William suggested. "Perhaps some prospecting equipment on one side for William and a washtub or some other household item of that era on Antonia's side of the stage. That way when only one of us is speaking to the audience, the other can be 'off stage' by engaging in another activity."

"Perfect," Sadie exclaimed. "I'm sure we'll be able to borrow some prospecting tools from the American Mining Museum and I have a vintage washtub from that era in my shop."

Roz nodded. "I like that idea. We'll already be in costume, so the historical props will add to the authenticity of the reenactment."

They rehearsed twice more, with Roz doing a better job of acting more naturally. Sadie timed the last reenactment at twenty minutes, which she thought was just the right amount of time to keep some of the younger audience members at the picnic from getting restless.

As they finished up for the evening, Alfred and Roz helped her move the dining room table and chairs back into place. Then Alfred took his leave, planning to be at the picnic early next Saturday in case there were any last-minute changes he needed to know about.

Roz lingered by the front door, slipping her jacket on. "That was fun. Alfred is a wonderful performer."

"So are you," Sadie told her. "I'm glad we're able to showcase both William and Antonia. They were a fascinating couple."

"Speaking of couples, what have you decided about Edwin's invitation?"

"Nothing yet," Sadie said, a nervous knot forming in her stomach. "I've been thinking about it, though, and weighing the pros and cons."

"Maybe it's time to stop thinking and just do it." Roz placed her hands lightly on Sadie's shoulders. "You like Edwin and he likes you. We're talking about one date here, Sadie, not a months-long journey into the untamed Colorado Rockies like William and Antonia undertook."

Sadie laughed. "You have a point."

"Of course I do." Roz opened the door and stepped out onto the porch. "Call me tomorrow and tell me how it went."

Sadie watched her best friend walk to her car, and then waved as she drove away. She stood in the open doorway, enjoying the peaceful night. Maybe Roz was right, Sadie thought to herself.

She was putting too much importance on this one date. It would be fun to spend time at the picnic with Edwin and a great chance to dip her toes into the dating waters.

Before she had time to reconsider, Sadie grabbed her jacket and headed outside. She drove her Tahoe into town, the full moon lighting her way on the dark country road. As she neared Silver Peak, Sadie wondered if she should have called first or waited until tomorrow, but she knew if she turned back now that she might lose her nerve.

She turned onto Jefferson Avenue and the large Marshall home loomed in the distance. She smiled to herself, imagining Edwin's expression when he opened his door and found her on the other side, ready to accept his invitation to escort her to the picnic.

But as she neared his house, she saw a car in the driveway and breathed a sigh of disappointment. It looked like Edwin had company, which meant she'd have to postpone accepting his invitation. She slowed the Tahoe as she drove in front of his house, the headlights shining on the car in the driveway.

It looked all too familiar.

She recognized it as Laura's rental car, the numbers on the back license plate confirming that fact. Laura had never mentioned any plans to visit Edwin this evening. In fact, she'd specifically told Sadie that she'd be working at Arbuckle's.

All her doubts about the two of them came rushing back. Sadie pressed down on the gas pedal and sped away.

18

THE FOLLOWING MORNING, SADIE WALKED DOWNSTAIRS AND found Laura seated at the kitchen table, eating a bran muffin and drinking a cup of coffee.

"Good morning," Laura greeted her with a smile. "The coffee is ready and I picked up some muffins at the Market bakery last evening. They're on the counter."

"Ooh, I love the Market bakery." Sadie's gaze moved to the white cardboard carton on the kitchen counter. "Did you get your work done?"

"Yes, but my client sent me a long e-mail this morning, wanting some changes."

As Sadie poured herself a cup of coffee, she waited for Laura to mention that she'd stopped by Edwin's house last evening.

"How did the rehearsal go?" Laura asked.

"Fine." Sadie had gone to bed last night before Laura came home, needing some time alone to think, so she had no idea when Laura had returned.

Sadie split a lemon poppy seed muffin in two and added a small amount of the strawberry jam that Laura had left on the counter. "Alfred really embodied the character of William Tate and Roz is wonderful in the role of Antonia."

"I can't wait to see them perform."

Sadie carried her coffee and muffin over to the table and sat down. "Yes, I'm looking forward to it." She picked up the muffin and took a bite, trying not to let her distrust show. "Was Arbuckle's busy last night?"

Laura gave a small shrug, her gaze on the newspaper in front of her. "Not too busy."

Sadie still didn't want to believe that Edwin and Laura were keeping secrets from her. But what else could she think? Especially since Laura seemed to be sticking to her story of working at the coffee shop last evening.

So many questions invaded her mind. *Had Laura and Edwin known each other before coming to Silver Peak? Had they slipped when mentioning the mutual acquaintance who had moved from Chicago to Boston, showing a possible, earlier relationship between them?*

Could Edwin be Laura's fiancé?

That last question was one she'd considered before but didn't want to believe. Now she didn't know what to think.

"You're quiet this morning," Laura observed. "Is everything all right?"

Sadie met her gaze, ready to ask her about Edwin and her visit to his home last night. But then she changed her mind. If they *were* trying to deceive her, then it would be all too easy for Laura to make up some clever reason. "I'm just a little tired."

"Me too," Laura said. "And now I have to make some phone calls and then get to work on those revisions." She drained her coffee cup and then rose to her feet. "Are you heading into the shop soon?"

"Yes, in a few minutes," Sadie said. "Have a good day."

"You too." Laura walked out of the kitchen and a moment later Sadie heard her climbing the stairs to the second floor.

Sadie finished her breakfast, then began to read her daily devotional. The message soothed her troubled mind and a gentle peace settled over her as she read, the passage, Philippians 1:9–10, again.

And this is my prayer: that your love may abound more and more in knowledge and depth of insight, so that you may be able to discern what is best and may be pure and blameless for the day of Christ, filled with the fruit of righteousness that comes through Jesus Christ—to the glory and praise of God.

Sadie closed the devotional book and then closed her eyes to pray. "Lord, give me understanding and courage, wisdom and guidance. Help me to walk on the path You set before me and to discern what is best. Amen."

She remained in silent prayer and contemplation for the next several minutes, ending when the telephone rang. She walked over to the phone and picked it up. "Hello?"

"Good morning, Sadie. This is Rita. Doc asked if you have some time to come in this morning."

"I'll be right there."

Sadie sat in Dr. Conroy's office, waiting for him to come in. Baby pictures covered each wall, depicting every baby he'd delivered since he'd started his practice. She smiled when she spotted the photo of Alice. She looked so tiny and Sadie remembered how nervous she and T.R. were when they'd brought her home from the hospital. They'd had no idea how much love and happiness she'd bring into their lives.

The office door opened and Doc walked inside. "Hello, Sadie. I'm glad you could come in on such short notice."

"I'm hoping you received the DNA test back from the lab."

"I have." Doc took a seat behind his desk and then handed her a large, white envelope.

"You haven't opened it yet?" she asked, watching his expression.

"No," he said gently. "I thought you might want to look first."

Sadie smiled, appreciating his sensitivity. Those test results would prove if Laura was really her cousin and if the Wright family had been mistaken about Rachel's death for the last one hundred and seventeen years. She wondered how she'd feel when she saw the results. Either Laura was her cousin or she was lying. No matter the result, their relationship would change.

Doc stood up. "Maybe I should leave you alone . . ."

"No," she said. "Please stay."

Doc sat down again and folded his hands on top of the desk.

Sadie slid one finger under the sealed flap and tore the envelope open. Then she pulled out the one-page report inside. Her heart skipped a beat as she silently read the results. Then she looked up at Doc. "It says that Laura Finch is not excluded as the biological granddaughter of Rachel Wright Ellis."

He gave a slow nod, watching her.

"Does that mean what I think it means? Laura *is* Rachel's granddaughter."

"Yes," he said gently. "It means the DNA test showed at least ninety-nine percent probability that there was a direct maternal relationship between the two samples."

Sadie took a moment to let it sink in. *Laura was her cousin.* That meant Rachel didn't perish in that creek at the old silver mine. The legend of the runaway bride had an entirely different ending. "So the DNA from Laura's hair," Sadie said slowly, wanting to be certain that she understood, "was a match with the DNA from the wedding dress. And the DNA from the blood on the wedding dress matched my DNA too."

"That's right." Doc leaned forward. "Are you all right, Sadie? I know this must come as a shock."

"Yes." Her shock started fading as she realized the tragedy in her family hadn't been Rachel's death, but the fact that Grandpa Jacob never knew his sister had survived and, according to Laura, lived a long and happy life in Boston. "I'm fine. Really." She met his gaze. "I have a new cousin."

He smiled. "Life is full of surprises."

She nodded, rising to her feet. "May I keep this?" she asked, holding up the report.

"Yes, it belongs to you. So does the information it contains."

"Thanks, Doc." Sadie walked out of his office, placing the report in her purse. She nodded to a passing nurse and then entered the reception area, where Rita was watering a potted palm.

Everything seemed so normal, and yet her family history had changed, shifting to a new reality. Sadie was still trying to catch up, but she knew the opposite result would have made her feel much worse.

She took a deep breath, feeling a little more grounded now. Then she approached Rita, not wanting to miss this opportunity to check in with her.

Rita looked up at her. "This plant keeps wanting to die, but I refuse to let that happen. It might be bad for business around here."

Sadie smiled. "So how's the Children's Games and Toys committee coming along?"

"Just great," Rita exclaimed. "Beth is a wonderful chairperson. I had no idea she was so creative." Beth Armstead was the wife of Dr. Ben Armstead and mother to Lacie. Beth ran a successful daycare in her home and hoped to someday open a preschool in town.

"Good. I've seen some of her plans for the picnic. The kids will have a great time."

"The adults too," Rita said, smiling. "We've got a few fun games planned for them, as well."

"Wonderful." They chatted a few minutes more before Sadie made her way out the door, her step lighter than when she'd come in. *God truly does work in mysterious ways*, she thought to herself. Laura and Edwin might still might be keeping secrets from her, but at least she knew now that Laura was a member of the Wright family.

"So it's true?" Roz said, her brown eyes wide behind her orange cat's-eye glasses. "Laura is your cousin?"

Sadie had invited her to lunch at the Depot, a restaurant and ice cream shop located north of Lincoln Street in the former train depot. She'd shared the news about Laura as soon as they'd sat down. "Yes. Doc made it clear that the test results prove Laura is Rachel's granddaughter."

Roz searched her face. "You seem to be taking the news rather well."

Sadie smiled. "I am. Actually, I'm thrilled that Rachel had a life outside of the legend. That she made a new home and family for herself in Boston. I just wish the family she'd left behind would have known about it, especially Grandpa Jacob."

"He knows now," Roz said gently.

Tears stung her eyes, but Sadie blinked them back. "You're right. He does."

"Have you told Laura the results yet?"

"No," Sadie replied, "she's working at the library again today. I thought I'd wait and tell her this evening. She won't be surprised, though. She knew it all along."

"But now you know it too."

Before Sadie could reply, a young waitress appeared at their table and asked for their order.

"I'll have the tuna salad, please," Sadie said. "And a glass of iced tea."

"And for you, ma'am?" the waitress said, turning to Roz.

"What are your specials today?" Roz asked, tilting her head toward the girl. The movement didn't escape Sadie's notice. Neither did the fact that Roz stared intently at the waitress's face as she spoke.

"We've got vegetable quiche," the waitress replied, "chicken pot pie, or a French dip sandwich with potato soup on the side."

"The French dip and soup for me, please," Roz said, handing the woman her menu. "And a glass of iced tea, as well."

After the waitress walked away, Sadie thought about the rehearsal the night before, as well as Roscoe's concerns about Roz's behavior and his complaint that Roz often ignored him.

"I'm so glad you invited me to lunch," Roz said. "I've been thinking about adding those props for the reenactment and now I'm not sure it's such a good idea. They might distract the audience."

Roz's words barely registered as Sadie remembered the way Roz had been watching Alfred so intently during the rehearsal. At the time, Sadie thought Roz had been overacting. Now she realized the reason might be something else entirely.

"Roz," she began, searching for the right words.

"Yes?" Roz said, leaning forward.

"Are you having trouble with your hearing?"

Roz stared at her for a long moment. "What makes you think that?"

"I've noticed some things. Like the way you were watching the waitress's mouth just now when she told you about the lunch specials. You did the same thing last night when Alfred was speaking. You even tilt your head slightly when someone is talking to you, like you're doing right now."

Roz leaned back, straightening her pose. "I have been having a little trouble hearing," she admitted, "but I think it's just due to that cold I had a couple of months ago. I probably still have some congestion in my ear canals."

"Maybe," Sadie replied. "Your father had a hearing problem in his later years, didn't he?"

A tremulous smile curved her mouth. "Are you telling me I'm getting old?"

"Not at all," Sadie assured her. "You know I love you. I'm just concerned."

Roz reached over and gave her hand a warm squeeze. "I know and I truly appreciate it. Don't worry, I'll take care of it."

Sadie wasn't sure what that meant, but she decided to let it go for now. If the problem worsened, she could say something to Roscoe about it. And she supposed it was possible that a bad cold could cause a temporary hearing loss. "Are you sure you're comfortable with performing the historical reenactment?"

"Of course!" Roz replied. "I can't wait to hit the stage again. And I didn't have any problems with my lines last night, did I?"

"No, you had every one down pat," Sadie conceded.

Roz smiled, fingering the long red turquoise necklace that adorned her white peasant blouse. "Well, there you go."

The waitress appeared with their food and set the plates and glasses down on the table. Roz picked up her fork. "So have you talked to Edwin yet?"

Sadie told her about going over there yesterday evening to accept his invitation and finding Laura's car parked in his drive-way. Her cheeks warmed as she recounted the story, feeling as foolish now as she had last night. "I don't know what's going on between them—if anything. But it made me change my mind. I called Edwin this morning and told him that I wouldn't be able to attend the picnic with him. I used the excuse that I'd just be too busy with my duties as the director."

Disappointment flashed across Roz's face. "And what did he say?"

Sadie sighed. "He understood and was very charming about it. I didn't stay on the phone long." She stabbed a chunk of tuna with her fork and pushed it around on her plate. "Do you mind if we change the subject?"

"Not at all," Roz said with a compassionate smile. "So tell me what you're going to do about Laura and the wedding dress?"

"That's a good question. As Rachel's granddaughter, Laura, I believe, is the rightful owner of the wedding dress. But Wade is suing me for it. And I'm not sure Laura wants to stick around Silver Peak to fight over the dress in court."

"Wade doesn't want that dress," Roz said. "He wants the treasure he thinks he'll find with it."

Sadie nodded as she chewed thoughtfully on her tuna salad. "You're right, he does. We know one part of the legend of the runaway bride was wrong. Maybe the part about the stolen treasure is wrong too."

"Too bad there's not a test for that," Roz said wryly.

There might not be a test, Sadie thought to herself, but there could be a public record. But since Rachel had secretly found her way out of Silver Peak, maybe those stock certificates had too.

––––––––––

That evening after dinner, Sadie told Laura the results of the DNA test.

"So we're cousins," Sadie said, handing the DNA report to Laura.

Laura grabbed it and then enveloped Sadie in a big hug. "I told you so!"

Sadie chuckled, giving her a warm squeeze. "Yes, you did. I'm sorry I didn't believe you."

Laura stepped out of the hug. "Don't be sorry. We both know we're cousins now, and that's all that matters."

Sadie breathed a huge sigh of relief that Laura wasn't offended by her actions.

Laura looked down at the report in her hands. "Maybe we should have this framed."

Sadie smiled. "The news that runaway bride, Rachel Wright, escaped to Boston and lived a long and happy life will come as a big shock to a lot of people around here."

"I'd love to be here to see it," Laura said wistfully. Then her eyes widened. "Maybe I should move to Silver Peak. After all, I have family here."

"You do," Sadie said with a careful smile. "But how would your fiancé feel about it?"

Unless he's already moved here himself.

Laura deflated. "Oh, right. What was I thinking?"

"The question now is what to do with the wedding dress," Sadie told her. "The problem is . . ."

"I'd like to have it," Laura interjected. "If you don't mind, that is. Nana meant so much to me and that wedding dress . . ." Her voice trailed off and she was silent for a long moment. "Well, it's important to me."

"Of course," Sadie said, struck by the strange expression on Laura's face. She sensed now wasn't a good time to talk about Wade Marley's lawsuit. "We'll figure something out."

———

On Tuesday afternoon, Sadie sat at her desk in the Antique Mine, several library books open in front of her. She'd picked them up this morning and, between customers, spent her time researching information about how stock in silver mines was handled, both publicly and privately.

Sadie had never believed the accusations that Rachel had stolen jewelry and stock certificates when she'd run away from her wedding. But now she wondered if Rachel had needed them to fund her trip from Colorado to Boston. If so, she would have needed to cash in those stock certificates at some point.

And, according her research, all stock transfers and sales were supposed to be recorded by the company, which were included in reports to their stockholders. And since Moose Creek Industries was a public company, transfers and sales were available to the public too.

Sadie looked up the phone number for Moose Creek Industries, once known as Moose Creek Mining Company before they started expanding into other industries. Then she dialed the number.

"Moose Creek Industries," said a pleasant female voice on the other end of the line. "This is Tracy. How may I help you?"

"Hello, Tracy. My name is Sadie Speers and I'm looking for some information about a possible sale or trade of stock certificates for Moose Creek Mining Company. Do you have that information?"

"We do," Tracy said. "Year, please?"

"1897," Sadie said, hoping their records went back that far.

Tracy chuckled. "My goodness, that's a long time ago. Please give me a minute to bring up the records on my computer."

So far, so good, Sadie thought to herself, growing more nervous with each passing moment.

"Here we go," Tracy said at last. "There was only one sale that year of two hundred shares of stock in the Moose Creek Mining Company."

"Can you give me the name of the person who sold the stock?" Sadie asked.

"Wallace Marley."

She blinked. Had the jilted groom really stolen the stock certificates from his own family? "You're sure that's the name of the seller?"

"Yes," Tracy said. "His name is right here in black and white."

Sadie's mind whirled. "Can you tell me the date of the sale?"

"June 20, 1897."

That was only two days after Wallace Marley and Rachel Wright were supposed to be wed. Perhaps Wallace had sensed that Rachel was planning to flee, Sadie thought to herself, or had even learned of her plans. Fearing he might lose the Wright wealth, Wallace may have tried to derail those plans by convincing his nephew, Marley Hopkins, to start the fight with Rachel's older brother. When that failed to keep his bride from running away, Wallace had stolen the Marley family stock certificates for himself and sold them a few days later, all the while letting the blame fall on Rachel.

"Would you be able to fax me a copy of that sale?" Sadie asked, knowing she might need the proof in court. She hoped it wouldn't come to that, but she doubted that Wade Marley would take her word for it.

"Sure," Tracy said. "I'll send it right away. Just give me your fax number."

After Sadie ended the call, she only had to wait a few minutes for the fax to come through. She smiled to herself, grateful that she finally had proof that her great-aunt wasn't a thief—or at least, that she hadn't stolen the stock certificates. But if that had been a lie, it was doubtful that she stolen any jewelry either.

Sadie scanned a copy of the stock sale into her computer just before an older couple walked through the door. The legend of the runaway bride was about to change again.

19

ON WEDNESDAY MORNING, SADIE PARKED IN FRONT OF THE office for *Marley Vacation Rentals* on Water Street. The office was housed in a log cabin-style building that had been built ten years ago when Wade expanded his business. He'd built and leased two other log cabin-style office buildings on either side of him, one called Material Girl, a quilting and fabric store owned by Lynette Kovacs. The other was a ski shop named Slopes, owned by Colt Malloy, a former snowboarding Olympian. Slopes sold and rented skis, snowboards, and snow mobiles, and even dog sleds, along with other sports paraphernalia and winter wear.

Sadie climbed out of the Tahoe and headed up the walk, her purse slung over one shoulder. She was ready to do battle, fortified by a jumbo cup of coffee and a piece of cinnamon streusel coffee cake that Julie had brought into the Antique Mine that morning.

She'd left Julie in charge at the shop, wanting to put a stop to this lawsuit nonsense before it went any further. Then she could give her full attention to the Founder's Day Picnic coming up in three days. After that, Laura would be heading back to Boston.

Sadie wondered if Edwin would go with her or if they'd conduct a long-distance relationship.

Sadie shook that unsettling thought from her head as she opened the door to the office and walked inside. Wade Marley sat at a wide pine desk, typing on his computer keyboard. He looked up at her and stopped typing, a scowl creasing his face.

"Here to rent a vacation home?" he asked.

Sadie smiled. "No, I'm here to put an end to your lawsuit."

He pushed back his office chair and settled his hands on his stomach. "Does that mean you're going to give me the wedding dress?"

"It doesn't belong to me." Sadie sat down in the chair opposite his desk. "The dress belongs to Laura Finch, Rachel Wright's granddaughter."

His scowl deepened. "What are you talking about?"

Then Sadie told him the story of the runaway bride and how she'd escaped marriage to Wallace Marley to make a new life for herself. When she was finishing, Wade's mouth hung open.

He took a moment to gather himself, then closed his mouth and sat up straight in his chair. "That can't be true."

"It is," Sadie replied. "And I have proof." She drew a copy of the DNA test result out of her purse and laid it on his desk.

He slid the paper toward him, his mouth gaping again as he read the results. "I don't understand. How did you get Rachel's DNA?" Then he narrowed his gaze on her. "So you do have Rachel's wedding dress."

"I do now. The first time you asked me, I'd sent it to a lab to have the blood on it tested. It turns out that Rachel faked her death, even using her own blood to make it appear that she'd shot herself."

"So she was diabolical *and* a thief," Wade said with a sneer, tossing the DNA report back toward Sadie.

"You're wrong." Sadie placed a copy of the sale report from Moose Creek Industries on the desk in front of him. "Rachel didn't take those stock certificates, but I have proof that Wallace did."

He studied the report. "This has to be a fake."

"You can call the company to verify it for yourself," Sadie said, her anger rising. "Or better yet, let me bring it into evidence in court. It's the least I can do after you smashed my car window and shot a bullet through my window."

He held up both hands. "Whoa, there. I never did any such thing. I'm not a violent man, Sadie. We might not always see eye to eye, but I'd never try to hurt you."

His words had a ring of truth to them, but Sadie knew he was an excellent salesman. "You made it clear you wanted that wedding dress and would do almost anything to get it."

Wade stared at her, a muscle flexing in his jaw. "I didn't care about the wedding dress," he said at last. "I never believed there was any treasure either, despite the legend."

She met his gaze, confused by this sudden turnaround. "Then why did you come into my shop and demand the dress?"

He shifted uncomfortably in his chair. "Because a man named Nathaniel Green offered me a deal I couldn't refuse. He knew all about the legend of the runaway bride and wanted to display that wedding dress in his museum. He promised free advertising for my vacation rentals to all the tourists who pass through his doors."

Sadie nodded as all the pieces began to fall together. "So that's why he served me that court summons. Because he had a deal with you for the dress."

"Exactly," Wade said. "I told him that lawsuit went too far, but he insisted that we play hardball. If you want to point the finger at someone for trying to intimidate you, look at Green."

"He didn't do it either. The day of the first incident, he was in the hospital in Breckenridge, recovering from food poisoning."

Wade shook his head. "Then you've got an enemy somewhere, Sadie. And you'd better figure out who it is before he strikes again."

"Thanks," Sadie said, hating to admit he was right. She sensed that her initial instincts had been right all along—and the blame probably lay at the feet of Laura's fiancé, a man she'd never even met.

She left Wade's office and drove back to the Antique Mine, satisfied that she'd set Wade straight. Still, it bothered her that Laura might be engaged to a man who would stalk her all the way to Silver Peak and try to cause trouble and intimidate her into returning to Boston. So far it hadn't worked, but Laura planned to leave Silver Peak after the picnic.

And what about Edwin?

As much as she didn't want to believe it, could he have been the one to break the back window of her Tahoe and fire a warning shot through her window? Every fiber of her being rejected such a ridiculous notion.

And yet . . .

She couldn't forget the three times she'd found Edwin and Laura together. First, at the library, then the coffee shop, and then at Edwin's house. How many other times had they met when Sadie was unaware?

She'd solved the mystery of the wedding dress and proven that Laura was truly her cousin, but questions still remained—including the reason for the mysterious brass key that had been found with the dress.

"Deal with it after the picnic," Sadie murmured to herself as she pulled onto Main Street and headed in the direction of her shop.

She intended to wait until after the picnic to confront Laura and Edwin about their relationship too. Sadie just hoped she didn't lose both an old friend and a new cousin in the process.

———

The next two days were a whirlwind of activity. Sadie worked in the shop all day on Thursday and then she and Roz led a final meeting with all of the Founder's Day committee members. To Sadie's surprise and delight, Roz's hearing seemed to have improved. She was more like her old self, laughing and talking with friends and having no trouble understanding anyone or exhibiting any of the behaviors Sadie had noticed at the rehearsal.

That good news enabled Sadie to give her full attention to Friday's preparations. As with most big events, small things cropped up that needed attention and, by Friday evening, Sadie had helped set up tables and chairs in the park, decorated the bandstand for the picnic entertainment, created a sign for Marge's silent auction, and made sure that Beth Armstead had all the assistants she needed for the children's crafts and games, along with a dozen other errands that left her dragging herself into bed shortly after midnight.

Saturday dawned clear and bright, a perfect day for a picnic. The weather forecast predicted a light breeze and an afternoon temperature of seventy degrees. Sadie ate a quick breakfast with Laura and then they both headed to Centennial Park. She'd closed the Antique Mine for the day, not wanting Julie to miss the celebration.

The picnic started at noon and by one o'clock it looked as if most of the 5,800 people living in Silver Peak had turned out to commemorate the founding of their hometown. The large park was filled with people of all ages, from the bandstand on one end to the municipal hot springs pool on the other. Jared Marley, a cousin to Wade, was planning to run for mayor and handing out campaign buttons. Spike Harris was playing the fiddle under a large aspen tree, much to the delight of the young children gathered around him.

The park sported picnic tables and outdoor grills in the middle, along with a playground and a hiking trail that ran through the thick stand of evergreen trees surrounding the park on three sides.

"Grandma, look at us," Sara called out, catching Sadie as she carried the vintage washtub from her Tahoe to the bandstand. Sadie turned around to see Sara and Mia wearing long calico dresses and matching bonnets. They even wore the sturdy shoes that laced up high on the ankle.

"You two look great," Sadie exclaimed. "Like you walked straight out of the history books." She shifted the washtub to her other arm as she turned to Mia. "Your grandma is an excellent seamstress."

"Thank you," Mia said shyly. "She made the patterns herself by looking at old pictures."

"Are you two enjoying yourselves?" Sadie asked as Alice and Theo walked up to join them.

"We're having a great time," Sara said. "Aren't we, Mom?"

Alice smiled. "We sure are. Theo and I were just at the antique car show in the swimming pool parking lot. I can't believe how many cars are on display."

"Isn't it wonderful?" Sadie exclaimed. "The nice weather brought out even more people than we expected." She'd kept an eye out for Edwin, but hadn't seen him yet. Then she realized she hadn't seen Laura for a while either and found herself wondering if they were together.

"Here, Grandma," Theo said, walking up to her and taking the washtub from her arms. "I'll carry this for you. Just tell me where you want it."

"On the bandstand, please," Sadie told him, grateful that she had such a thoughtful grandson. She chatted with Alice and the girls for a few more minutes, then followed Theo to the bandstand. The historical reenactment was scheduled for three o'clock and Alfred and Roz were changing into their costumes in the swimming pool locker rooms.

Don Sweeting walked up to her with a smile on his face. "I just talked to Jeanne and told her the picnic is a huge success. She's thrilled and asked me to thank both you and Roz for all your hard work."

"Well, you're both welcome, but Jeanne made it easy for us. I'm just sorry she's missing the fun."

"So am I," Don said. "But she's enjoying the time with her mother and I've been sending her pictures from my cell phone. I even promised to videotape the historical reenactment so she can enjoy it as well."

"Wonderful," Sadie exclaimed. "Do you mind sending me a copy too?"

"Not at all, I'll make one for Professor Daly and Roz, as well. I can't wait to see them on stage."

Sadie checked her watch. "They're scheduled to go on in one hour. I'd better make sure everything is set up."

He smiled. "Tell them to break a leg."

"I will." She went to the bandstand and asked Theo to place the washtub on the right side of the stage they'd set up, then she looked out over the rows of folding chairs, which were already filling up with people.

"*Pssst!* Sadie, over here!"

Sadie turned at the sound of Roz's voice and saw her best friend, hiding behind one of the bandstand's large white columns.

Sadie hurried over to her. "What is it?" Her gaze moved over Roz's period costume. It was a perfect fit and Sally Henderson had done a magnificent job with Roz's hair and makeup. "You look wonderful!"

"Oh, Sadie," Roz cried. "We have a big problem."

Sadie took another step closer to her, now out of sight of anyone in the audience. "Roz, what's wrong?"

"This." Roz held out her hand. An old hearing aid lay in her palm, broken into two pieces.

Sadie's gaze moved from the hearing aid to Roz's distraught face. "Is that why you've been hearing better the last couple of days? You were wearing a hearing aid."

Roz nodded. "I saw an audiologist a few weeks ago, when I thought that cold had caused a problem with my ears. He said I have a condition called presbyacusis, which is just a fancy way of saying that I have a hearing deterioration that happens to some people as they get older. He wanted to fit me for a hearing aid, but I wasn't ready to admit I had a problem."

"Oh, Roz," Sadie murmured, her heart going out to her friend.

Roz drew in a deep breath. "When you noticed the problems I was having, I decided to start wearing my dad's old hearing aid that I'd kept after he passed away. Only it never quite fit right and fell out this morning and broke." She tugged lightly at the vintage cameo choker circling her throat. "What if I don't hear all of Alfred's lines, Sadie? What if I miss my cues and mess up the whole thing?"

Sadie reached out to give Roz a reassuring hug. "You won't. I'll make sure of it."

Roz stepped back and looked into her eyes. "How will you do that?"

"Easy," Sadie said. "You've memorized that script word for word. So all you need is a cue every time it's your turn to speak. Just look at me if you're not sure and I'll tap my finger on my cheek when it's time for your line."

Roz's eyes widened with relief. "That just might work."

"Of course it will," Sadie said, giving her hands a reassuring squeeze. "Just watch me, Roz, and everything will be fine."

"I hope so. On Monday morning, I'm going to get fitted for a new hearing aid." Roz took another deep breath and slowly released it. "But first I need to get through this performance. I guess if Antonia Tate can travel west to the Rocky Mountains, survive the hardships of a prospector's wife, and build a town, then the least I can do is get on this stage and tell people about it."

Sadie's grinned. "That's the spirit!"

"Okay, I'm going to find Alfred and fill him in on the plan," Roz said. "Maybe he can give me some subtle signals too."

They separated, with Roz going in one direction and Sadie headed in the other. She climbed down the stairs of the bandstand and found Edwin waiting for her at the bottom.

"Hello, Sadie," he greeted her. "You've done an amazing job here. Everyone seems to be having a marvelous time."

"Thank you," she said, warmed by his compliment. "Would you mind doing me a favor?"

He met her gaze for a long, lingering moment. "Anything."

"Could you save a seat in the front row for me, right in the center of the row?"

"Absolutely," he said, smiling. "I'll see you there."

———

Ten minutes later, Sadie joined Edwin in the front row. The rest of the seats had all filled up and there were people standing behind the chairs to watch the performance.

Alfred and Roz took the stage to enthusiastic applause. Then silence descended as Alfred took two steps toward the audience. "Our destiny awaits, Antonia," he began in a loud clear voice. "The silver in Colorado is calling our name. Are we ready to answer?"

Sadie lightly tapped her cheek, signaling to Roz, who stood at the washtub, that it was her turn to speak.

"The dirty laundry is calling *my* name," Roz said, to the delight and amusement of the audience. "And I hear that prospecting is a dirty business, which means more laundry for me."

Sadie laughed along with the rest of the crowd. Roz and Alfred had great chemistry on stage and the cue system that Sadie had suggested seemed to be working like a charm.

"Soon, we'll be awash in silver, my dear Antonia," Alfred intoned. "The laundry can wait, but our fate cannot."

The rest of the play continued as it had started, with wonderful acting and timing between the two performers. The balanced blend of drama and comedy kept the audience enthralled until the very last line.

Sadie breathed a sigh of happy relief as Alfred and Roz took their bows, and then she joined Edwin and the rest of the audience in a long, standing ovation. She watched as dozens of people approached the two performers to offer their praise and congratulations. Then she saw Lance Ely walk up to them for an interview.

She looked around for Edwin, but found that he had disappeared in the crowd. Then Roz caught her eye and winked. Sadie winked back, thanking the Lord for her best friend and for William and Antonia Tate, who had built such a wonderful place to live.

————

On Sunday morning, Sadie returned home from church to find Laura asleep on the living room sofa. Hank was snuggled by her feet at the end of the sofa. He lifted one eyelid as Sadie walked into the living room, then closed it again.

She and Laura had planned to go to Campfire Chapel together, but a migraine headache had kept Laura home and now Sadie crept over to cover her with the vintage, log cabin quilt that was folded over the top of the sofa.

Laura stirred a little as Sadie placed the quilt around her, but she didn't awaken. A notebook lay open on the coffee table, indicating that Laura had been working before she fell asleep. Sadie saw the words *Campaign Strategy* written at the top of the page, followed by a list of phrases that included *respected Chicago judge* and *hometown boy*. She stared at it for a long moment, something niggling at her brain. Then Edwin's words echoed inside her head.

"Silver Peak gave me such a wonderful start in life. I'd really like an opportunity to give something back."

"He campaigned for a judgeship there and said Laura was instrumental in his winning the election."

Was it possible that Edwin and Laura didn't have a romantic relationship? Sadie asked herself. That they simply had a *business* relationship? In high school, Edwin had always talked about his dream of going into politics someday. Perhaps meeting Laura and knowing how she'd helped his friend win an election had motivated him to try the same thing.

There was only one way to find out. Sadie grabbed her purse and headed out the door.

20

SADIE FOUND EDWIN SITTING ON HIS FRONT PORCH SWING. IT was the same swing they'd sat on over forty years ago, when they were two young kids in high school with their whole lives ahead of them.

"Hello, Sadie," Edwin said as she walked up the porch steps. He rose to his feet. "Have you recovered from all the picnic activity yesterday?"

She smiled. "I think so. It was a great day." Then she cleared her throat. "Do you have time to talk?"

"Sure. Do you want to go inside or talk here?"

"Here is perfect," Sadie said, joining him on the swing. They gently rocked the swing back and forth together, just like old times. "I have a confession to make."

He turned to look at her, curiosity shining in his blue eyes. "Oh?"

"I saw some notes in Laura's notebook and it made me wonder . . . are you planning to run for mayor of Silver Peak?"

He chuckled. "My secret is out. I didn't want to say anything to you until I'd made up my mind." He hesitated, then met her gaze. "I was afraid you'd think me presumptuous."

"Presumptuous?" she echoed in disbelief. "I think you'd make a wonderful mayor."

He arched a silver brow. "Really? Even though I've just moved back to town?"

She smiled. "Edwin, you were born and raised here. You know Silver Peak as well as anyone. And you can bring some new ideas and experiences here that you've learned in your career and during your life in Chicago." Sadie's voice softened. "We'd be lucky to have you."

"Thank you," Edwin said. "That means a lot coming from you." Then he smiled. "My decision is made—I'm going to run for mayor. And maybe I should ask you to lead my campaign."

"Not if you want to win," she said, smiling. "Besides, I thought Laura already had that job."

He shook his head. "I believe Laura's planning to give up campaign work when she returns to Boston. Her advice has been invaluable, though. She's an interesting woman."

Sadie could hear a friendly affection in his voice, but nothing more serious than that. She'd assumed the worst—and even thought Edwin might be trying to scam her. It all seemed so ridiculous now, although she'd had some reasons to doubt him.

"I still can't believe she's my cousin," Sadie told him. "And that Rachel survived past her wedding day."

"It amazes me that a sixteen-year-old girl could execute such a plan so perfectly," Edwin mused. "And that it wasn't discovered until over a century later."

"I know," Sadie agreed, enjoying the warm September breeze and the comforting sway of the porch swing. "She would have needed money and clothing and food just to make it to Breckenridge on foot and catch a train."

"And she must have worn some type of disguise so she wouldn't be recognized," Edwin added, "especially after the news spread of her escape by horseback from the wedding."

Sadie thought back to the story her family had told her, during those rare times they had talked about Rachel Wright. "She rode bareback to the mine that day, so she didn't have any saddlebags to store things like clothes or food."

"And yet she managed to make it out of Colorado and all the way to Boston without anyone catching sight of her."

Sadie pictured herself in Rachel's place, desperate and willing to do just about anything to avoid marriage to Wallace Marley. But why go all the way to the silver mine to do it?

"Maybe she stored her supplies at the mine ahead of time," Sadie said, thinking out loud. "Along with a spare set of clothes and possibly even a horse. That would certainly get her to Breckenridge much faster than traveling by foot. She might have been on a train out of Colorado before the search party even found her wedding dress and the revolver lying beside it."

Edwin gave a slow nod. "That sounds plausible. Likely, actually."

"Perhaps the original plan had been for Jacob to meet her at the mine," Sadie continued. "He might have helped gather those supplies for her and taken them to the mine to avoid raising any suspicion."

"It makes sense. Her plan worked, so it's apparent she left no stone unturned in her quest to escape from Silver Peak without a trace."

They fell into an easy silence, watching two young boys ride their bikes past the house and a large hawk soar overhead. After a few minutes, Edwin turned to her. "Sadie, it means a lot to me that we've renewed our friendship. I'll be honest, though. I'd like us to be more than friends." He gazed into her eyes. "I'd like us to start dating, if you feel the same."

Her pulse picked up at his words and she drew in a deep, calming breath. "My feelings are so hard to describe, Edwin. I'm so happy that you moved back to Silver Peak, and I really like you . . ." She twisted the silver wedding band on her finger, searching for the right words. "But I'm not ready for a new relationship. Not yet, anyway. I hope you understand."

"I do," he said gently. "Thank you for your honesty."

She smiled. "And thank you for yours. I hope we can still spend time together, as friends."

"Absolutely," he said, then a mischievous twinkle gleamed in his eyes. "After all, I may need your vote."

She laughed, and any tension between them melted away. "You've got it."

———————

As Sadie drove home that afternoon, her thoughts kept returning to the logistics of Rachel's escape from Colorado. The runaway bride had managed it well, fooling everyone. But were there some clues that Sadie had missed? Something at the mine that might have proven Rachel's real intentions that day?

On an impulse, she turned the Tahoe left instead of right, taking the mountain road that would lead her to the old silver mine. When she arrived there twenty minutes later, she parked under an aspen tree and climbed out.

The sound of clear mountain water gurgling over the rocks must have sounded the same in 1897 as they did today, Sadie thought to herself. She looked around, trying to put herself in Rachel's shoes and knowing the girl would need to have acted quickly, certain that someone from the wedding would be on her trail.

Sadie supposed that Rachel could have hidden a change of clothing and even a horse at the opening of the mine. But what about money, which she would have needed to finance the trip? Even if Rachel had stolen some jewels, as Hester had claimed, it would have been risky and time-consuming to try to sell them in Breckenridge.

No, Sadie thought to herself, it was more likely that she'd hidden cash up here too—at least enough to purchase a train ticket east.

Then her gaze fell on the two flat-topped stones at the mouth of the mine. She remembered now that Laura had referred to them as sentinels. Sadie walked over to the mine and knelt down in front of the nearest stone. She pulled away some of the brush that had grown over it and saw a rough engraving on the top of the stone. It looked like the work of a child and soon she realized that it resembled the letter *R*. Then she walked over to the other stone and cleared away the brush there too, only to find a small, crude engraving of the letter *J*.

Rachel and Jacob?

Sadie had heard Grandpa Jacob talk of going to the mine with his father to check on the miners, but he'd never mentioned Rachel going along. Then again, Grandpa Jacob *never* mentioned Rachel.

She realized now that the two of them must have gone up there together. They'd probably sat outside the mine on those stool-shaped stones, each claiming one as their own while they'd waited for their father to return.

Maybe that was why Rachel had come here on the day she ran away, Sadie thought to herself. Maybe she'd had a ready-made hiding place.

Sadie wrapped her arms around the stone in front of her and used all her strength to pull it out of the ground. When it finally dislodged from the soil, she was able to roll it a few feet from its original spot.

A small dirt hole, about the size of a cigar box, had been concealed by the stone. The hole was empty, but just its existence lent credence to her theory. She walked over to the other stone, the one with the *J* scratched into the surface. This one was harder to move and Sadie had to rest several times and wedge some branches underneath before it finally began to loosen from the soil.

With a grunt of exertions, she pushed it away. That's when she discovered another hole, about the same size as the first one, that had been hidden beneath the stone. Only this hole appeared to have something in it. As she brushed loose clumps of dirt away, her fingers brushed something that felt like cloth. She lifted it out of the hole and soon realized that it was some kind of box wrapped in a thick layer of canvas-like material.

Her heart beat in her throat as she quickly unwrapped the cloth to reveal a tin box underneath. The outside had rusted so much that there was no way to tell what the original exterior had looked like. She tried to lift the lid, but it was stuck.

Then she saw the keyhole on the front.

"It's not stuck," she said out loud. "It's locked."

Sadie set the box on the ground and then jogged over to her Tahoe. She reached into her purse and dug around until her fingers found the brass key. Then she raced back to the mine, her heart pounding now.

She took a deep breath as she inserted the key into the lock, wiggling it a little when she encountered some resistance. But after a moment, she heard a satisfying *click* as she turned the key and the lid popped open.

Then Sadie saw something she never expected.

21

"LAURA," SADIE CALLED AS SHE RAN INTO THE HOUSE. She carried the rusty box in her hand, still amazed by her discovery.

She entered the living room, wondering if Laura was still asleep, but the sofa was empty and the notebook was gone from the coffee table. Turning toward the kitchen, Sadie called out again. "Laura? Hank?"

Silence permeated the house. Disappointed, Sadie set her purse and the tin box on the dining room table, assuming that Laura had taken Hank for a hike. But when she walked into the kitchen, she saw a half-full carton of milk standing open on the counter with an empty glass beside it.

A cold chill passed over her as she looked around the kitchen, listening intently for any noises coming from the floor above. Then her gaze fell on the table and she saw a note.

She picked it up, her heart dropping to her toes as she began to read it.

If you want to see Hank alive again, bring the treasure back to the old family mine. Don't call the sheriff or anyone else. I saw you take something from there that belongs to me.

—*Laura*

The harsh sting of betrayal made her gasp for air.

After taking a moment to gather herself, Sadie read the note again, more slowly this time. She recognized Laura's handwriting and then she noticed the paper itself, sensing something familiar about it. It was ash-gray, the same color as the paper Lance Ely had used when he'd interviewed her for his article.

Sadie held the paper up to the kitchen light. In one corner, she saw the same recycling symbol that had been on the cardboard cover of Lance's notepad.

Either Lance Ely was Laura's fiancé—or he wasn't really Lance Ely. What better way to maintain contact with your fiancée than by hiding in plain sight and posing as a travel writer? It gave him the perfect opportunity to gather information and ask questions of anyone in town.

Sickened by their deception, Sadie realized one of them must have been following her and watching from a distance when she'd unearthed the tin box from beneath the stone.

But how had they gotten back to the house so quickly? Or perhaps Laura had been here all along and her fiancé, Lance or Ray or whatever his real name might be, had followed Sadie and then put his kidnapping plan into action.

It didn't matter at this point. Right now she needed to save Hank.

Sadie ran for the door, grabbing her purse and the tin box on the way. She didn't want to turn over the treasure, but the ransom note had made it clear that it was the only way to get her dog back.

————

Fifteen minutes later, Sadie drove up the steep road leading to the mine. She'd driven faster than usual on the mountain roads, praying all the way and fearing the worst with each passing mile. She'd also placed a quick call to the sheriff's office to report Hank's kidnapping, ignoring the admonition in the ransom note. She wasn't going to play by anyone's rules but her own.

Any hope that this was all some sort of sick prank quickly died when she saw Laura standing in front of the mine with Ray Johnson, the man who had introduced himself as Lance Ely. Hank sat behind them, his leash hooked around a narrow tree trunk. He happily chewed on a rawhide bone, seeming blissfully unaware of what was happening.

She climbed out of the Tahoe with the tin box in her hand, praying that they'd let her and Hank go as soon as she handed it over.

Then Sadie saw the gun in Laura's hand. It was pointed directly at her.

"Happy you could join us," Ray said, tossing a small stone into the creek beside him. "And even happier that you brought the treasure box. I can't wait to see what's inside."

He started walking toward her.

"Stop," Laura shouted.

Ray glanced back at her and all the color drained from his face when he saw the gun now pointed at him. "Laura, what are you doing?"

"The right thing, Ray," she said firmly. "Finally, I'm doing the right thing. Now go sit over by that tree."

He took a step toward her. "Laura, baby . . ."

"Now!" Laura ordered, her harsh tone brooking no argument.

Ray slowly backed away from her, his hands half-raised in the air. "You aren't thinking straight, honey. Our plan worked. The treasure is ours."

"*Your* plan," Laura countered, not taking her eyes or the gun off of Ray. "It was always your plan. Coming to Silver Peak and telling me to make friends with Sadie. Wanting me to ply her for information about the wedding dress and the treasure. I hated every minute of it."

"You're crazy," he spit out. "We can go back to Boston now. We can have it all!"

"I'm not going anywhere with you," Laura said evenly. Then she glanced over at Sadie. "Do you still have that tow rope in your Tahoe?"

———————

A short time later, Laura's sputtering ex-fiancé was seated on the ground, his back against a tree trunk and Sadie's bright yellow tow rope tied tightly around him.

Sadie and Laura sat by the creek watching Hank frolic in the clear water while they waited for Sheriff Slattery to arrive.

"I can't imagine what you must have thought when you found that ransom note," Laura said. "Ray forced me to write it."

"So his real name is Ray?" Sadie clarified. "He's not Lance Ely?"

"Actually, his full name is Bentley Ray Johnson. He only wishes he could write as well as the real Lance Ely." Tears gleamed in her eyes as she looked at Sadie. "I don't know what I ever saw in him. He was so charming at first, and then little by little, he'd convince me to do things I didn't want to do."

"Like lie to me?" Sadie asked softly.

Laura closed her eyes. "Yes." Then she opened them again and drew in a deep, shuddering breath. "Ray had heard me talk about the treasure in Nana's wedding dress and he became obsessed about it. I'd already shared my genealogy research with him and everything I'd learned about my family in Silver Peak."

"Then one of you must have found the *Chatterbox* blog on the Internet."

"Ray did," Laura said. "When he read the bit about finding Rachel's dress, he bought us two plane tickets to Denver the same day. I thought it was a romantic gesture, giving me a trip to Nana's birthplace to meet my family there." She sighed. "Then he told me his plan."

"Of course she went along with it," Ray called out, obviously overhearing their conversation. "Until it was finally ready to pay off."

Laura looked over at Sadie. "He's wrong. I *never* willingly went along with it. In fact, I told him that I was done—that our engagement was off. And that's the night he smashed your car window."

"As a warning to you," Sadie surmised.

Laura nodded. "The next day he sent me a text message, warning me that much worse would happen if I didn't continue to play along."

Sadie could hear the despair in her voice and see the tears rolling down her cheeks.

"I was so weak," she murmured. "I should have known I couldn't trust him when he made me keep our romance under the radar in Boston. Part of me understood, since he worked for a public figure, but he wouldn't even let me put an engagement announcement in the newspaper."

Sadie wondered if Ray had been in trouble before and tried to avoid the spotlight.

"And then I'd hear the tales of the courage and strength of the Wright women," Laura continued, "and feel so foolish—like I wasn't worthy of my heritage."

"You weren't weak," Sadie said, hearing a police siren in the distance. "You made a brave stand today, when it really mattered, to protect both me and Hank. That's something I'll never forget."

"Can you ever forgive me?" Laura asked her.

Sadie smiled. "I already have."

———

Later that evening, Sadie joined Laura in the living room, holding the tin box in her hand. "You never asked me about the treasure."

Laura sighed. "To tell you the truth, I'd rather pretend you never found it."

"You might feel differently when you see what's inside of it." She sat down next to Laura on the sofa and lifted the lid on the box.

Laura stared at her. "Letters?"

"That's right," Sadie said with a smile. "Would you like me to read them to you?"

"Please." Laura watched Sadie lift the first one from the box.

Then Sadie cleared her throat and began to read out loud.

Dear J.,

I know you have not abandoned me, as my stepmother claims. She is gleeful on this wedding day, ready to tether me to her odious family forever.

However, I have other plans. When you did not meet me for our rendezvous three days ago, I concocted another way to gain my freedom. It will not be easy, but it is the only hope I have left.

Do not worry when you find me gone, for I shall flourish once I'm free of my stepmother and her nephew. The only thing of value I take with me is our mother's diamond necklace, which I will need to sell to fund the escape we planned for me.

We both know our mother would rather see me safe and happy without her necklace than in a miserable marriage with it.

No one can ever know what really happened to me. Wallace Marley is a vengeful man and will never stop look-ing for me if he believes I am alive somewhere in the world.

Be safe and well, my dearest brother. And know that you shall live forever in my heart.

Yours,
R.

Sadie lowered the letter and saw tears streaming down Laura's face.

"So my nana and your grandpa Jacob," Laura said, "had planned her escape to Boston together."

Sadie nodded. "I found out that Grandpa Jacob was jailed shortly before the wedding and languished there for a week. By the time he was released, Rachel was gone."

"So he never knew?"

Sadie smiled. "There's one more letter in the box." She pulled it out and began to read it.

Dear R.,

Although you may never see this letter, I must write it before I leave Silver Peak. The Marleys have been spreading ugly rumors about you and it has taken all my strength to keep from revealing the truth to clear your name.

That is why I must leave here for a while. You know James has agreed to keep the key to our secret hiding place, so if you ever return to Silver Peak and I do not, I know you will be able to open this box and find this letter.

I love you and I pray every day for your health and happiness. My greatest wish for you is that you surround yourself with a lifetime of love and family, growing old with a deserving husband who adores you and filling your life with the laughter of children.

We shall meet again someday in heaven. Until then, your secret shall always be safe with me.

Yours,

J.

"So he knew," Laura said, sounding as awestruck as Sadie had felt when she'd first read her grandpa's letter. "He knew she didn't die that day."

"Yes," Sadie said, her own eyes tearing up now. "And he kept her secret all those years, just as he'd promised. He did it to protect her and safeguard her happiness."

"Oh, Sadie," Laura breathed. "We're so blessed to have found these letters."

"And to have found each other." Sadie reached out to give her a hug. "The treasure with the wedding dress is the importance of family—and the love that is expressed in every word of those letters."

"Amen," Laura said.

"Amen," Sadie echoed, knowing she'd keep that treasure in her heart forever.

Epilogue

LOYAL READERS OF THE *CHATTERBOX* WILL KNOW THAT THE Legend of the Runaway Bride has taken many twists and turns over the last few weeks. The man posing as travel writer Lance Ely will now be able to write about his adventures in the Blake County Jail as he serves his sentence for vandalism, extortion, and other misdeeds.

Meanwhile, the granddaughter of hometown girl and escape artist, the late Rachel Wright Ellis, is moving from Boston to Silver Peak to rediscover her roots. Laura Finch will be staying in the Antique Lady's third-floor apartment above the Antique Mine and is offering marketing and promotional services to local retail establishments and other businesses.

Silver Peak keeps the *Chatterbox* hopping, so stay tuned for the latest news around town. You never know what's going to happen next!

Yours truly,
The Chatterbox

About the Author

CAROLE JEFFERSON IS THE PEN NAME FOR A TEAM OF WRITERS WHO have come together to create the series Mysteries of Silver Peak. *A Mountain of Mystery* was written by Kristin Eckhardt. She is the author of more than forty books, including nineteen of them for Guideposts. She's won two national awards for her writing, and her first book was made into a TV movie. Kristin and her husband have three children and live in central Nebraska. Kristin enjoys quilting, traveling, and spending time with family.

Nobody's Safe

"Don't know if we need a man so citified to be our mayor," a voice called out. "You don't look like anyone who lives in Silver Peak."

Sadie Speers turned her head and searched through the crowd packed into Arbuckle's Coffee. The popular shop was filled to the brim with residents wanting to hear why they should vote for Edwin Marshall as their mayor. There was only one person on their feet besides Edwin. Sadie frowned at Marge Ruxton. It pained Sadie to admit that Marge was somewhat of a busybody, the type of person who seemed to have an opinion about almost everything and everyone. Sadie tried hard to like her, to give her the benefit of the doubt, but sometimes it was difficult. She looked back at Edwin. How would he handle her critical comment?

Edwin looked very distinguished in his oxford shirt and flat-front Dockers. At Sadie's urging, he'd left his usual sweater vest at home, which for him was a big step toward making his appearance more casual. He was a large, well-built man with silver hair and steel-blue eyes that hinted at intelligence and kindness. At only five foot four, Sadie felt small when she stood next to him. And she liked that. Edwin had been her steady boyfriend in high school until he left Silver Peak to go to college. He'd spent many years as a circuit judge in Chicago before moving back to Silver Peak after his wife died. A lot of time had passed since those days, yet when Sadie looked at him, she could still see the handsome young boy she'd been so crazy about.

Edwin smiled at the sharp-faced woman. His deep baritone voice boomed with confidence. "You're right, Marge. As a judge, I grew used to dressing rather formally. If it brings you any comfort, my friends are working on me." He looked over at Sadie and gave her a quick wink before turning his attention back to Marge. "Be assured that I am fully committed to Silver Peak. I grew up here, and my roots are firmly planted in its soil. I love this town, and I intend to represent you the best I can."

Sadie felt a surge of emotion as she watched Edwin. Although they were just friends, more and more she'd felt drawn to him, especially as his attraction to her became more obvious. Even though her husband, T.R., had been gone for several years, in many ways she still felt like his wife. They'd had a wonderful marriage, and Sadie wasn't sure she was ready to imagine herself with anyone else.

She shook herself out of her reverie and refocused her attention back on the meeting. She smiled as Marge, who wasn't used to being told she was right about anything, looked flummoxed for a moment, then shrugged and sat down, seemingly satisfied.

Another hand shot up. Edwin nodded at Doc Conroy, Sadie's physician. Doc was a longtime Silver Peak resident. He'd delivered Sadie's daughter, Alice, along with a lot of the people gathered inside Arbuckle's. Doc was seventy years old but had the energy of someone twenty years younger. The gray-haired doctor stood.

"I think it's safe to say that all of us are committed to making Silver Peak better, but most of the folks who live here aren't interested in changing the personality of this town. We want to make Silver Peak the best it can be without losing what makes us unique. So what are your plans for our future, Edwin?"

Doc sat down to a round of applause.

Edwin smiled. "I completely agree with you, Doc. For one thing, the Silver Peak Historic Preservation Council is working hard to restore the fine old buildings in our town. I'm proud to be a part of that." His eyes swept the group. "As many of you know, we've been approached by several developers interested in Silver Peak. Unfortunately, their plans for us aren't in line with our vision."

"And what is our vision?" someone called out. Sadie couldn't see who spoke, but it sounded like Doc's receptionist, Rita Dodd.

"To maintain and preserve our heritage." Edwin responded instantly. "We're blessed to live in a special town that is nestled in some of the most beautiful country in the United States. Silver Peak has a rich history. We should work hard to protect that."

Another wave of applause broke out. Sadie was pleased to see that her friends and neighbors supported Edwin and his ideas. She glanced at her watch. The meeting had already gone twenty minutes longer than scheduled. Edwin had handled his speech with

amazing composure, skillfully managing all the inquiries put to
him by the residents of Silver Peak. She needed to get back to work
and hoped the discussion was finally coming to a close.

"Any other questions?" Edwin asked, gazing around the
packed room.

No one responded to his query, so Jesse Wilson, Edwin's campaign manager, jumped to his feet. "Thank you all for coming,"
he said. "Before you leave, I'm supposed to remind you that the
Antique Mine has just gotten in some beautiful handmade quilts
from all over the state. Stop by and take a look before you leave.
And please see me for handouts you can pass around to your
friends and neighbors." He flashed a practiced smile at the assem-
bled group.

After one more enthusiastic bout of applause, conversation
broke out all over the room.

Sadie waved good-bye to Edwin, who was still answering
questions from those lingering behind, and she began to make
her way toward the door that joined Arbuckle's and the Antique
Mine. She'd only gone a few feet when someone put their hand
on her arm. She turned around to find Jerry Remington standing
behind her.

Jerry and his wife, Jane, owned Silver Peak Bed and Breakfast, a charming inn housed in a renovated Victorian home owned
by one of Silver Peak's early residents. Jerry reminded Sadie of
Harrison Ford. Not only was his coloring the same, he had a sideways
smile that was an almost perfect match to the well-known actor.

"Hi, Jerry," Sadie said. "I'm happy you and Jane could come today."

She noticed Jane having an animated conversation with Edwin.
Always the picture of elegance, Jane wore her silver hair tucked

into a smart-looking white wool hat with gray fur trim. Her coat matched her hat, and the outfit was set off by black leather boots that came to just below her knees. Jane was tall and slender and carried herself like a model. Even though she was in her seventies, she could easily pass for a woman twenty years younger. However, one of the things Sadie loved most about Jane was that she didn't seem to realize how beautiful she was.

Jerry laughed. "Jane's determined to get the word out. She's very vocal about her support for Edwin."

"I'm glad."

"I hope you and Edwin still endorse our goal for establishing a dinner theater in the old opera house," Jerry said.

The Silver Peak Opera House was undergoing extensive renovations, and a lot of people had ideas about what to do with it when the work was done. Jerry, the chairman of the historic preservation committee, had suggested the idea of a local dinner theater made up of Silver Peak residents. In the same manner of the plays that had once graced the opera house, Jerry and Jane had suggested the troupe act out stories about the early days of Silver Peak. The plays would not only be entertaining, they would be educational, helping to preserve Silver Peak's history.

"We're still excited about it, Jerry. I wouldn't worry. Luz is a very reasonable woman. I think she'll come around. I hope you and Jane are still willing to head up the troupe. You're the only couple we know with acting experience."

Jerry laughed. "That's true, but it's been a long time since those high school plays, Sadie. Not sure my skills are what they used to be."

After saying good-bye to Jerry, once again Sadie headed toward the door that led to her shop. She glanced back at Edwin, but he was in a deep conversation with a man she didn't recognize. As she tried to place him, the man turned his head and looked right at her. He was a small man, who wore large glasses that made his eyes look too big. He smiled at her as if he knew her. She returned his smile but still couldn't figure out who he was. Turning her attention away, she continued to wend her way through the crowd. She stopped several more times to greet friends. Eventually she made it through the door and into her shop, which was already crowded with people checking out the new quilts. But there were other displays that also attracted attention, just as Sadie had hoped. She pulled the door closed behind her and gazed lovingly at her shop. Every time she entered her unique store, a feeling of contentment filled her. From the high pressed-tin ceiling, the polished wooden shelves that held all her beautiful antiques, to the rich mahogany desk that helped to make up her front counter, the Antique Mine had a charm that most antique shops didn't possess. Every item in the store was displayed with pride, and nothing was ever allowed to gather dust or grime. Sadie treated her treasures with the respect she believed they deserved. Antiques were a part of history, and Sadie, a retired history teacher, treasured the past.

With the shop already bustling, people drifting in from Arbuckle's to see the quilt display made things hectic.

"Do you need help, Sadie?"

Sadie looked up to see her best friend, Rosalind Putnam, standing in front of her. Rosalind, whose nickname was Roz, stared at Sadie through large bejeweled eyeglasses, her gray bob framing an intelligent face. Like Sadie, Roz was a retired teacher.

"I think we'll be fine, Roz," Sadie said with a smile. "But thank you for asking."

"Well, if you change your mind, let me know." She nodded her head toward several customers perusing the quilt display. "Looks like you're going to sell some of those quilts today."

"I think we will," Sadie said. "Aren't they beautiful?"

Roz nodded. "I've got my eye on that Native American Star Quilt. If someone doesn't buy it soon, I think it will have to come home with me."

Sadie smiled at her tall friend. Roz was decked out in her usual bohemian style. A long-sleeved cream-colored peasant-styled blouse was tucked into her long turquoise skirt, and ankle-length fringed boots peeked out from underneath her skirt's scalloped edge.

"I know I said we'd try to have lunch today," Sadie said. "But it might be too busy for me to get away."

Roz waved her hand at her friend. "Not a problem. I'll stop by and check with you before we leave. If you can't go, we'll do it another time."

Sadie smiled. "Thanks, Roz."

Roz scooted off to check on the star quilt while Sadie helped a customer who had a question about a sterling-silver candle snuffer. They were discussing price when the phone rang. Sadie looked around for Julie, but she was talking to a couple interested in a large wedding quilt.

"I'm sorry," she told the woman. "Do you mind if I take this call? I promise I'll be quick."

"Not at all." The woman put the candle snuffer down on the counter. "I also wanted to check out your collection of teapots. I'll meet you back here in a few minutes."

"Thank you so much." Sadie grabbed the phone as the woman walked away. "The Antique Mine," she said loudly, trying to be heard over all the chatter around her.

"Sadie, is that you?" a man said. "It's Ardis. Ardis Fleagle."

Ardis Fleagle was the contractor in charge of the renovations at the Silver Peak Opera House. Although Sadie was on the Historic Preservation Council, Jerry Remington was the chairman and was overseeing the work. "Are you looking for Jerry?" Sadie asked.

"No, I'm looking for you, although you might want to let Jerry and the rest of the council know what I found over here."

"What you found?"

"What did you say?" Ardis asked. "Sounds pretty noisy over there."

Sadie took a deep breath, then cupped a hand around the receiver to block the sounds of her busy shop. "Yes, we're very busy. I'm sorry, but did you say you found something?"

"Yes. We started tearing down an old wall and discovered something inside that I think you might be interested in."

Something inside a wall? What in the world could be inside a wall that had anything to do with her?

"It's a safe, Sadie. And it looks very old."

A Note from the Editors